"Adam, you don't want to start something we can't finish."

"We can finish this." The seduction in his voice was almost her undoing.

"No," Rosa said, a little stronger. "I'm only here for the summer."

Adam watched her a moment. Rosa wanted to drop her eyes, but she didn't. Wouldn't.

"You're afraid of me," he stated.

"Why would I be afraid of you?"

"Like you said, afraid of starting something you can't finish. I know what you're thinking."

"You do?"

"I've been there. Always moving, having no time to make lasting friendships, and relationships are out of the question. But there comes a time when you have to stop," he said. "Miss that plane. Stop and be a part of what's going on around you." He tugged at her arm and she fell a little closer to him. "We won't say we're starting anything. We're just two people enjoying a morning on a Montana mountain."

His mouth was close to hers, and Rosa could feel his breath on her lips. His free hand went around her back and he pulled her close.

"Tell me to stop," he whispered.

Also by Shirley Hailstock

On My Terms
The Secret
You Made Me Love You

Where There's A Will
(with Margie Walker, Bridget Anderson,
Shelby Lewis, and Donna Hill)

Last Night's Kiss

SHIRLEY HAILSTOCK

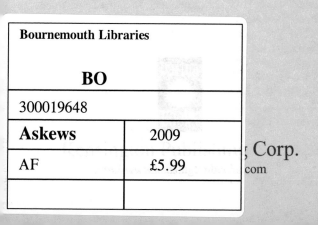

Corp.
com

DAFINA BOOKS are published by

Kensington Publishing Corp.
850 Third Avenue
New York, NY 10022

All Kensington Titles, Imprints, and Distributed Lines are
available at special quantity discounts for bulk purchases for
sales promotions, premiums, fund-raising, and educational
or institutional use. Special book excerpts or customized
printings can also be created to fit specific needs. For details,
write or phone the office of the Kensington special sales
manager: Kensington Publishing Corp., 850 Third Avenue,
New York, NY 10022, attn: Special Sales Department,
Phone: 1-800-221-2647.

Dafina and the Dafina logo Reg. U.S. Pat. & TM Off.

ISBN-13: 978-0-7582-1352-5
ISBN-10: 0-7582-1352-2

First mass market printing: September 2008

10 9 8 7 6 5 4 3 2 1

Printed in the United States of America

To Richard J.

Only he and I know why.

Chapter 1

Adam Osborne scanned the baggage claim area of Waymon Valley Airport. He was looking for the out-of-place beauty queen dressed as if she were going to a dusty Montana ranch in the 1800s, only her clothes would be new, pressed, with razor-sharp seams and pointed-toe boots. New boots, he added.

With a grunt he lounged against the wall near the entrance. Everyone getting off a plane had to come through those doors.

The airport was busy. People rushed by him, running into the arms of loved ones, kissing hello and hugging each other as they walked off toward the parking lot. Adam remembered when the place had only one terminal with a few planes coming in each day. Now it had a full complement of aircraft taking off and landing.

Checking his watch, he wondered where she was. He didn't know Rosa Clayton. Had never set eyes on her, unless you consider her staring back at him from a magazine cover. He was here in Mike's place, or rather in Vida's place. He was doing a favor for a friend of a friend. It was complicated, and the short of it was, Vida couldn't come and Mike had been called away, so he'd been pressed into car service.

Rosa Clayton was a supermodel. Few men under 105 wouldn't recognize her face. Or her body for that matter. She'd been on magazine covers and in television ads. She had a body to die for, but Adam had seen his share of beautiful women. A pretty face did nothing to turn him on. In his experience, there was nothing behind it but unused air, Vida excepted. Rosa Clayton was no different. Yet she was one person he'd never interviewed. He frowned, wondering why that was. When he'd been a correspondent in D.C. everyone who was anyone passed through the capital and he'd interview them for a segment on the news.

Then he'd gone into the field. Doing hard news. Stories that mattered. At least he thought they mattered.

Checking his watch again, he wondered where she could be. This wasn't Dulles or National Airport. It didn't take this long to get from the plane to the street. He had several things to do this morning and chauffeuring a beauty queen around was not high on his list.

"Are you waiting for me?"

Adam heard the voice from his left. Pushing himself away from the wall, he looked into her dark brown eyes and nearly drowned. She was tall and thin, too thin, he thought. Her face, while more than beautiful, was drawn. Circles, smudged eyes fringed with lashes as long and luxuriant as silk fringe. Rich, sable-colored hair was pulled back from her face and secured in a thick, curly ponytail. Adam had no doubt who she was. He was just surprised that she didn't look as if she'd stepped off the pages of the latest fashion magazine. And more surprising was the way his stomach clenched at the sight of her.

From the corner of his eye, he noticed the men in the area turning to look at her. The women looked, too, but Rosa didn't give any indication that she knew they were there. Years of practice, he thought. Only royalty could ignore the gawkers and curiosity seekers rubbernecking to get a glimpse of someone famous and beautiful the way she was doing.

"This is you, right?" She held a photo out to him. He took it and wondered where she'd gotten that one. He was used to seeing his publicity photo, a smiling professionally taken picture with all the right lighting to show off his best features. Although he hadn't been the big-time journalist for two years now, this photo was a candid shot taken several years ago during a winter vacation. It showed him astride a horse, his hat in his hand, and a smile on his face as he leaned forward to speak to Mike Holmes.

He nodded and handed it back. "Welcome to Waymon Valley," he said. "Vida's looking forward to your arrival."

She smiled. It wasn't the bright, white, sell-toothpaste smile. This one was more tired and in need of nourishment.

"She told me she couldn't get to the airport and e-mailed the photo so I'd recognize you."

"Luggage?"

She turned and looked at the rollerbag behind her.

"Is that it?" He couldn't help frowning. Vida

traveled with enough suitcases to fill her own freight car. Rosa had a small bag that looked as if it would hold only a single change of clothes. According to Vida, Rosa was here for the summer.

"That's it," she said.

He took the bag from her, his hand brushing across hers. Turning toward the exit, not waiting for her to follow, he left her behind. What was wrong with him? He was being intentionally rude and he rarely, if ever, did that, but the brief touch of his skin to hers sent a shiver up his arm. He could still feel it.

She said nothing on the way to his truck. He walked faster than he normally did. She kept up with him. He didn't bother thinking whether he was trying to leave her behind or get away from her. The one thing he did know was he regretted agreeing to come here and pick her up. She was beyond beautiful, the kind of woman Adam had interviewed more than once, and several times been involved with. He had no desire to go through that again. But the jolt that went up his arm when he touched her told him that this could be the beginning of something. He was going to make sure it wasn't.

He opened the door and she climbed into the pickup. She wore a simple pair of khakis, a light sweater, and tennis shoes. The uniform was the same for most of America, either jeans or Dockers, but on Rosa it was a combination that warranted a second glance.

"When you were on the news in D.C.," she said after they were situated and he was pulling onto the main road, "you weren't this quiet."

So she knew who he was. That surprised him. "Sorry, I have a lot to get done today."

"And picking me up cut into your schedule," she stated.

He sighed. She was perceptive, he thought. But that wasn't the whole story. And he wasn't reporting the part that he'd edited out.

"Vida is excited about your visit." He changed the subject. "She said the two of you worked well together."

"We did."

"She gave up her day job several years ago. You're still at it."

"Is that your way of telling me I'm getting old and losing my looks?"

"I would never say such a thing." He refused to fall into the trap of giving her a compliment, telling her how beautiful she really was. Even in her state of obvious distress, she could still stop traffic.

"How long is the drive to Vida's?"

"About twenty minutes. I'll have you there in no time. You look tired. Was it a long flight?"

"Fourteen hours in the air just to get to American soil. Then another three to get here."

"Where did you come from?"

"Vida didn't tell you?"

"I only got the time you were arriving."

"I flew to San Francisco from Australia."

"With only that one suitcase?"

"I don't usually carry a lot of clothes. Or makeup."

She wasn't wearing much makeup. Her face had the remnants of lipstick that must have been applied before she crossed the international date line. Yet there was something about her mouth, something that found a place inside him that years earlier he'd closed tighter than a can of unexposed film. Swinging his attention back to the road, he drove as quickly as possible toward Vida's.

"I forgot," he said flatly. "Other people do the carrying for you."

"And you," she said. "I'm sure you didn't sprint through the airport with a suit bag over your shoulder pulling a suitcase when the next breaking story needed your personal brand."

He could tell he'd gone too far. Her back was up now and her fangs were coming out.

"Vida tells me you live here now," she said.

"I've always lived here," he said. "I was born here. I came back a couple of years ago."

"Weren't you up for the anchor's job in D.C. about that time?"

"I turned it down." He'd been offered the job on the national news, but the timing was wrong. His father needed him. And he'd come home, but that wasn't the only reason.

"Why? I thought reporters lived for getting that anchor desk."

"You were misinformed."

"Sorry. I was just making conversation."

Adam took a deep breath. He was out of character. He did have things to do today and this trip *was* slowing him down, but that was no reason to be rude. There was something about her that brought back memories of everything he'd left behind. "I have an aging father," he finally said.

"Is he ill?"

"Not according to him."

"Is he part of the things you need to be attending to?"

He nodded.

"If you need to stop somewhere before taking me to Vida's, go right ahead."

Adam relaxed his hands on the steering wheel. Rosa Clayton was turning out to be different from his preconceived notion of her. She was dead tired. He could see it in the way her eyes drooped. She was a supermodel, a celebrity in her own right, someone whom people catered to, yet she was putting his needs ahead of her own. Where was the vain character he was sure she was harboring?

"We get to Vida's first," he told her as he turned onto the road leading to Vida's house. The subdivision was new. There was a section at the far end of the street that was only skeletons of new houses.

Vida lived on a cul-de-sac at the end of the street. Her house was a modest development property like those that had sprung up across America in the last couple of decades. Adam was surprised to see them here since there was so much open space in Montana. People didn't need to live on top of each other like they did in the ten-mile tract that limited the District.

Of course, the space between properties here was wider than it was in the major cities, but still it was a development. Adam lived on his father's horse ranch. From fence post to fence post it covered five thousand acres. As a boy, he'd loved to camp out in the woods. As a man, he knew how hard it was to run.

As he stopped the truck, Vida came hobbling out the door, crutches under her arms. Her right leg was encased in an air cast. She'd fallen down the back stairs several weeks ago and sprained it badly. She was lucky it wasn't another break. Because she couldn't drive, she'd asked Adam to pick Rosa up. No one would know Vida had once been a model, too. Not as super as Rosa Clayton, but she'd traveled the world and had her picture in a large share of magazines. Like Rosa, she'd gotten a few contracts over her career to be the signature model for a specific company or product, but her career didn't have the same identity as her friend's. Rosa Clayton's name was a household word.

"Rosa," Vida said, her arms resting on the top of the crutches. She opened them as Rosa jumped down from the cab.

"Davida," she shouted with a huge smile on her face. Adam hadn't seen that in the time the two of them had been together. The two women hugged like long-lost friends while he took Rosa's suitcase from the truck bed and set it inside the door.

"No one calls me that here," she said. "I'm plain old Vida from Waymon Valley."

"You look great," Rosa said. "This fresh air must agree with you." She took a moment to sniff the air.

Vida looked nothing like the stick-thin model today. She wore jeans and a long shirt that stopped just short of her knees. Her hair hung straight down her back, only curving upward on the ends. And, according to her own words, she'd gained twenty pounds and didn't fit into any of the clothes she'd worn on the cover of *Cosmopolitan* or during her entire career. After the accident she'd given up that career three years ago and returned to Waymon Valley. She was now a junior studying design at the University of Montana's extension in nearby Butte. She planned to open her own firm.

"Adam, aren't you coming in?" Vida asked as

the two women turned toward the door. "I made a big breakfast."

"Gotta go take care of Dad," he said, shaking his head.

"I suppose I'll just have to eat it, then." She grinned as if the prospect was appealing.

He passed them without a backward glance.

"Adam," Rosa called. Her voice struck him like the words of a song. A love song. He clamped his teeth together and turned around. "Thank you. I know I was an inconvenience."

"Don't worry about it," he said, and shrugged as he pulled himself into the driver's seat.

"Well," Adam said out loud, "she ought to stir up trouble around here." But he wasn't going to be part of it. He'd had his fill of beautiful women. He amended that. He'd had his fill of women.

Rosa stopped a moment and watched the truck pull out of sight. Adam Osborne was nothing like she expected him to be. She'd been through the nation's capital often enough to know that he was being groomed for the anchor's chair. Either he'd done something unthinkable and turned the political tide at the station or he'd turned the position down. And why would he?

"What's wrong?" Vida asked.

"Nothing," she said. She turned back to Vida with a smile.

"It didn't seem like you and Adam got on well. I've never known him to turn down one of my breakfasts."

"I'd say he has a chip on his shoulder."

"Adam?" Vida's eyes widened.

"Adam," Rosa repeated.

"Maybe he's worried about his dad. He said he had to go home and take care of him."

Rosa accepted that. For a moment her heart was heavy. She knew what it was like to be concerned about a sick parent. She was adopted. In fact, her entire family was adopted. They were brothers and sisters through the grace of loving foster parents. Their father had died suddenly, and years later their mother had a heart attack and lingered for several days before succumbing to eternal peace.

Rosa was tired from her long flight. She forgave Adam for being abrupt. He had his father on his mind. And family always took precedence where she was concerned.

"So, what's for breakfast?" she asked, smelling a flavored coffee permeating the air. She knew Vida loved hazelnut coffee.

Vida led her to the kitchen. The table was set for three and covered with food. Rosa recognized strawberry blintzes and crepes filled with ice cream and blueberries; a plate of bacon sat next to a bowl of southern-style home fries. Fried apples and grits rounded out the entrees that were complemented with toast, muffins, and an assortment of spreads: apple butter, marmalade, jellies and jams.

"Wow," Rosa stated, her eyes as wide as dinner plates. "If I eat like this I'll never be able to walk down the runway."

"There are no runways in Montana," Vida informed her, stretching her legs out as she took a seat and poured herself a cup of coffee from the carafe on the table.

Rosa didn't want to mention the weight Vida had gained, but then the model was no longer working in the business. The weight looked good on her. And she was wearing a cast from her knee down. From the looks of the table, Rosa could see the cast wasn't the only way she'd acquired extra poundage.

Vida had fallen off the stage during a rehearsal in Paris a few years ago. Her leg was broken in two places and they discovered she had a rare form of osteoporosis. She'd laughed it off saying it gave her a reason to get out of the rat race, but she confessed to Rosa that she thought she'd have a few more years before she had to quit. Yet in the past three years, she seemed to thrive on her new venture. Her e-mail messages were always full of excitement.

"We don't eat like this every day," Vida said. "I know you're dead from flying forever to get here, so I wanted your first moments to be satisfying before you fall asleep. Of course, I thought Adam was staying and he eats like a starving man."

Rosa sat down and began filling her plate. The room reminded her of her home in Texas. Her mother making breakfast for the horde of children she fed three times a day. The table had been filled with food, the meals noisy and boisterous, and the love unconditional.

Looking around the table, she wondered which seat Adam took when he ate here. She also wondered if Adam and Vida were a couple. Why the thought even entered her head surprised her. What did she care where Adam sat or if he was the new man in Vida's life? She dug into her food with zest. The airplane food in first class was a step above that in coach, but as her brother Brad who worked in a hospital said about hospital food, it was still airline food, processed and squared into unnatural shapes. Vida's meal was fresh off the hoof.

"Do you miss the life?" Rosa asked.

"Modeling?" Vida's eyebrows went up and she waved a dismissing hand. "Not a single day." After a moment Vida relented and said, "I do miss some parts of it, my friends, the new clothes, but dieting, never being able to indulge in a good meal, always being on display at any event, that I don't miss at all. I'm too busy with school and my new business."

"How's that going?"

"I love it. I'm designing the kind of clothes I like and putting in all the ideas we used to complain about."

They laughed. Rosa could tell Vida loved what she was doing. Her face lit up when she said it and she went on to talk with enthusiasm about her classes and the designs.

"And you know it was Adam who got me interested in designing."

"Adam?" A small current went down Rosa from her throat to her belly.

"When he first came back here he spent some time at the local university. I think he taught a journalism seminar. One night we were out and talk got around to what to do with our lives from this point on and Adam suggested I try something that I liked and would love doing. I was going to go into psychology, but after one class I knew it wasn't for me. When I stepped into the design room, it was like coming home. In a few years, I hope to have my own label."

"What does Adam do now other than care for his father?"

Her frown opened a question, but Rosa didn't

know what it was. Obviously Vida and Adam had a bond, but Rosa was unsure if it was friendship or something more. "Bailey isn't doing too well."

"Bailey?"

"Adam's dad. He used to run the ranch, but Adam's taken that over. Bailey still rides his horses, though."

"Is that what it is? A horse ranch?"

Vida shook her head as she put a forkful of eggs into her mouth. "It was a horse ranch, but most of them have been sold. They have a few horses for riding. It's no longer a working ranch. And that doesn't make Adam or his father the best of companions."

Rosa seized the word *companion*. Vida had mentioned Adam before, when they were on the road and sharing living space, but it was because he was an up-and-coming newsman, not to mention eye candy, and Rosa hadn't got the impression that they were lovers. She was getting it now. "Do you and Adam have a . . . a . . ." She trailed off. "A special relationship?"

Vida laughed. "You could say that. But if you mean are we lovers? The answer is no. And we never have been. Adam is a special friend. I could always count on him. I feel about Adam the way you feel about your brothers." She paused. "I thought about having Mike pick you up from the airport," Vida continued hesitantly. She'd just started dating Mike.

"And you decided not to. Why?"

Vida shrugged. "It's the kind of request you make to a *boyfriend*. I don't want him to know I feel that way about him."

"Then it's serious?"

"Only on my side. Not totally sure of Mike yet,

but he's coming along." Vida's expression was bright, almost glowing. She was in love, Rosa thought as she bent her head and drank from her coffee cup.

She thought about Adam and Vida's comment that they were very good friends, not lovers. Rosa couldn't believe she actually felt relief at hearing that. She didn't like Adam. Even though she'd forgiven him for his rudeness earlier, he wasn't her type. She did like the rugged-ranch-cowboy look, but she also went for polish and class. Adam Osborne had it. He could turn a head. That was a contributing reason why the TV station had put him on the screen more times than not. He had an honest quality about him, but he was straightforward and concerned in his presentations. And in Rosa's case, rude.

Glasses clinked and the splatter of sporadic laughter cut through the general noise of the party. Rosa smiled and mingled, making associations to remember the names of everyone Vida had introduced her to. This was a technique she'd learned during that long-ago Italian summer when she'd fallen into modeling. At least this time she could do it in English.

Sipping her ice water, she saw Liam Wilkerson across the room. He wore a belt with a huge silver buckle sporting the letter L, an indication that he hadn't won it in rodeo competition. As Liam was an unusual name, she had no difficulty remembering it, or the fact that he towered over everyone else in the room. He was as tall as he was wide, with a booming laugh. He also told her he was a Realtor and handed her a card.

Loretta Stanton was of model height, at least six feet tall before slipping her shoes, or rather her boots, on. She wore white, custom-designed boots that skirted up her thighs, where they almost met the hem of her short dress. Just shy of an inch of skin was visible unless she made the mistake of bending over, which for the last half hour she'd never done. Trying not to think of her as "long legs, short skirt," Rosa associated her last name, Stanton, with "stands tall" and her first name with "nothing low."

Rosa was used to meeting people. It wasn't long before she'd shaken hands, kissed, hugged, nodded to, smiled at, or bobbed her head toward everyone in the room. That is, everyone except Adam Osborne and the man with him who'd come through the door ten minutes ago to much fanfare. Adam was obviously the favored son of Waymon Valley. And he was lapping it up like a cat with a fresh bowl of milk. The smile he apparently reserved for friends, of which she was not, split his face to show his even white teeth. His brown eyes crinkled at the edges and women flocked to him as if he were a money tree. Wearing a soft brown sweater and Dockers, he moved with ease through a crowd as familiar as family.

A man walked toward her. He was huge, bald, with arms the size of small trees—a mountain of a man was the only phrase Rosa could think of to describe him. Everything about him looked tough and solid except his smile, which showed gleaming white teeth, and his eyes, which crinkled into his temples.

"Hello," he said. "Name's Mike Holmes and I'd told Vida I could pick you up from the airport. Sorry I didn't."

So this was Mike Holmes. Rosa would never have put him and Vida together as a couple. But as his big hand enveloped hers, she could feel that his size and strength were controlled.

"Rosa Clayton," she said, sure he already knew her name. "Adam Osborne took your place."

Both of them glanced in Adam's direction. He was talking to at least three women.

"My loss," Mike said.

Vida joined them. Her arm went around Mike's waist and she planted a kiss on his mouth. "I see you two have met," she said, turning back to Rosa, but continuing to hold on to Mike.

"I'm the county engineer for the Valley," he said. "We had a bridge collapse the day you arrived. I had my hands full."

"I hope no one was hurt."

Mike shook his head. "There was no one on it at the time. I got the call when Joy Stapleton-Jones—she's the librarian—couldn't get to work that morning."

"And if you know Joy," Vida said, rolling her eyes to the ceiling, "not opening the library is tantamount to the earth stopping its rotation."

"I'm going to get a drink," Mike said. "Can I get you two something?"

"Not for me," Vida said. Rosa raised the glass in her hand, showing she had a nearly full glass.

"You should stay off that leg," he told Vida.

She nodded.

"So, that's Mike?" Rosa said as they watched him walk away.

"Yep," Vida said proudly. "That's Mike. He's a big man, but he's a teddy bear."

Vida had told her about Mike, and that the two of them had renewed the friendship they'd had before she became a model. Rosa envied her friend. She looked happy. And while Rosa wasn't unhappy, there was no one in her life like Mike.

"Excuse me a moment," Vida said. "More guests are arriving."

Rosa sipped her drink and walked toward a window. The room was full of people. They hailed each other, hugged and kissed as if they hadn't seen each other in years.

Her eyes went to Adam Osborne. He was clearly the best-looking man in the room. She felt drawn to him, felt a tingle inside her that was unfamiliar and scary at the same time. She refused to analyze it, even give it a name. He had a harem already. He didn't need her to join it and he'd made that clear.

"A rose for Rosa."

Rosa shifted her gaze to the man who now stood in front of her. She'd been concentrating so hard on Adam, she hadn't seen him approach. He'd come in with Adam, and Rosa was in no doubt that this man was Adam's father. Adam wasn't a replica of the older man, but there was enough of a resemblance to defy objection.

"Thank you." She accepted the bud vase, its sole content a single-stem rose surrounded by baby's breath and tied with a long red ribbon. Raising the flower to her nose, she breathed in the fragrance. Rosa had received flowers before. She'd accepted them from many men, but none more elegant, none more sincerely given than that from the silver-haired man standing in front of her.

"Bailey Osborne," he introduced himself.

"Rosa Clayton," she said.

"You need no introduction. I think everyone in the Valley knows who you are."

Bailey was the same height as his son. He stood tall, with a rugged face that spoke of years of experience, his eyes as brown and intelligent. Rosa felt as if he were looking into her mind. She would have said he was the picture of health, but both Adam and Vida mentioned he needed care.

"My son said you looked like your photos, but he withheld the full and complete truth."

Rosa held her smile but was unsure of his meaning and distrusting of his son's assessment of her.

"No way does a picture tell the whole story," he continued.

Rosa blushed, something she couldn't remember doing in a long time. Bailey Osborne was a character. Rosa liked him immediately. Despite his words, she understood that when he looked at her, he saw more than the runway model.

"How do you like our Valley?"

"I haven't seen much of it. But I'll be here for the summer and I'll let you know. So far, it's beautiful. I love the openness, the green grass, and those stunning mountains in the distance."

"Vida could use someone around until she's fully back on her feet."

"Vida is extremely self-sufficient." Rosa had learned that the first day she arrived when she saw Vida's foot in a cast and the breakfast table covered with food. She didn't mention that the house was also immaculate. In the three days since, she'd witnessed Vida doing what was needed. The only thing she didn't do was drive. Rosa had been her chauffeur to the doctor's office yesterday, where the air cast had been removed and instructions given for her to take it easy.

Easy didn't seem to be in her vocabulary, since

this party was planned for just twenty-four hours after removal of the leg brace. Rosa helped as much as she could and Vida had hired a caterer to prepare the food.

"I'm not planning to stay the entire summer with Vida. I'm taking a house," she told Bailey.

"Oh," he said, clearly surprised at this revelation. "Where?"

"I don't know yet. Liam tells me there are several properties in the area I can rent for a few months."

Bailey glanced over his shoulder at Liam. He was talking to Wes Gilchrist, the owner of a local dry cleaning business, whose image Liam nearly obliterated. He nodded as if thinking of something, but decided not to say it.

"Bailey," someone called. "Good to see you."

A man no taller than Rosa approached them. He had gleaming white teeth, and was near to Bailey's age. His hair was equal parts black and white.

"Well, Sam, when did you get back?" Bailey smiled and the two men pumped each other's hand. Rosa didn't know how long their separation had been.

"Moments ago," he said. "Came straight here."

"Sam Stone, meet Rosa Clayton, our guest of honor. Sam consults for a company in Seattle and spends a lot of time in airplanes."

Sam looked at her, his smile as big as the sky. Saying hello, he shook her hand as if she were a one-arm bandit.

"Vida's done nothing but talk about your visit for a month," he said. "Glad you made it."

"Thank you." She looked from one man to the other knowing they wanted to reacquaint themselves. "Excuse me, I'll put this away." She indicated the bud vase she was still holding.

With a nod she left them, going to the kitchen and placing the flower on top of the refrigerator. She took a moment to breathe. The kitchen was momentarily empty. The caterers were seeing to the tables of food in the other room.

Rosa raised her arms above her head and stretched. The kinks in her back and neck eased. The kitchen door swung inward and she turned. Adam Osborne faced her. His presence surprised her as did the current of electricity that bolted through her when she saw him. Rosa wanted to say something, but could think of nothing. Falling back on her manners, she asked, "Can I get you something?"

She regretted the words the moment she saw his eyes sweep her form from tip to toe.

"Water, juice," she offered, her tone letting him know she was not part of the available menu.

"Water will do," he said.

Turning to the refrigerator, she pulled the door open and took out two bottles of water. Her throat suddenly felt parched and dry. Handing him one bottle, she twisted the top from the other and drank thirstily. Adam held his, but didn't drink.

"Feeling a little overwhelmed?" he asked.

She shook her head, but she was lying and she knew he could tell.

"You know it's strange to think that someone so used to being stared at and admired could have crowd phobia."

"I'm not afraid of the crowd."

"What is it, then?"

Rosa wasn't sure she wanted to tell her secret

to this man. Yet she heard her own voice saying it. "I'm tired of being stared at only because of what I look like."

"You think that's how they view you?" He took a step toward her. Rosa held her ground.

She nodded. "How do you think they view you? Your legion of fans? Do you think they look past your face and into an intelligent mind?" She doubted it. The man had a raw sexuality that radiated from him. Any woman in his realm couldn't resist it, except her. She'd seen this kind of man before. She had brothers with the same attributes, an aura that drew women. And Rosa wasn't about to let the superficial outer layer of a man sway her. Yet she admitted to herself that her blood pressure had gone up a notch or two when she saw him standing in the doorway.

"I can't control what people think."

In lieu of speaking, she nodded. It was a good answer. One she'd adopted herself. It didn't mean she didn't want to show off her brain, but her face and body preceded her and men mostly didn't listen when what they were seeing took precedence. Vida told her she'd constructed an invisible wall around her feelings and she wouldn't let anyone get close to her. Rosa pushed the notion aside. She moved around too often to commit to a relationship. Of course, she had friends all over the world, but no one special.

"I'd better get back." Rosa took a step toward the door. Adam moved in front of her, blocking her way. Without thinking, she instinctively moved back. She hated herself for doing it, but somehow she didn't want him to touch her.

"I'm sure you're missed out there," he said. "But I have a question for you."

"What is it?" Her throat was dry and she opened the bottle of water again and took a drink. Although it was wet, it didn't seem to satisfy her thirst.

"Why are you here?"

"Here?" Her heart beat faster. She didn't know what he meant. From what she'd heard from the people in the other room, everyone had known for months she was coming. "I came for the waters. I hear they have healing powers."

Adam didn't take to the joke. His face went dark. She could see the blood paint a dark undertone below his brown skin.

"You don't look broken to me," he said.

"Looks can be deceiving. And I know the proper use of light and makeup."

"You can stop being sarcastic," he said. "It doesn't suit you."

"What do you want to know?"

"Vida doesn't need someone she's going to have to wait on. She had a bad fall and she needs to heal."

"Vida's not an invalid. And you don't need to worry about her waiting on me."

"And why is that?"

"I'm taking a rental. Liam says I might find a house."

"What? When? Where?" Vida stood in the doorway. She hobbled inside, letting the door swing closed. "I thought you were going to spend the summer with me. When did you decide this?"

"Staying with you would be fine for a weekend, even a week, but I'm here for the summer."

"So? We were roommates on the road. What's the difference?"

Rosa smiled and looked at her friend. "We're

not on the road, Vida. On the road we were working ninety hours a day. We hardly did anything in those rooms but fall into a tired sleep and shower. At our age being roommates is like having dead fish in your kitchen." Rosa spread her hands to encompass the room. "After three days they smell." She smiled. "And we'd probably be ready to kill each other long before that."

"But where will you live?"

"I don't know yet. Liam is showing me some places tomorrow afternoon."

"I know I'm not going to be able to change your mind," Vida said. The two of them had spent enough time together to know their minds. "But see if you can find something close by. There are things about Montana you don't know. Dangers that could get you hurt."

"Like bears," Rosa joked.

"Like bears," Adam stated without the hint of a joke in his voice. "Coyotes, snakes—"

"How about werewolves?" she asked, staring him directly in the eye.

Adam peered at Rosa from across the room several minutes later. She had to be the most beautiful woman he'd ever seen. What was she doing in Waymon Valley? Okay, she had a friend here, but this was a nowhere kind of place, a way station, a pit stop on the way to somewhere else. People didn't come here for the season. They had no tourist industry.

Butte, a stone's throw away, was a day trip. People came to see the defunct copper mines. Take the tour. They took pictures in western garb, drank Coca-Cola, and piled back into their vans or SUVs and hurried off to Glacier National Park, Yellowstone in Wyoming, or back to their RVs at one of the local campsites. They didn't hang around for the entire summer.

Rosa Clayton was hiding something. The journalist in him knew it. She was a story in the making. He'd give Ben a call. Suddenly Adam stopped. He was no longer a journalist. He'd left that life behind in Washington, D.C. He was a rancher now. And Rosa Clayton was none of his business.

"So, Adam, what do you think? Is she as pretty as her pictures?"

He glanced at Vida, who'd sidled up beside him.

"I can feel the friction between you two, but you have to admit, you can't keep your eyes off her."

"You shouldn't spend so much time on that leg," Adam said, distracting himself from Vida's all too true comment.

"I'll take care of it," she said. "Now answer my question."

Giving his full attention to Vida, he was surprised to find that he didn't want to look away from Rosa. There was something fascinating about her. Something that commanded not only his attention, but every man's in the room.

"If I didn't know better," Adam told her, "I'd say you were into a little matchmaking."

"It wouldn't hurt you to get serious about a woman."

"It wouldn't help me, either."

Since Vida had returned to her childhood home, she and Mike Holmes had picked up their relationship just where they'd left it when the three of them were back in high school. Vida thought Adam had put his life on hold and that finding a mate would do him good. She was wrong.

"Besides, she's way too beautiful for me."

He lifted the drink he was holding and sipped the glass of champagne. They rarely had champagne at parties. Waymon Valley was more a beer and pretzel place. They had a couple of white-tablecloth restaurants, but their parties were mainly barbecues. Glancing at Rosa Clayton, he understood the reason for the drink. She moved through the room like a queen.

"I don't think so," Vida said. "She's more than a pretty face. She's got a brain, too. Wait until you get to know her."

"I'm not going to get to know her. I don't expect our paths to cross more than a few times the entire summer if she stays that long." He clearly didn't see it happening. "Come September she'll be off to Paris or Rome or Australia and I'll be tending horses and making sure my father takes his medicine."

They both looked toward Bailey Osborne. He was talking to Rosa. She laughed at something he said. Bailey was a charmer, Adam thought. Even at his age, women still vied for his company.

"What's she doing here?" Adam asked. He wasn't one to skirt an issue. As a reporter, he needed the facts and baldly asked Vida.

"Vacationing, visiting a friend, finding a place to unwind. Being a model is hard work and no one works harder than Rosa."

"Why here? And for three whole months. This sounds more like hiding out than just spending time with friends. You heard her. Staying with friends for longer than a few days . . ." He trailed off.

Vida laughed. "You've been a reporter too long," she accused. "This is not the naked city or the nation's capital. Stop looking for conspiracy theories around every corner."

"The problem with that," he told her, "is there usually *is* a conspiracy around every corner."

Chapter 2

It must have something to do with the curvature of the earth, Rosa thought as she look up at the sky from her new patio. She'd met Vida in Greece during a photo shoot, and naturally the two had talked about their origins, their families, and where they lived. When Vida told her how big the sky was in Montana, Rosa took it with a grain of salt, but today she understood. It was something you had to see. It couldn't be filmed or photographed, at least not with justice to the splendor and vastness. She needed to be able to stand in the space and bathe in the limitless light.

Rosa place a bowl of fruit on the table. She'd moved into her rented house three days ago, two weeks after she'd stepped off the plane. It was freshly painted and had two stories. Unlike Vida's development house, this place was rustic with a loft bedroom on the top level. She'd divided the space into two areas, using a third of it as an office. She'd found an old fax machine downstairs. Bringing it up, she put it on a makeshift desk and left a place to sit the computer she'd ordered. She used to

have video conferencing equipment her brother
Dean insisted everyone use for family meetings. In
the past few years the Internet had replaced the
need to carry that equipment from place to place.
And it had come in handy with the six of them
living and moving so far from one another.

The bottom floor was one big room. The walls
had been painted a deep dark mahogany, making
the white molding around the doors and windows
stand out. One wall was decorated with pictures of
national parks. Rosa was thankful there were no
stuffed animal heads staring at her through glass
eyes. Because the ceiling was so high, a system of
invisible wires had been strung across the room.
Suspended from them were small lights with a lot
of illumination. To further disguise the lights, an
array of figures hung from or balanced on the
wires. They added a bit of whimsey to the formal
room and Rosa liked the touch.

The floors were hardwood, a rich brown with a
hint of red that reflected the walls. The furniture
was overstuffed and comfortable, two large sofas
flanking a fireplace that spoke of use on cold
Montana nights. Islands had been created in the
large space using area rugs and group placement.
There was a living room area and an alcove perfect for reading. The kitchen counter defined the
cooking area, which was long and spacious.

The upstairs had a railing that ran the length
and breadth of the room. Standardized spindles
composing the structure had been rejected, with
the builder opting instead for an intricately
carved mosaic that had one blending into the
next. From a distance the carvings told a story.
Rosa could see horses and wagons in one area
while industry had grown in others. She made a

mental note to read it or find out what it meant later. A king-size bed dominated the only bedroom. No stereotypical longhorns adorned a headboard or stared down from the walls. A serene scene of snow-capped mountains hung next to a historic map of the Montana Territory.

Rosa spun around. The place was masculine, dark with touches of light here and there. She loved it.

She signed the lease and moved in the same day.

When she'd told her family she was spending the summer in Montana, they'd immediately thought something was wrong. Workaholic that she was, she was always off to the airport heading for the next destination. And Waymon Valley was a small town, not a major metropolis where she usually lived and worked. But she was older now and living on planes and out of suitcases was beginning to wear thin. Vida had done it three years ago. Rosa was twenty-seven. She had many years left on the runway. Her skin was smooth, unmarred by even the hint of a wrinkle, and she could pick and choose her contracts. Money wasn't an issue. With more time for saving than spending, she'd amassed a nest egg large enough to take into the next millennium.

The one missing item in the place, Rosa noticed, was a television. She hadn't been able to see the news since she'd arrived. Vida told her the mountains blocked cable signals and there were places were cell phones were iffy. Rosa could get DIRECTV, which bounced off satellites, but this house wasn't equipped with it.

Rosa was a news junkie and her family suggested she wean herself off it during this rest period. She'd give it a try. Taking this house over the others she'd seen was because it had no access to WNN, the twenty-four hour news station she was addicted to watching. The most she could get would be from the local Waymon Valley television station, but the absence of a television solved that issue. It wasn't going to be easy. She already missed being able to find out what was going on in the world.

A knock came on the door as Rosa was putting the finishing touches on the patio table. She wasn't expecting anyone, but Vida's leg was better and she was now allowed to drive short distances. Waymon Valley wasn't that large, so driving anywhere posed no problem. Maybe she'd decided to drop by and see Rosa's new place.

On her way to the door, Rosa checked her watch, or where her watch had been. Wearing one was another thing she was weaning herself from. She'd left it on the end table upstairs. There was no schedule she was on while she was here.

She opened the door and froze when she saw Adam Osborne standing there. A moment later, she looked behind him, scanning the space left and right for Vida.

"I know," he said, placing his hands on his hips in a purely casual way, but her eyes followed the action. "You weren't expecting me."

"No, I—"

"You have a package," he interrupted. "Or I should say packages."

Adam picked up a large box and moved to pass Rosa. She stepped aside, allowing him access to the house.

"Where do you want it? It's heavy so you should put it where you're going to open it."

It was the computer equipment she would use to talk to her family and search the Internet. She wondered if it would work here. The mountain blocked cable signals. Maybe they would block the Internet, too.

"Upstairs," she said.

He took the steps two at a time, running with the box as if it weighed no more than empty air. Rosa watched him with interest. He was a strange man. He did favors for people, but with an air that he'd rather not. At least that's how *she* saw it. He walked along the loft, passing her bedroom, and put the box in the area she'd set up as an office. Good, she thought. She could open it there and set things up. She'd call her brothers in Texas tonight and see what was going on in the world.

When he returned to the bottom floor, she was frowning at him.

"What?" he asked.

"How'd you get these?"

"I was in town and thought I'd save Matt a trip."

"Matt?"

"He runs a package delivery service," Adam said. "I had some business in town and ran into him." He left her to go to his truck. Returning, he carried three more boxes. "Same place?" he asked.

Rosa nodded. As he disappeared up the steps, Rosa didn't even try to resist turning to stare. The man had the best ass she'd ever seen. Despite his attitude, his jeans fit in all the right places. There were several agencies she could recommend him to if he wanted to model the sexy jean look. Rosa turned away. She wasn't about to go dry-mouthed over someone she didn't like and who didn't like her.

"These weigh a ton," he said, straining. What's in them? Books?" Adam spoke from the loft.

"Clothes and some computer equipment," Rosa corrected. "The packing weighs more than the equipment."

Adam came down the stairs. He brushed his hands together, then swept away invisible lint from his pants.

"Thank you," Rosa said, "but I don't expect you to run errands for me."

"No problem. It wasn't out of my way."

"I see," she said. She'd learned that his father's ranch wasn't far from her house. In fact, it was the next property. Rosa had yet to see the house. As Liam had driven her here, he'd pointed out the different properties. Mostly what she could see was a driveway and a sign designating the name of the ranch. The last one they'd passed before reaching the house was Bailey Osborne's place.

"Do you need any help opening them?" Adam brought her back from her musings.

She shook her head. She knew he didn't like her, and she wondered why he went to the trouble of bringing her packages. "I can handle it," she said, relieving him of the displeasure her company would cause.

He nodded and shrugged at the same time. Then headed for the door.

"So deliverymen do that out here?"

Adam stopped and turned back.

"Isn't it against the law for them to allow someone else to deliver packages sent through their service?"

"It's not against the law. It might be against

company policy, but there's no law governing package delivery by nonfederal agencies. And yes, that's the way things are done out here. We help each other when necessary."

"You say that like you're a native."

"I am a native."

"Not anymore. You've been back for two or three years. Prior to that you were roaming around the world, doing the news from every hot spot there is. Your experiences have made you a foreigner in your hometown."

"What makes you think that after being here for two minutes?"

"You get the same reception I do."

"So?"

"So when you're not an outsider, people just say hello and keep going. For you they stop, flock around, like you were an outsider."

"They only do that because of what I've done."

"Exactly," she agreed. Rosa didn't wait for another reply. She passed him and moved to open the door. With her hand on the knob, she turned back. She would never understand what happened next. She'd intended to open the door and usher him out. Maybe it was his dislike of her that intrigued her or the fact that she'd been so rude. She didn't usually act like that. And men didn't usually react as if she carried the plague. She wanted to know what it was about her that Adam found so unpalatable.

"Adam, I apologize. I'm not usually rude to people. I was about to eat. If you haven't eaten yet, I'm willing to share my lunch."

Her admission was unexpected and she could see surprise reflected in his eyes. "The food is already prepared," she said, gesturing toward the terrace. She hated eating alone. Manners forced her to offer him something for his troubles, but she had other reasons.

Adam swung his gaze in a lazy fashion toward the open door leading to the wood-planked patio that held a picnic table and bowls of food.

"Are you expecting someone?" he asked.

She shook her head. "I don't often cook. When I do it's usually for a lot of people. So I haven't got the hang of cooking for one."

She went to the kitchen and got a second place setting.

"Okay if I wash my hands?" He spread them out as she pulled silverware from a drawer.

"Sure," she said.

He went to the bathroom and she set a place for him on the table.

"It's not much," she said, when he joined her. "I mean I don't do cow often."

"And you're from Texas? Isn't that against the law?"

"Only in Texas." She relaxed, smiling at him. She hadn't told him where she was from and she had no Texas twang. She'd studied hard to get rid of it before doing commercials. Vida could have told him. She was quickly learning that everyone knew the story of everyone else's life in the Valley. "When I'm in Texas, I eat it, but there I have sisters-in-law who are wonderful cooks."

Rosa spooned salad onto her plate. She'd made a spinach salad with mandarin oranges and raisins. Topping it were julienne strips of chicken, ham, and roast beef she'd bought at the grocery store. Because she loved lemonade and never got any freshly made except at her sister-in-law Erin's house in Cobblersville, Texas, she'd made a pitcher. The day, which was unseasonably warm, called for it.

"Sisters-in-law," Adam said. "How many?"

"Two that live in Texas. I have one in Philadelphia and one in upstate New York."

"You have *four* brothers?" He sounded surprised.

"Four brothers and a sister." Rosa poured lemonade into their glasses.

"Six children. Parents didn't believe in birth control?"

"They believed in birth control. They also believed in adoption."

"You were adopted?" His voice changed slightly. The accusation she read in it disappeared for a moment.

She nodded. "We all were."

"All six of you?"

"By the best parents in the world," Rosa assured him, popping a leaf of spinach into her mouth.

"You were lucky. I covered more than a few stories where foster children were abused."

"We were. Lucky, I mean. Our parents took in the hard-core, unadoptable kids and we all turned out okay."

"You were unadoptable?" He leaned back in the chair and smiled his skepticism.

"I was four. Abandoned by my mother at a hospital. My adoptive mother was the doctor on call who found me."

He leaned forward and suddenly became serious. "Did you ever find out why she abandoned you?"

"She died." Rosa said it without emotion. Devon and Reuben Clayton were the only parents she'd ever known. Her biological mother had no face in her mind and no attachment to her affections. "The police tracked her down. She was an alcoholic. When they found her, she was very weak. She didn't live long after they got her to the hospital. She did ask for me once. She called me Rosa. My parents kept the name."

Adam ate and drank without commenting. Rosa had the feeling he wanted to say something, but didn't.

"What about you?" she asked. "Are you an only child?"

"I like the way you put that," he said. "Only children are usually self-centered and spoiled."

She let the comment hang in the air. From what she'd seen he had all the earmarks of exactly that.

"I used to wish I had brothers and sisters, but I don't." He paused. "And I don't think I'm spoiled or self-centered." His eyes came up and bored directly into hers. "You, on the other hand, have to be the baby of the family."

"Why would you say that?" Obviously he'd assessed her as she had done him. He hid it better than most men.

"There's a certain amount of spoiling in you, too."

"Not with my brothers around." Rosa shook her head. "They made me work for everything."

"You mention your family a lot."

She became conscious of the smile on her face and the memory of growing up with a houseful of people. "I do," she said. "They're the best family in the world. There's always someone to argue with, someone to laugh or cry with, someone to tell your stories to."

Adam dropped his head a moment. Then he sighed.

"I'd opt for a large family. They're so much fun in the long run," Rosa continued.

"There's nothing I can do about that. If my parents had had more children, maybe the siblings would be here to help out with my father."

"You mentioned him before. He didn't look ill. I pictured a bent-over man leaning on a cane."

"He has a heart condition and he won't take care of himself. He insists on riding every day and I have to make sure he takes his medicine regularly."

She looked down with a tiny smile, remembering the older version of Adam Osborne and the rose he'd presented her with during the party at Vida's. She hadn't seen him since. And suddenly she missed the older man.

"Why are you smiling like that?" Adam asked.

"Are you sure he's not doing it on purpose?"

"What do you mean?"

"My older sister is a child psychologist and she says it's not unusual for children to act helpless just to get attention."

"My father's not a child."

"You're taking care of him. You have to get home to make sure he takes his medication. I bet you check to see if he's eaten, too. And if he's in bed at night." She stopped and checked his expression. He gave her a quick nod. "So, who's the parent and who's the child?"

He didn't answer. Rosa knew he wasn't ready to concede that his father was running his life, and she wouldn't push it.

"I thought your sister was the psychologist."

"She is. I used to date a psychologist. I guess

some of both of them rubbed off on me. Disregard everything I said."

Adam checked his watch and stood up. His face showed that he'd spent more time with her than he expected to. "I'm sorry I have to cut this short," he said. "I have several errands I need to run."

Rosa knew he was going to check on his father. She stood, too, and cleared the food from the table, taking it into the house. When she turned, Adam was behind her holding his plate and glass.

"Thank you," she said, accepting the dishes. For a moment their hands touched. Rosa moved hers away quickly. She placed the dishes in the sink, knowing that her hands had suddenly lost the ability to perform simple tasks. Yet it appeared that every nerve ending in her fingers was on fire.

"When I left town I didn't expect food," Adam said as Rosa walked him to the door.

"Next time, maybe I'll make you a real meal."

"Next time?" He raised his eyebrows.

"Yeah," she said. "As soon as you get over your dislike of me."

The natural progression from being a model to life after the runway was either to open an agency or become a photographer. Rosa opted for the camera. She loved taking pictures and had quite a portfolio. Looking through the lens and selecting exactly which slice of life she wanted to preserve gave her power.

Montana was perfect for the camera. Like the sky the state was so famous for, the land went on forever, too. Rosa sat astride a horse. The groom at the stable had called the filly Leah. Rosa hadn't been on a horse in a while and tomorrow she would pay for the exercise today. Lifting the camera that hung around her neck, she scanned the land before her. The mountains in the distance were spectacular. They were farther away than they looked and she used a telephoto lens to pan their height.

Sliding off the horse, she tethered it to her belt using a slipknot in case something spooked it and she took off. At least she wouldn't take Rosa with her. It was a technique her brother Digger had taught her one rainy afternoon. She didn't think she'd have a use for it. She just liked the way the knot would come apart by pulling either end.

Raising the camera, she focused and took a shot. Moving about, she continued taking picture after picture. It was early morning, before breakfast. The daylight changed by the minute. Like the Grand Canyon's changing of color throughout the day, the morning light here provided a panorama of color just as spectacular. And what she could do with it on her computer screen might not be art, but it was pleasing to her eye.

Rosa took a shot and stopped. She heard something. It was a horse. The cadence was rhythmic and coming toward her. Squinting in the morning light, she tried to see who was approaching. For a moment she thought it was Adam. Then she recognized Bailey Osborne. The tiny flip of her heart somersaulted to her stomach. Had she hoped it was Adam? And then become disappointed to find it was someone else?

Bailey pulled up in front of her and dismounted with the agility of a man half his age.

"You're a morning person," he stated.

"After a lifetime of having to be at some place before the day woke up, I suppose sleeping late is something my body hasn't learned to do."

"That's great. I love seeing the sunrise." He looked toward the horizon. "It's the best part of the day. Clears your mind and gets you ready to do what's gotta be done. And"—he paused—"it's one of the few times I get away from Adam."

"He's very worried about you," Rosa told him.

"I know. He thinks I'm going to die on him." He tapped on his chest. "Bad ticker. I suppose everyone has to die someday, but I'm planning on beating the clock for a lot more years." He smiled at her, giving her a grin that was so like his son's.

"So, are you playing games with Adam?"

"Games?" He frowned.

"Not taking your medicine. Riding alone. Things like that."

"I'm not an invalid. And I do take my medicine. I just kinda wait for him to show up to do it. It gives us time to talk."

"I see," Rosa said. It was time he wanted with Adam. She raised her camera and looked for a good shot.

"You're a model and a photographer?" he questioned.

Rosa faced him, still looking through the viewfinder. "Not really," she said, snapping a picture. "There's a lot of time between takes when you're on assignment. I picked up a camera one day and starting taking snapshots to show my family. I enjoyed it enough to keep doing it. Now I'm rarely without a camera."

Lifting the instrument again, she took a shot of Bailey.

"There's not much to see around here. You should go to some of the parks. Maybe you can get Adam to take you. He used to be a summer guide before he went off to college."

"Maybe I will," Rosa said, knowing she had no intention of asking Adam anything. He'd shown his dislike for her and Rosa didn't want to be in anyone's company if they didn't want her around. "There's a lot around here, though," she said. "It might be commonplace to you, but it's all new and gorgeous to me."

She panned the area with her camera, then lowered it and looked directly at Bailey.

"Have you always lived here?"

"Every one of my sixty-nine years." He said it with pride. "I spent time in the Army. Vietnam. Traveled some when my wife was alive. But the bulk of my time has been right here." He pointed toward the ground.

"You love it here."

"Like Texans love Texas," he agreed with a smile. "And if you stay here long enough, you'll love it, too."

"I already do," Rosa said. "I have an apartment in New York and I grew up in Dallas, but I love small towns much better. Waymon Valley is small and big at the same time."

"I know what you mean," he said. "In town, where Vida lives, everything is practically within walking distance. Yet out here there seems to be so much room. My great-grandmother came out here in the 1890s. She was a teacher named Clara Winslow Evans. Clara moved from Virginia to Montana to teach school and help my great-great-aunt Emily Hale run a boardinghouse for the miners. Copper mining was big back then.

Since then our family has always lived here. I've got more cousins and aunts and grand-aunts here than any family in Georgia."

Rosa laughed as his voice displayed both consternation and pride when he spoke of his heritage. She thought of her own family, her siblings, and how their heritage would begin with them. "That must be wonderful," she said. Rosa had no cousins or aunts or uncles. No grandparents. Only her brothers and sisters and the promise of nieces and nephews.

"It's great country," Rosa finally said. "I think I'll ride over there." She pointed toward a distant outcropping of rocks. "And take some more photos."

Bailey stopped her as she pulled the reins from her belt. "Not today," he said. "And not alone. There are some dangers to this country, too. Why don't we ride back to the stables and I'll get you breakfast?"

Rosa smiled. "I'd like that." Her stomach growled as if on cue. "It must be the air out here. I'm suddenly very hungry."

Rosa was surprised half an hour later when they turned in the horses and Bailey stopped his pickup at the ranch house instead of a restaurant.

Her heart began to pound as she knew Adam was on the other side of that front door.

"I thought we were going into town," she said.

Bailey got out and came around to open her door. "Got the best food in the county right here," he said.

She slid out of her seat. "It's just that I have an appointment in town and thought I'd get a ride."

They were on their way to the door. "I'll have Adam drive you after we eat," he said.

"That won't be necessary. I'll give Vida a call. I haven't seen her in a couple of days. We can get together."

"Nonsense," he boomed. "Adam's going to town anyway."

"What's that?" Adam spoke, and Rosa's entire body tensed at the sound.

"Rosa needs a ride into town right after we eat," Bailey explained.

Adam was freshly showered. Water still glistened on his hair. His face was clean shaven and he wore jeans and a polo shirt.

"Come on," Bailey said. "I can smell the coffee."

The kitchen was huge, a country kitchen with a wide table in the center and huge windows opening one wall. Several individual sections had jars with peppers or colorful foods suspended in oil or flowers in them. They made art out of the windows.

"This is Medea," Bailey introduced. "She rules the kitchen."

"And the house," Medea corrected.

"Medea, meet Rosa Clayton. I've invited her for the best breakfast in town."

"Good morning," Medea said. She was in her early forties, with a few strands of gray in otherwise jet-black hair that touched her shoulders. Only slightly overweight, she had a round face with a welcoming smile and dark eyes.

Rosa took a seat at the table and Bailey handed her a cup of strong black coffee. She added cream and chose a sugar substitute from a jar on the wide table.

"You're here for the summer," Medea stated. "Staying in Mr. Adam's house."

Rosa nearly dropped the cup she'd begun to lift to her mouth. "Adam's house?"

"It was empty. I haven't been there in a while," he said. "Liam suggested I rent it out." He spoke in a staccato burst.

"Liam never told me who the owner was. Just that it was for rent." And she never thought to ask, Rosa admonished herself. It was Adam's house. Adam's furnishings. Adam's *bed*.

"Adam was lucky." Bailey interrupted her thoughts. "He'd only put it up for rent a few days before you took the place."

Adam was her landlord.

Adam shifted uncomfortably in his chair. "What do you have to go into town for?" He changed the subject, but it was still on Rosa's mind. Why hadn't he told her when he was there? Memories seemed to replay in her mind now, like how he seemed to move through the rooms with a casual intimacy. He didn't ask where anything was. He'd gone straight to the space in her loft where she wanted the computer. When he washed his hands, he didn't ask where the bathroom was. He knew.

"Rosa?"

Startled, she looked up. She had her hands around the coffee cup and was apparently staring into space.

"Town?" he prompted. "You need to go into town."

"I've reserved a car. I need one to get around if I'm going to be here all summer." She'd made herself comfortable in the house and liked the surroundings, the scenery, and the proximity to the stables. The wide-open spaces were just that. Things were much farther away than they looked.

If she was going to spend a considerable amount of time here, she needed transportation.

Medea set a plate in front of her. It was piled with food. "Eat every bit of it," she ordered. "You're too skinny." She glanced at Adam, then back at Rosa. "But then, Adam likes his women skinny." She and Bailey laughed. Rosa's face went hot and she could see the anger on Adam's.

Rosa waved good-bye to Bailey and got into the truck. The door slammed shut and Adam thought she looked as if she were in prison. He climbed into the cab and jammed the key into the ignition. The engine roared to life, but he didn't touch the gearshift.

"Where are we going?" he asked.

"Town," she answered.

"There are no rental car agencies in Waymon Valley."

"Except at the airport," she corrected. "But all their cars are reserved. I'm going to Butte."

"You said you were going into town."

"Just drop me at Vida's. I'll go to Butte from there and rent the car."

He gave her a long look before throwing the gear into drive. He hadn't intended to try and break it, but that's what he'd done before roaring away from the house. Moments later, without saying a word, he passed the turnoff leading to Vida's development.

"What are you doing?" Her head swiveled back and forth as she looked through the back window and back at him. In the rearview mirror the distance grew longer and longer from where she expected them to head. "Where are you going?"

Adam gave her a look that said *be quiet*. "I'm taking you to Butte."

"Why?"

"Because Vida cannot drive that far. And you know it."

"Vida wasn't going to drive me. I was going to borrow her car and drive myself."

"Then how were you going to get two cars back?"

"I figured they would deliver the other one."

"You're not in New York. This is Montana. We don't deliver cars here."

"Unlike packages."

Adam gave her a withering look. She held it.

"Who would have known this was the back of beyond? I bet they haven't even heard of the telephone this far from civilization," she said.

Adam should have thought of it. There she was thinking that everything was the way it was in the big city. Yeah, Butte was big, but it wasn't New York. There weren't all-night anythings in Butte. Maybe a drugstore, a fast food place here and there, but for the most part people lived normal lives and went home at reasonable hours.

"The packages were a favor for a friend, someone here in the Valley. Butte is miles away and with those eyes of yours, I have no doubt you could convince them to deliver a car to you."

Rosa turned away, staring out the window.

"Where'd you find my father?" Adam asked, changing the subject.

"I met him on the range. The same way he told you we met. Why, do you think I have an ulterior motive in speaking to your father?"

"No."

"He's a charming old man." Rosa smiled to herself. "I like him."

She left the sentence hanging as if saying she liked the father, but the son was another matter. He knew that. He knew she didn't like him. He didn't want her to.

"Why didn't you tell me?" she asked suddenly.

"Tell you what?"

"Tell me that the house I was living in was yours?"

"Would it have made a difference?" he asked. "You were already there. Your clothes were there. Your computer boxes were there. You'd made yourself at home. Why did you need to know who owned the house? If you were interested you should have asked before you signed the lease."

"Yes, that's true. I just never thought that you wouldn't tell me that I was about to live in the house that you used to live in."

"I didn't live there for very long. I got out of school. I bought the house. I worked the ranch for a little bit. Then I got a chance to work for a news agency and I was gone. Minneapolis. I left. From there—"

"From there you went on," she interrupted. "Other places, other worlds, other cultures, around the world. Seven, eight, nine times?"

"Maybe. I didn't count."

"I'm sure you didn't."

"How many times did *you* go around the world?"

"More than I can count," she said. "But I enjoyed every minute of it. I enjoyed all the cities I was in, everything I saw, all the people I met. And I didn't have to tell their life stories on the news."

"I never interviewed anyone who didn't want to be interviewed."

"You know, I don't get you," Rosa said, leaning back against the window to stare at him.

"Get me? What do you mean, get me?"

"You act like you don't like me and I believe you don't. For some reason you've decided I am the devil incarnate. Or close to it. Why? I don't know why and I don't care, so don't bother explaining. Then you go and do something nice for me. You came to the airport to pick me up. I'm sure Vida has a lot of friends who could have come. But you came. Then you bring my packages and place them where I want them. And now you're driving me to Butte when I only said I wanted to go into Waymon Valley. Why is that?"

"It just so happens I have business in Butte today and I can just as easily do it this morning as later in the day. So you're really not taking me out of my way."

"Thank the Lord for that," she said. "We certainly wouldn't want to interrupt a schedule as packed as yours."

"You didn't."

"There you go again. You weren't planning on going to Butte this morning. Now you are. So why is it that you don't like me, then would do something nice for me, your father asked. Is that it?"

"Could be," he said. "Could be something else."

"What something else?" she asked.

"Nothing," he said. He'd already said more than he planned to. That had just slipped out. He didn't intend to say it out loud. Rosa Clayton wasn't anybody he wanted to be around for long periods of time. Especially, long periods of time in the confines of the truck's cabin. He could smell her perfume, or was it bath soap or just the essence of her? He didn't know, but it was doing strange things to his mind *and* his body. She had on jeans, but he knew she had long beautiful legs. He knew exactly what they looked like. He'd seen them in countless magazines and on television commercials. She was definitely beautiful, but he'd had his fill of beautiful women. He knew how they were. How they acted. And how they were no good for a man.

Rosa Clayton was more than just a beautiful woman. There was something about her that had men turning their heads. She had a certain amount of class mixed with a body that could make a man beg. There was an aura about her that couldn't be duplicated. It was something you had to be born with. And Rosa Clayton had it.

But Adam had a certain amount of resistance to beautiful women. And Rosa was testing it to the limit.

Chapter 3

The Butte Airport was on the far side of the city. Rosa phoned there looking for a rental, but opted for the downtown office. As they approached Butte, Adam swung the truck off the highway and headed into the city. Rosa found everything spiraled off Main Street and sprawled for miles around. Apparently, people out here got more than their forty acres and a mule and were holding on to it. Butte looked much like it had in the 1800s when copper was king.

The city wasn't a mass of high-rise buildings. Most were made of brick and few were higher than a few stories. Like most of what Rosa had seen since arriving, the imposing mountains in the distance lorded over everything.

Adam parked and jumped down from the driver's seat. The agency's door was a few steps away. Coming around the front of the truck, he pulled Rosa's door open. She noticed him glancing at her legs. Although she wore pants, they fit like gloves. She didn't move to get down, but she sat watching him until he raised his eyes.

An invisible fissure seemed to open, connecting them. Their eyes met and held. Rosa couldn't have moved if she wanted to. She expected a reaction from Adam, but she wasn't expecting to find her insides shaking as if she'd been dropped from a helicopter.

It had been there all the time, Rosa realized, a certain chemistry that drew people together. Unfortunately, people didn't get the choice of whom they wanted to have chemistry with. It was just there. And it was between her and Adam. There was also a certain amount of physics between them in the form of friction. As he took her hand and helped her down, she realized friction produced heat and fire. Both of which were making themselves known within her.

"You should be all right from here on," he said, dropping her hand as if he felt the heat flashing through her.

"I have several appointments to attend to," he said.

"I'll be fine." Rosa nodded. She felt awkward and thought Adam did, too. They both wanted to get away from each other. She stepped back and went though the glass doors of the rental car agency. She didn't breathe until the doors closed and Adam was no longer close to her.

Rosa stood a moment with her hand on her heart. It was beating faster than normal.

"May I help you?" a man said from behind a counter.

Rosa looked up. It took her a moment to regain her composure.

"You're Rosa Clayton," he stated, awe evident in his voice. Often she wanted to reply to that

question, saying, "I know that." But she only
smiled and nodded.

He reached across the high counter to shake
her hand. "Welcome," he said. "I'm William Har-
rison. I have everything ready. Although . . ." He
trailed off.

Rosa looked around to see what it was that ar-
rested his attention. Several men across the
room quickly averted their eyes. Rosa knew they
were staring at her, but she didn't mind. She
smiled pleasantly. A woman farther down the
counter smiled back at her.

"What is it?" she asked. "Is there a problem
with the Jeep?"

"No, there's no problem. I just wondered if
you want the Jeep you asked for."

"Don't you have it?"

"Oh yes, we have it, but we also have a different car that I think you might be interested in.
Would you like to see it?"

The expression on his face was as intriguing as
that of the Cheshire Cat. Rosa nodding, thinking
she wanted to see what he thought was her kind
of car.

She gasped when she saw it, gleaming in the
sun, blood-red with rounded fenders that begged
to be touched. It was a Corvette and looked out
of place on the dusty lot filled with pickup trucks
and SUVs. Sliding her hand along the car's door,
she could only think about how it would drive.
Sex on blacktop sprang to her mind.

"It did that to me, too," William said. She had
forgotten he was there.

"Would you like this one instead? The price is
a little higher than the Jeep."

Rosa didn't care. She opened the door and

slipped into the driver's seat. The control panel called to her, her foot going immediately to the accelerator, her hands to the steering wheel. Breathing in, she recognized the new car smell. Rosa checked the odometer. It read ten miles. The car was brand-new. It didn't matter what it cost, she thought. She wanted this one.

She understood she would stand out in Waymon Valley. Among the trucks, pickups, and SUVs she'd seen during the party at Vida's and along the roads, this car would surely be noticed. But then she didn't have to tell people who she was. The car was something people would expect her to drive. At least she rationalized this as she said, "I'll take it."

A few minutes later, Rosa heard the swish of the glass door opening behind her. Out of the corner of her eye, she saw Adam enter the small room and advance toward her. She took a long, slow breath and gathered herself for the emotional onslaught his presence predicted. After the encounter getting out of his truck, she was unsure how her own body would react to his.

Apparently, she wasn't the only one who noticed the heralding of his arrival. A noticeable intake of air came from a woman farther down the counter. He strode over to Rosa with the ease of a man who walked through familiar territory. Nodding at the woman, he stopped next to Rosa.

"Everything all right?" he asked.

"We're just finishing up," she said, taking note that the woman down the counter was openly staring at him. He'd been back in Waymon Valley two years and this was a small community. Rosa thought that by now the citizens would be used to his presence, but then Adam Osborne would cut a striking figure any place on earth.

He looked at the man at the counter. "William, how's it going?"

"No complaints," he responded. The two men shook hands and Adam leaned against the high counter. "I wanted to make sure everything was in order before leaving."

Rosa didn't comment.

William handed her a copy of the paperwork and dangled the car keys in front of her. Rosa took them, along with a map of Butte and its surrounding area. Coming through a half door next to his workstation, William said, "I had it cleaned and moved around to this door." He raised his arm and pointed to a side door. As Rosa and Adam started for it, she heard a rustle behind her. Several women who had joined the clerk at the counter. Obviously they were trying to get Adam's attention. He glanced back and smiled.

Rosa stopped and looked at them, then at Adam. "Tell me," she asked, "what is your technique?"

"What?" He frowned.

She glanced at the small group. "Bread crumbs? Do you leave a trail and they just follow?"

"It doesn't seem to work with you," he commented.

Rosa couldn't speak. Her mouth went as dry as the sand in Death Valley. Adam held the door open and she passed through it, unable to ignore the smell of him. He wore no cologne she recognized, but there was an essence about him that was unmistakable and not at all unpleasant. Rosa understood it as charisma. She'd seen it on the television screen when he delivered his news reports and she saw it now in person.

Outside sat the red Corvette, its convertible top already down.

Adam let out a low whistle, the same type Rosa had heard whenever she passed a congregation of men, usually those at a construction site, sporting big guts and no shirts. He walked around the car, taking in the smooth lines of it.

"Good thing you're traveling incognito," he said sarcastically.

"You like it?" she returned. Suddenly she wanted his approval.

"It's gorgeous." His eyes were on her when he said that. Rosa colored under her skin. She felt the warmth penetrate her face.

Slipping into the driver's seat, she closed the door. She felt the rich upholstery against her back. The car felt great, as though it already belonged to her. She remembered the first time her brother Digger had gotten a car. It looked like a reject from the junkyard, but he restored it over a long, hot summer and she was right there to help him. Or get in his way. She wasn't sure which.

"You gonna follow me back?" Adam asked.

"I thought I'd look around before going back. Maybe do some shopping, find a Starbucks, get some coffee and watch the news for a few minutes before heading back. You needn't worry. I have a map." She picked it up from the passenger seat. "And a cell phone."

"No Starbucks in Butte, but there's a coffee shop owned by one of my aunts not far from here," Adam told her.

No Starbucks, Rosa thought. She liked coffee, but she didn't crave it the way she did the news.

"Your father said he had a lot of relatives in this area."

"Hundreds," he agreed. "The shop is a few

blocks from here, on the corner of Grant and Elm."

He reached over her and grabbed the map. Rosa's intake of breath noted her surprise. Moving back, he hunkered down and pushed the paper in front of her. "You're here." He pointed to the spot on the map that had a red arrow indicating the car rental agency. "Grant and Elm is right here."

Rosa took the paper. "I'm sure I can find it."

"Okay," he laughed, apparently at her discomfit. "If you're not there by tomorrow, we'll send a posse."

"I've been around the world, remember? I'm sure I can drive five blocks."

"I'm sure you can," Adam teased. "But just for your reference, the Valley is that way."

The shopping area was easy to find after Rosa left Adam. She pulled the car away from the curb and noted how easy it was to drive. It took her mind off the reason for her rapidly beating heart. She was sure there were malls close by, but the downtown had survived the suburban sprawl and its subsequent contraction. Rosa didn't buy much. Mainly she looked in the windows. She'd shopped in some of the best boutiques in the world. She wasn't looking for haute couture here. In Butte she would supplement the clothes she needed for this area. She could use some boots and long-sleeved shirts for the cool nights.

However, what Rosa found herself buying was souvenirs to send to her family and an evening gown. It was a beautiful dress and stood in the window of a small store. Going inside, she got the dress and, after the clerk got over who she was, tried it on. It fit as if a designer had made it for her to model in his next collection. The dress label was from a competitor, but Rosa let that go and bought it anyway. It was scarlet, strapless, and fitted in the front. However, the back portion of the skirt was full. It made her feel elegant, the way she did each time she put on evening gowns to model. This one wasn't for modeling. It was for some special occasion yet to be determined. She smiled knowing that finding a place to wear it in Waymon Valley was as practical as renting a red Corvette for the summer. But practicality wasn't on her mind today.

Storing the dress and other purchases in the car's trunk, Rosa spent another hour looking in the windows and picking up some personal items. Her stomach told her it was time to find that coffee shop.

She couldn't help smiling as she took the driver's seat. She wished she could get the car in front of the computer so she could show her brothers, live and in color, what she'd rented, but she supposed a photo would have to do. She pulled away from the curb and started driving, not really looking at the direction she was taking, more interested in the traffic and the architecture of the buildings.

When her stomach growled again, she started looking for Grant and Elm. She passed the coffee shop before she saw it and drove around looking for a parking space. Finding one, she parallel-parked and patted herself on the back as she left the vehicle. She hadn't parallel-parked in years, but she got into the space on her first try.

"Well, well, what have we here? Where are you going, pretty lady?"

Rosa looked up as a guy spoke to her. There were four of them and she could see they had trouble on their minds. The oldest one couldn't be more than seventeen. They eyed her up and down, giving her chills.

"Not in the mood, boys. It's time you went home. I'm sure you're missing your Similac fix."

"Similac," one of them said in a deep voice that had obviously changed years ago. He started toward her.

"Hey!"

The guy stopped. All of them turned at the sound of the voice that came from Rosa's left. Adam was across the street, striding toward them.

Rosa raised her hand, palm out, stopping Adam. "I've got this one," she said, then turned back to the four guys in front of her. "Okay, guys, split up. Go home."

"Guys, I got this one," one of them mimicked her. He was tall, thin, muscular, beautiful. He took a step toward Rosa. Adam did the same. Both of her hands went up, one toward the young man, her would-be attacker, one toward Adam. She'd been in situations like this before. Her brothers had trained her how to handle them. Unfortunately, the four young guys in front of her, and Adam on the edge of the street, didn't know that. "I told you," she said to Adam. "I got this."

She turned back to the young man. They checked Adam out and dismissed him. After all they had strength in numbers. Or so they thought.

"If you'd like to have children at any time within the next fifty years, I'm warning you," Rosa said. "Turn around and go home."

He laughed. His friends laughed and they took another step forward. Rosa looked him straight in the eye. Her face showed no humor. She took a step in his direction. She stood with her legs apart, her weight balanced evenly in the center of her body. A moment later he broke into a run. Just before he got to her, Rosa moved. Too late, he couldn't stop. Momentum propelled him forward like a guided missile. As he reached her, she rolled her body, scooping him over her back. He landed with a thud on the hard ground. His friends gasped. He sucked air into lungs that had expelled it in a fast whoosh.

The rest of them came toward her. Adam moved, too. Without looking in Adam's direction, she stopped him with an outstretched hand. The three attackers advanced on her. She grabbed one of their hands and wrenched it around. His body somersaulted in the air, then went down. He hit the ground with a moan of pain. The second propelled himself into the air. She stopped him with a well-placed kick with her booted foot. The impact had him hopping backward and wheezing in pain. Tears sprang to his eyes and his knees buckled. The last one looked at her and the carnage on the ground. Raising his hands in defeat, he ran off.

Rosa turned and looked at the three remaining young men. "*Men*," she said, shaking her head. "You never listen." For a moment she watched the writhing group. Then she turned and walked into the coffee shop, not even looking at Adam, missing the huge smile on his face.

* * *

"Make that two," Adam told the clerk serving Rosa coffee.

"Hi, Adam." A wide smile appeared on the clerk's face.

"Pandora," he acknowledged. "Meet the newest resident of Waymon Valley, Rosa Clayton." To Rosa he said, "Pandora Ellis. She's my cousin."

"I know who she is," Pandora said. She looked at Rosa and smiled shyly.

"Pandora is a very intriguing name," Rosa said.

"My father claims it was because I was born to keep secrets."

"More intrigue," Rosa said.

"I have no secrets, so I have no need to expose them."

Pandora set their coffees on the counter and Adam pulled out a bill to pay for them.

"You're coming to the party, right?" Adam asked.

"Sure," she said. "I wouldn't miss it."

"See you later," he said to his cousin. "Tell Aunt Marge I say hello."

Pandora nodded and moved to help the next customer.

Adam took both cups.

"Whose party?" Rosa asked.

"Dad's." He moved toward a table near the windows. "It'll be his seventieth and apparently the whole town is getting into the celebration."

"That's wonderful," Rosa said. "I'm sure Bailey is loving all the attention."

"Is he ever?" Adam agreed. "It's in August. I'm sure he'd like you to come."

Rosa smiled. "I'd like that."

Adam set the cups on the table. Rosa picked hers up. "I'm not staying," she said.

"I thought you wanted to watch the news." Adam glanced at the overhead television that was set to WNN. He recognized the newscaster, a former colleague and friend. "From what Vida tells me, you need regular fixes of world news. I suppose that's why you know so much about me."

"I thought you had things to do today," Rosa said, ignoring his comment. "Don't you need to hurry back to Waymon Valley and get them done?"

"They can wait." Adam had a ton of things to do. The ranch didn't run itself. He knew his father would take care of whatever needed doing. Why was he lying to Rosa Clayton?

Following her through the door, he waved good-bye to Pandora. "I'll walk you to your car and follow you back."

"I don't need you to take care of me," she said.

"I know. I've seen you in action. Maybe I need you to take care of me."

"I doubt that," she said, taking a sip of her latte.

"Where'd you learn that?" he asked.

She didn't pretend to misunderstand him. "I told you. I grew up with brothers. You said I was the baby of the family. I am, and that meant I had to learn to hold my own."

"You can certainly do that. I was impressed at how well you handled yourself. Did you take self-defense classes?"

"In many parts of the world," she answered. "I was a woman alone. Fairly good looking."

"Absolutely beautiful," he contradicted.

"I'll take that," she said. Adam saw her color darken. "All women like compliments. After one of the models was mugged in New York, we all enrolled in self-defense courses."

"Have you had to put the learning to practice?"

"More times than you would think," she said. "Many men think that because I look this way, I owe them something and if I'm not agreeable to their demands, then they are free to take what they want. It appears the world is not a safe place. But those were only kids today." She glanced at the shop windows as if they were still there.

"Yeah, kids, six feet tall and outweighing you by at least fifty pounds. Not to mention there were four of them."

"Well, I had surprise on my side. And a little bit of training."

"Are you going to be all right from here on?" he asked. He didn't just mean on the road back to the Valley. He meant from here *on*. He knew seeing her further was trying the promise he'd made himself, but Rosa was proving she wasn't the stereotype he'd assumed she would be.

"I think so. I don't expect to run into four teenagers again and if I do, I'm sure the story of what happened today will have permeated the entire town, or at least the high school, within half an hour. Now I have fear on my side."

She smiled the smile he'd seen countless times from billboards. At the time he didn't know who she was, but with eyes three feet wide and that tantalizing smile, she'd gotten his attention. Back then she was just paper, cardboard at most, unknown and safe. Now she stood less than a foot from him, and the animated flesh-and-blood woman was inconceivable as a comparison to a paper figure.

Rosa got into the car and placed her cup in the car's cup holder.

"You don't look very fearsome." He brought his

attention back to the present. "Especially sitting in that decadent car."

"It is decadent, isn't it?"

He looked at it again, his eyes running along the side from front to back, before coming back to rest on her.

"But you wouldn't want to meet me in a dark alley," she told him. "Or a lighted street for that matter." She laughed at her own joke. The tinkling of her voice aroused him.

"All right, drive on," he said. Standing up, he stepped back from the car.

Rosa turned the key and the engine roared to life, then purred. His hands itched to drive the mighty beast. He wanted to tame it, show it who had the real power.

"Be careful," he told her. "It's a powerful car. You don't want it to get away from you."

"Remember those brothers of mine? They taught me to drive, too."

"I'll have to meet these brothers one day."

"Maybe," she said. She pulled out. Adam stared after her. The car wove through the early afternoon traffic. She didn't look back. Adam knew she wouldn't. He stared after the car, looking at the path she'd taken long after she'd turned the corner and was completely out of sight.

Rosa Clayton had hidden talents. A couple of them came out today. Adam found himself wanting to know what the others were. And how pleasurable it could be to discover them one at a time.

Rosa felt every one of the four hundred horses kicking their front legs up and raring to burst through the starting gate. Pressing the accelerator, she opened the gates and let the horses have their way. Getting off the highway, which would take her straight back to the Valley, Rosa noticed a side road on the map. It was straight and deserted. She pressed her foot on the accelerator. The car responded with erotic pleasure, needing only a soft touch to have it purring. Inching the speedometer up past the legal limit, she let the wind whip her curls about her face.

She couldn't help the rodeo yell that came from her mouth. It went with the car. Behind her, a tail of dust defined her route. She felt as if she were about to be airborne, launched into the sky, although the car hugged the road solidly. It cornered with the lightness of a slow walk and took a curve as if car and road were engineered as one tandem unit.

By the time she pulled up in front of Vida's house, the need for speed had abated by only a minuscule amount. However, she was careful to reduce the volume of her radio to normal hearing decibels and drive under the residential limit.

Vida met her at the door. "I thought you said you were renting a Jeep." Her eyes looked past Rosa to the car in her driveway.

"I was, but this one is so much more fun."

"It's just like you," Vida said. "Take me for a ride. And I wanna drive, too."

Vida disappeared for a moment, grabbing her purse and a hat from the table, before returning to the door. Vida loved hats and rarely went out without one. Within minutes they were riding along.

Vida scanned the dash in front of her. "I always wanted to own one of these." Her hands ran over the soft leather like a caress.

"Why didn't you get one?" Rosa knew they'd both made a fortune modeling.

"Practicality," she said. "On the road there was no need and out here it's not a practical car."

"Screw practicality," Rosa said. "If you want it, get it."

Vida smiled. "How would it look for a poor, struggling designer to be driving around in a red Corvette?"

"You're not poor. And why would it look strange? You'd look prosperous. And why shouldn't you?" The two women glanced at each other, sharing a knowing smile.

Rosa pulled the car to the edge of the road. She threw the gearshift into neutral, pulled the parking brake up, and got out. "Your turn," she told Vida. Vida didn't hesitate. She got out and rushed around the front of the car. Her limp was nearly gone, yet she put her hand on the car for support several times.

"Fasten your seat belt," Vida said, and pulled onto the road. Within minutes they were out of town and Vida was speeding along the road leading past the Osborne Ranch.

"Doesn't she drive like a dream?" Rosa asked.

"Oh yes," Vida agreed. "I have *got* to get me one of these."

"Practicality aside."

"Practicality can go take a leap," she said, without any malice in her voice.

As they passed the Osborne Ranch, Adam was turning into the driveway. Vida blew the horn and waved but didn't slow down. Yet Rosa had a clear view of the anger on his face.

"Are the two of you getting along any better?" Vida asked as if they'd been discussing Adam.

"I try to steer clear of him." Rosa didn't tell her that the effort wasn't working well.

"Was that before or after you two had lunch? And breakfast from what I hear?"

Rosa stared at her. "Am I being followed or something?"

Vida shook her head. "I ran into Bailey. He told me the two of you met on horseback this morning and that Adam had taken you to get the car. I suppose Adam told him about lunch."

"Pull over," Rosa said. "You're only supposed to drive short distances."

"I'm fine."

"I know. But let's not push the leg." She knew what Adam's expression had meant. And while she wanted to tell him to jump off the nearest mountain, it was Vida who would be hurt if she pushed herself too hard.

Although Vida no longer limped, he'd been adamant in reminding her that Vida couldn't drive as far as Butte. Speeding along the road wasn't good for her, either.

"This car is so easy to drive, the touch so light, I could go all the way to North Dakota."

"Pull over," Rosa said.

Vida slowed the car and stopped. There was no shoulder to speak of, so most of the car sat on the one-lane road. Again the two switched seats. Rosa took the wheel and headed back to town. Her own house was along the way.

"Can we stop a moment?" Vida asked as they neared her driveway. "I haven't seen your place."

"Sure," Vida said. "I thought, since it was Adam's, that you'd been here before."

"I have, but I want to see what you've done with it." It had to be the designer in Vida. She was forever discussing how she would have decorated any room the two of them were in.

Inside the house, Rosa poured the leftover lemonade into two glasses and took them to the living room. Vida looked around. She took in the floor and walls and paintings. "The house looks great. It hasn't changed much. I'm sure you'll add a few touches of your own. And it's time someone lived here."

"How long did Adam live here?"

"Not long. He moved in and almost immediately got an assignment. Like us, he was always on the road. He maintained an address in D.C. We were all surprised when he showed up here, suitcases in hand, planning to stay."

Rosa knew about the condo in D.C. She'd seen a spread on him in *GQ* a few years ago. The place was upscale, using a thirties theme of black-and-white art deco. She wondered if he still owned it.

"Maybe his dad was the reason he returned."

"Bailey can use some looking after, but Adam could have hired someone to do that."

"A nurse is no replacement for family."

"He has a lot of family here. Any number of his cousins would have moved in with Bailey. Adam was about to get the job of his life. Then suddenly he's back in Waymon Valley."

"You think there's another reason for him being here?" Rosa thought about that. Usually that meant a woman.

Vida was nodding. "He hasn't said what, but I know Adam. And he's not telling us everything."

"You two have a very special relationship."

"The Osbornes and I have a special relationship. I learned to ride horses on their ranch. Medea taught me how to make the best corn bread in the West. Bailey told me stories about the settlement of Waymon Valley that were more alive than anything I learned in a school history class. And Adam and I practically grew up together on roads that are now streets."

"I understand a little more now."

"What do you mean?" Vida sipped her lemonade.

"He's extremely protective of you."

"Not just me." She smiled. "It's his nature. He's a sucker for a woman in jeopardy. He'd do the same for anyone."

Rosa wasn't so sure—although he had come to her aid in Butte when he thought she needed it.

"Have you lost your mind?" Adam nearly shouted when Rosa pulled into the driveway after dropping Vida off at her house. She opened the door and he brushed by her, walking into the middle of the room. He stopped as if he hadn't decided what to do after getting inside.

"Not to my knowledge," Rosa answered, her tone as soft as his was harsh.

"Why did you let Vida go roaring down the road like that? If she'd hit something, she could break that leg again, not to mention breaking your pretty little neck."

"Welcome," Rosa said, acknowledging his lack of manners. "Won't you come in?" She closed the door.

He glared at her but didn't bother saying hello.

"Vida may have been roaring, but it wasn't down the road. And her leg was not broken. *And* in case you haven't noticed, she'd not an invalid.

She seemed to do very well taking care of herself without you around for several years to my *personal* knowledge. You're acting like her father and even if you were she's way too old for you to make decisions for her."

Rosa moved to the counter that separated the kitchen from the large living room. "Why are you really here? This is no longer your house. You don't have the right to come barging in here reprimanding me as if I were a child."

He took the time to look her up and down, slowly as if he were deciding something. "I can see you're no child." His voice was low and sexy.

Rosa's body flashed hot under his stare. After a moment of enduring it, she said, "What is it about me that you don't like?"

"You're beautiful," he replied. "Too beautiful."

It was the last thing she expected to hear. Adam certainly wasn't like other men she'd met. Most of them followed her around like a lapdog. Adam followed her around, but only to get a rise out of her. And she seemed to play right into his hands.

"Beauty isn't something I can do anything about," she said. "My looks were determined by my parents, the ones I never knew. But it's worked for me. And it worked for you. Don't think your face didn't get you into places where others would have been turned away." She paused a moment. "But you're not here to talk about my face." She looked at him a moment. His expression was unreadable. "Why don't you tell me about *her*?"

"Her? Who?"

"The other woman. The beautiful one. The one who was too beautiful."

His shoulders dropped a second later. Rosa

knew she'd touched a nerve. She moved around the kitchen counter. Opening the refrigerator, she took out a carton of ice cream and filled two bowls. Adding chocolate syrup, nuts, and cherries to one, she took them to the living room.

"Well, follow me," she said, using her arm to wave him over.

She handed him a bowl along with the syrup, nuts, and cherries and sat down on one of the huge sofas in front of the fireplace.

"Am I in therapy?" he asked, tasting his ice cream.

"Not today," she said. "Therapy involves lying down, with soft music in the background and hot oils."

"I'll keep that in mind. What does ice cream indicate?"

"Friendship . . . maybe."

"Maybe?" he questioned.

"You don't like me, remember?"

He nodded. "Why'd you come here for your vacation? With all the cities open to you, why Waymon Valley?"

She stopped him. "Oh no, this is your floor show, not mine. You're going to do the talking."

"Did I agree to this?"

"Of course you did. It's healthy. It'll make you less cynical."

His look said he didn't believe her, but he took a seat and laid his head back against the upholstery. For a long time he said nothing. Rosa didn't think he was going to. He seemed to have drifted back in time to a place where only he and his demons knew the address.

Chapter 4

It was unusual for Adam to come across someone like Rosa. Her name indicated delicacy, someone who needed and wanted pampering. And heaven knows her body spoke of the type of woman who needed caring for. But her disposal of four healthy teenagers in the "male out for trouble" category proved she'd passed the shrinking violet period long ago.

Adam admired her ability to keep her head and protect herself. She reminded him a lot of Maureen. The two women were radically different in looks and personality, but Adam hadn't had to worry about either. At least that's what he thought, until the police knocked on his door at 3:00 AM and took him to the morgue to identify the body of camerawoman Maureen Carter.

Squeezing his eyes shut, Adam closed off the mental image of Maureen lying naked under a sheet, her face gray with death. And the aftermath of her passing. He'd seen worlds torn apart. Witnessed the worst that man could do to himself, but when that cruelty touched him, he never knew how deeply it could cut, how much it could change his life.

Purposely he pulled the image of Rosa Clayton to mind. She was sitting across from him, but he visualized her in the car—her hair a mass of long curls pulled into a swinging ponytail, her face clear, unadorned by a frame of hair, her makeup flawless, and her smile inviting his mouth to ravish hers.

His eyes flew open. She stared at him. Standing up, he moved to the fireplace. Abruptly he dropped thoughts of Rosa, although his body, aroused from mental pictures, took longer to resume a normal state.

Rosa was about to say something. He could feel it, but the ringing of the telephone stopped her. Both of them turned to look at the white instrument on the table next to where she sat.

She picked up the receiver and a moment later, her eyes met his. She hadn't said anything beyond hello.

"I'll give you some privacy," he said. As he started to move, she stood up.

"It's for you."

When he turned, she was holding the phone out to him. Who could this be? Adam hadn't lived here in years. Who had this phone number other than his father and people in the Valley? But none of them would call him here.

Putting the phone to his ear, he said, "Hello."

"Adam, good to hear your voice."

"Not interested," he said, recognizing the deep bass tone of Benjamin Masterson. Ben was a producer at WNN, his former employer. He'd called Adam several times, always with a more lucrative offer to get him back to D.C. and a news job.

"You haven't heard what I have to say," Ben said. "At least give me a chance."

"It doesn't matter what you're offering. I'm not interested."

Adam could imagine Ben in his big office overlooking the Potomac. He knew Ben had deliberately used this line. Adam had been home for a few weeks one summer and done some work from here. He'd called Ben and left the number for him to return the call. Apparently, he'd kept it. If he'd called on Adam's cell phone, his name and number would display on the tiny screen and Adam wouldn't answer the call.

"It'll make your career," Ben insisted.

"I don't have a career," Adam said. "Get someone else. I'm out of the business. Good-bye."

Without waiting for Ben to ring off, Adam hung up. Turning around, he saw Rosa staring at him perplexed. He could tell she wanted an explanation. But he wasn't ready to explain himself.

"Why?" she asked.

"Why what?"

"Why don't you have a career? You were the fair-haired boy, moving up the ranks, the anchor's chair practically had your name stitched into the fabric. And without warning you're gone."

"How do you know so much about me? You aren't even in the business."

"According to my family, I'm a news junkie. I watch the news. And I read. You know, inquiring minds . . ."

"My life isn't exactly written up in grocery store rags."

"No, it isn't. On the road, one of the models read a lot of *Variety* and news magazines. She had a brother in sportscasting and he'd fill her in. So of course, she'd tell the rest of us all the juicy gossip."

He didn't nod, but Rosa could see agreement in his actions.

"I have to go now," he said.

"Coward," Rosa said when he began walking toward the exit.

Adam stopped in midstride. He turned back to her. "I am not a coward."

"Touched a nerve, did I?" She smiled and he understood why men thought she was delicious enough to eat.

"You've dodged two of my questions by retreating. Sounds like a coward to me."

Adam's life was personal. He didn't have to answer to anyone. His reasons for leaving the rat race behind were his own. And the beautiful women in his past had let him down. But when he saw Rosa standing there, he could think of nothing to say. Only something to do. Before he knew what was happening, he'd crossed the room and cupped her face in his hands.

He saw the flash of surprise in her eyes, quickly replaced by awareness. Adam's heart was racing, and his mind was on sensory overload. In one fell swoop he lowered his mouth to hers. Adam intended to satisfy an itch. He understood as soon as their lips touched that the itch was greater than he'd known. His arms went around her slender body and he gathered her close. His tongue dove into her mouth, the two mating and dancing the ancient tango. Rosa relaxed in his arms. He felt her body melt into his as if they were made for each other. The thought should have had him forcing her away, but the truth was he wanted her close. He hadn't felt anything so good in years. She wasn't enamored by his looks or his celebrity. She'd just as soon throw him out as she would feed him ice cream.

Lifting his head slightly, he repositioned it, still holding her as close as possible. He felt her push back, but they didn't separate. Her eyes were closed. They opened slowly like someone waking from a pleasant dream. Adam lowered his mouth and took hers again.

What had gotten into him? He was holding fire in his arms and he knew it. The flame was bright, beautiful, enticing, but he'd dealt with fire before and he knew better than to put his hand in the flame. So why did she feel so good? Why did her mere presence send his hormones into overdrive? Why did her mouth tantalize his like a drug he couldn't get enough of? Adam had no answers. Maybe he did, but he was unwilling to let them have a voice. At least not now. He pulled her even closer, never thinking two people could withstand this much closeness without passing through each other.

His head bobbed with hers. Their mouths danced in unison. Every inch of them touched. Her arms were around him, his circumventing her. He could feel her heart beating, his own thundering in his head. Knowing this was a different experience for him, Adam didn't consider stopping. He deepened the kiss, his hands running long, slow strokes down her back, gathering her closer, caressing her, feeling her muscles contract and relax under his touch. It aroused him just to feel her, smell the exotic scent of her hair and body.

Suddenly he lifted his head, breaking contact as if they'd been forced to separate.

Adam wanted to hold her, to put her head on his shoulder and stand like this for the rest of the day. But logic caught up with him. He stepped back, putting some distance between them. He wasn't sorry he'd kissed her. He'd wanted to kiss her since she came off the plane, looking tired and worn. She no longer looked like that. Her face was healthy, her eyes drowsy, and he could think of nothing other than the huge bed in the loft and carrying her up the stairs.

But this was wrong. She was the wrong woman.

The thought of taking a jacket occurred to Rosa when she left the house. After Adam's exit, she couldn't stay there. Her mind kept replaying the kiss, the feel of his arms around her, the imprint of his body aligned with hers. She got in the car and started driving. She would have gone to Vida's, but her friend would have known something had changed and within minutes Rosa would have been pouring out all the details.

So she headed the car away from Adam and let the engine take her as far as it would go without leaving the state. She was in the mountains. The air was thin. She'd forgotten how far above sea level she was. Her lungs labored to maintain breath. Rosa stopped and looked out. The scenery was awesome. Dark mountains in the distance were as imposing in height as the Grand Canyon was in depth. Slipping out of the car, Rosa leaned against a boulder.

She took a deep breath and closed her eyes. Instantly Adam's image surfaced against her closed lids. She could see his face coming toward her, blurring as it lowered to kiss her. Her body went hot against the chill in the air. Her eyes flew open, and she pushed herself away from the rock. She swallowed to wet her throat and took several deep breaths.

Rosa remained there until she started to shiver. She walked back through the paths to the place she'd left the shiny new car. Starting the engine, she turned on the heater to dispel the coldness that seemed to seep into her bones. It was irresponsible to come out without a jacket and drive into the hills. Rosa hadn't been thinking rationally at the time. She was running, getting away from Adam and the memory of the scene in her living room.

The Corvette drove like a dream. Being raised with older brothers had its rewards. They'd taught her about cars. The four-hundred-horsepower engine with 542 foot-pounds of torque purred with the smoothness of water running down a straight glass pane. Rosa sped along the road, the speedometer needle well past the limit. With the top down, the wind ripped her hair back from her face.

She gave it no thought. The radio blared a country-western song and she belted out the lyrics as if she were on the stage of the Grand Ole Opry.

She was almost home when she saw a truck parked along the side of the road. It had pulled over, too far over, she thought. In fact, the pitch of the truck must have been forty degrees off normal. She slowed down. Usually she would have passed it without a backward thought. She was a woman alone and while she could defend herself, there was no need courting danger. But this wasn't one of the major crime capitals of the world. This was Waymon Valley where crime was low and people helped each other.

As she was passed the truck, she saw a man inside. He was slumped against the steering wheel. She recognized him. Stopping, Rosa jumped from the car, not bothering to stop the engine or close the door. She ran back to the truck and pulled at the door. It was locked. Tapping on the window, she called to the man inside. Slowly he raised his head. His body fell back against the seat as if it were a grocery bag shifting from a sudden stop.

"Bailey," she shouted. "Open the door." His movements were sluggish, but he eventually touched the button and she heard the click as the locks released. Yanking the door outward, she touched his head and looked him over, trying to see if he had any visible injuries. "Are you all right?"

He opened his mouth, but nothing came out. A moment later he tried again, but the words came out garbled. She remembered quickly that Adam had told her he'd had a heart attack. And Bailey had said he had a bad ticker. He was having another one now. Rosa recognized it. Her mother had had a heart attack, too. Rosa hadn't been in the room when it happened, but she knew the symptoms. Her mind raced as she tried to remember what to do. She had a brother and a sister-in-law who were doctors, but none of their medical training had rubbed off on her. *What should I do?* she asked herself. Then she remembered her sister-in-law Stephanie. Aspirin. Rachel had given her mother aspirin. Rosa didn't have aspirin. She usually took Tylenol and she had none in the car.

"Medicine, Bailey?" She controlled her voice, forcing herself not to shout. "Do you have any medicine?"

He said nothing. She rifled through his pockets frantically, but came up empty.

She needed to get him to a hospital. And fast. Seconds could mean the difference between living and dying.

"Move over," she ordered.

He didn't budge. He couldn't. She wasn't going to be able to lift him or carry him or get him around to the other side of the truck. And she couldn't get him out and into her car. Releasing his seat belt, she pushed him over as far as she could, then climbed into the driver's seat, thankful that she was a *skinny girl.* Rosa turned the key. The engine groaned, but didn't catch. She tried it again. This time it started, but the moment she moved the gearshift, it sputtered and stopped.

"Come on," Rosa coaxed, trying to get the truck to start by the force of her will. She tried the key again. The motor roared loudly. Rosa tapped the accelerator several times, giving gas to the engine.

Gingerly putting the truck into gear, she pressed the accelerator. The tires spun on the unpaved surface; then suddenly the truck leapt forward.

Rosa quickly moved her foot from the gas pedal. She didn't want the truck to die on her again. She followed the uneven ground until she got the four tires on paved road.

She could drive anything. Growing up with her brothers, she and her sister Luanne had learned a lot about driving. Rosa had tackled everything from a minibike and a tractor to a big rig. Rosa pulled out of the ditch and scuttled around her own car, then headed toward town as fast as she dared.

The truck needed overhauling. The engine chugged and Rosa couldn't get much acceleration out of it. She pushed the pedal closer to the floor. The truck groaned in protest and she backed off. She couldn't afford for the engine to cut out on her before she found the hospital.

Her mind raced to remember where she'd seen the sign with the huge white H on it. Where was the hospital?

Bailey groaned. Rosa wasn't sure if that was due to the position he was in or if it was his heart. She spoke softly to him. "It's going to be all right," she said. "I'm getting help. Just hold on. We'll be at the hospital in no time." All the while she was praying the truck kept going.

She put a hand on his back and rubbed it soothingly while continuing to drive as fast as she could. Finally she saw the sign. Turning, she had to use both hands on the steering wheel of the big, unfamiliar truck. She pulled into the circular driveway below the lighted EMERGENCY ROOM sign. Jumping down, she rushed inside and yelled, "Heart attack! I need help."

Within seconds the place was filled with people rushing toward the door. Rosa followed them. She pointed to the truck.

"Bailey Osborne," she said. "He needs help. He's having a heart attack." She sucked in air as she spoke, giving each word a full breath. "I couldn't give him anything. I didn't know anything to give him. He had no medicine on him. I had no time to search the truck."

"We'll take care of him," a nurse said. Her voice was soft and calm, although their feet sped across the ground to the truck. Rosa knew the tactic was to calm her down. She took a long breath.

They got him out of the truck and on to a gurney. Immediately, he was hurried away. Rosa started to follow. A nurse turned to her. "Park the truck," she said.

It was the first time she'd thought of the vehicle. Rosa got back in the driver's seat. She hadn't turned the engine off. White smoke came from the exhaust system. The engine coughed. Biting her bottom lip, she eased it into gear, but it protested. It was hard to steer and as heavy as an eighteen-wheeler. Slowly it rolled into a parking space. Before she could turn the key, the engine died. Rosa gave it little thought. She left it, running back inside the sliding doors and searching for Bailey. Her head swung from right to left. She didn't see him. At the desk, she asked, "Where is he?"

"Exam room one," the nurse said.

Rosa turned to leave, but the nurse stopped her. "Do you need some information?" Rosa asked. "His name is Bailey Osborne and he lives at—"

The nurse stopped her. "We know who he is," she said. "We have all his information."

Rosa had forgotten how small this town was. Naturally, they would know who he was.

"You're not a relative, are you?"

Rosa shook her head. She must be the only person in the Valley who didn't know who Rosa was and why she was here.

"Could you tell us when this happened? The doctors will need as much information as possible."

"I don't know," Rosa said. "His truck was parked along the side of the road, not far from his ranch. I stopped when I saw it and found him."

"How long ago was that?"

"About ten minutes. When I didn't find any medicine, I drove straight here. It was all I could think to do."

"You did fine," the nurse assured her. "He's with the best doctors we have."

"When can I see him?"

"The doctors will let you know. In the meantime, we need to get in touch with a relative. There's a phone over there. You might want to call someone." The nurse nodded at a few chairs that were placed against a wall outside the area.

The woman, who was a fortyish blonde with deep wrinkles in her face from years of too much sun, assumed Rosa knew the Osbornes well enough to know where to find Adam. Rosa knew nothing. She didn't even have a phone number for the house. But she would start there.

She reached for her purse to get her cell phone and found the space on her shoulder empty. She'd forgotten it, left it in the car. When she saw Bailey, all other thoughts had gone out of her head. The pay phone stared at her. At least she didn't need money to make a call.

Adam's pickup skidded to a stop in front of the Corvette. Something was wrong. The door was open and the car was empty. Quickly he jumped down from his seat and strode back to the car. The engine was running. Rosa's purse lay on the passenger seat, her cell phone next to it. Picking the phone up reminded him of his own. He'd run over it when he finally calmed down enough to return home. He'd been cursing himself for going mad this afternoon.

Now he was scared. Where was she? He looked around, scanning the land for Rosa. She was nowhere to be seen. His heart stopped, then beat faster.

"Rosa," he called, hoping she was nearby. He couldn't think of a reason she should leave the car running and her personal items behind. He looked around, calling her name louder. There was no response. A coldness ran through him.

"Where is she?" he muttered. There was nothing here but open range. He could see clear to the mountains, his view unobstructed.

Reaching down, he turned the car off and pulled the keys out. Gathering her personal items, he opened her phone and dialed Vida's number. If anyone would know where she was, it was Vida. The phone was smaller than his hand.

"Vida," he said when she answered.

"Adam, I'm so glad you called. Rosa has been trying to find you."

"I'm at her car. Where is she?"

"The hospital."

"Hospital?" He stood up straighter, his throat closing, his body rigid as if it were waiting for a punch. "Is she all right?" His voice was tight.

"It's not her," Vida said. There was a long pause. "Adam, it's Bailey."

"Dad?"

"He's had another heart attack. Rosa found him along the side of the road. She got him to the hospital. She's been trying to find you for about an hour. I've been calling your cell phone, too."

"It doesn't work," he shouted into the phone. As soon as Vida had said Bailey, Adam had climbed into the truck and turned it around.

"I'm on my way." He clicked the phone shut

and spun the tires as he burned up the road leading to the Valley's only hospital.

In one fluid motion, as Adam pulled into the hospital lot, he was out of the truck and running toward the door. Rosa hung up the pay phone as she saw him come inside. She ran toward him. Adam grabbed her and pulled her against him. "Is he all right?"

"I don't know," she told him. "They haven't let me see him since we arrived."

Taking her hand, he went to the desk and spoke to the nurse. He had to leave Rosa behind when he went to ICU to see his father. Bailey lay pale and small in the bed. He was asleep and Adam was only allowed to stay ten minutes. Adam said nothing, knowing his dad needed to rest. They'd run the scenario before. Bailey had to take better care of himself. Anger leaked into Adam's thoughts, but he pushed it aside. There was plenty of time later to discuss Bailey's regiment of needs.

Returning to the waiting room, he looked for Rosa. She was gone.

Don't panic, Rosa told herself as she walked. Her shoes were flat and she was wearing pants. She was thankful she'd donned them this morning instead of the heels and skirts she wore to the point of them being a uniform. Darkness had fallen. That big sky was filled with stars, but no moon, and frankly at this point, it was scary. The beauty of it escaped her. She knew where she was. At least she thought she knew, but she'd just as soon have a bright light to steer her.

She could kill Adam Osborne right now. Her keys had been missing when she got back to the car. So was her cell phone and her purse. She was stranded. Seconds counted when she'd found Bailey. Thoughts of her own car and personal items hadn't entered her head. Finding the hospital, finding help was more important. But now she wished she'd taken her keys when she left the car. It still sat along the road like a shiny red paperweight.

Adam had gone in to see Bailey. The drama was over. Her frantic attempt to find him had pumped her system with anxiety. Now that he was here and Bailey was receiving care, her thoughts returned to herself.

And the car!

She'd left it running along the road. That was hours ago. She had to get back to it. Everything was in her purse, credit cards, cash, keys. She needed to get them. She had Bailey's keys. She'd drive back and pick up her own car. Rosa spoke to the nurse and told her to let Adam know that she'd left if he came out. In all likelihood, she expected to be back before he returned.

The moment she turned the key in the ignition, she remembered the engine had died. No amount of coaxing and praying would make it start again. Rosa got out. She looked at the hospital entrance and thought of going back in and waiting for Adam. Then she realized, it hadn't taken that long to get to the hospital and she really wanted to get her purse before someone found it. And in a car that obvious, it would be noticed.

The car couldn't be more than a few miles away. She'd been afraid for Bailey during the drive to the hospital and the truck wouldn't go very fast. At the entrance, Rosa looked for a taxi, but was reminded by the emptiness of any vehicles that this was Waymon Valley and outside was only sky.

She looked up as she continued to walk. The sky told her nothing about her location. She could only guess that she was walking in the right direction. No one had come along this road since she began walking. She wasn't sure if that was good or bad. She thought of her brothers and her sister. They gave her credit for being rational and sensible. What she was doing now was neither. The house was at least five miles from the car. But going back to Bailey's was farther.

Her legs were tired and her arms felt as if she were carrying thirty-pound weights, yet she held nothing but air. Rosa glanced around her. It hadn't been dark when she started out. Now the night noises, crickets, and cicadas played a symphony of sounds, but she thought of Adam's warning— bears, snakes, coyotes. She tried walking faster, but her legs wouldn't let her. She was too tired. She concentrated on putting one foot in front of the other. She couldn't stop. She remembered stories of people dying from exposure, freezing to death. It was summer, there was no threat of that, but the animals were a real possibility.

Don't panic, she thought again. *People who panic don't think rationally. You'll be home soon. Safe. You'll laugh about this in the morning. But that would be morning.* Right now her eyes played tricks on her. She could see bears in the darkness. The yellow eyes of coyotes or wolves formed in front of her. Her footsteps became starts and stops. Echoes plagued her from behind.

Lights swung around a corner, startling her. She didn't remember a corner. They seemed to come from nowhere. One minute it was dark; the next a flood of bright light brought the road into view. Instinctively, Rosa dropped to the ground, making herself as small as possible. As much as she wanted a ride, she didn't know who would be in the car or truck. It was better to be safe and alone than picked up by someone she might have to fight. She had no energy for fighting.

The truck passed her. It wasn't a car. Suddenly it slowed and stopped. A man got out and called her name.

It was Adam.

She stood up. "I'm here," she said. She wanted to run to him, run into his arms and thank him for finding her. But she was too tired, beyond tired, exhausted.

Adam ran.

He reached her, pulling her into his arms. Rosa was a rag doll, too weak to do anything but let him. Her arms flailed and she sagged against him.

After a moment, he roughly pushed her back. "You should be horsewhipped for a stunt like this," he said. "Why did you leave the hospital?"

His words were harsh, but his arms were caressing. She leaned against him, breathing softly, until he turned them both and led her to the truck. No seat ever felt so soft or so welcoming. She was safe. Adam had found her. Leaning her head back against the upholstery, she closed her eyes. A moment later, she felt him reach over and fasten her seat belt. He didn't say anything when he climbed into the warm cabin. He started the truck and pulled it back onto the road, completing a U-turn and heading in the direction Rosa had been walking. Rosa's eyelids felt as though they were cemented closed. She was finally safe.

She wanted to take Adam's arm and lay her head on his shoulder. She settled for the headrest.

"Wake up, Rosa." She heard Adam speaking. His voice seemed to be a long way off. She opened her eyes and closed them again. They felt as if someone had thrown sand in her face. "Wake up," he said. "You're home."

"Home?" She forced herself to keep her eyes open. "We're home?"

"You're home," he said.

Leaning forward, she reached for him. Her hands touched his shoulders and he lifted her from the seat and set her on her feet.

"I'm sorry," she told him, trying to steady herself. "It was a long walk."

Shaking her head to clear it, she looked at the sky. The stars were still overhead. They were high enough to see the curvature of the universe. "How's Bailey?" she asked.

"Probably better than you are."

He led her into the house. "I think you should get some sleep. Will you be all right?"

She nodded. He turned to leave, then stopped. Pulling something out of his pocket, he turned and placed her purse and cell phone on the counter.

"Adam."

He looked at her.

"Thank you. Thanks for finding me. I know you have Bailey on your mind, but thanks for coming for me."

He looked like he wanted to say something, then thought better of it. "We can talk about this later. You're dead on your feet. You need rest."

"I went to the car, but the keys were gone. I didn't take them with me."

"I know," he said.

"I wasn't thinking about the car when I saw Bailey was having a heart attack. I only thought to get help."

"I understand, Rosa." He seemed exasperated. He had other things on his mind and she was too tired to think about what she was saying. "Good night," he said.

Rosa stared at the closed door. She heard the motor of his truck start up. She felt sorry for what she'd put him through. His father was very sick, in the hospital, and he was driving around the country worrying about her. *Worrying.* The word stopped her. Was he worried about her? Or just angry at her?

Chapter 5

Pain sliced up Rosa's back. She moaned, but the sound that she heard when she woke the next morning *couldn't* have come from her. It wasn't her sound. It was something she heard from her brothers the morning after a game of basketball. She understood them now. Everything hurt. Every muscle in her body shouted in protest of yesterday's escapade. She groaned as she tried to sit up. Flopping back against the pillows, she took deep breaths. They hurt, too.

She needed a good soak in a tub of bubbles. There was no chance of her riding that morning. With effort she pushed herself up and went into the bathroom, where she filled the tub with soapy water and submerged herself. The hot water had to make her feel better, because she was unsure if she could get out of the tub if it didn't. After an hour and her filling the tub three times to keep the water hot, she pulled her pruning body out of the water and dressed.

She felt better. Her muscles still ached, but their screams had subsided, especially after she downed two aspirins. The car was still sitting out on the road. It was time to do something about it. She needed it and mentally went through several methods of her getting it back. Adam had left her purse on the counter. Her keys were probably in it. She could walk back to the car. The thought of doing that received protest from her body. She could walk to the stables and get a horse, then drive three miles an hour with it tethered to the car to get it back to the stable. Calling Adam came to mind, but she quickly rejected the idea. He had his father to think about, and more than that, she was unsure of her feelings when she was around him. He touched something in her. Rosa's initial reaction from years on the road was to protect herself by not allowing any emotions to take root.

That left Vida. Vida would come without a second's thought. The only thing about calling Vida was that Rosa would have to explain what had happened. And her friend was going to probe into every word she had exchanged with Adam.

But Rosa had no choice.

Gingerly she descended the stairs. She made a cup of coffee and spied her purse still lying where Adam had left it. She opened it. No keys.

"Damn," she protested, her shoulders dropping. She was stranded. Now she had to call him.

At that moment she heard a car pull into the driveway. Setting the coffee on the table, she looked through the window. Adam opened the door and got out of the Corvette. Behind him someone else pulled up in a pickup. She saw him drop her keys on the driver's seat and turn toward the truck. He wasn't even going to knock on the door.

For a moment she debated opening the door and calling to him. He didn't know she was there and apparently didn't care to find out.

Yanking the door inward, she went outside. "I could have gotten the car," she said, not bothering to acknowledge the morning.

He stopped and faced her. His eyebrows rose. "How?" he asked. "You weren't planning to walk, were you?"

She shook her head. "I don't think I could get to the end of the driveway if I tried to walk."

"Then it's good I brought it back."

"You're always helping."

Rosa glanced at the driver. She left the word reluctantly hanging off her sentence, but he knew it was there.

"Thank you for taking care of it for me," Rosa added.

Adam pivoted and headed for the truck. Rosa glanced at the driver. It was Medea.

"Hi, Rosa," she said, a ready smile on her face. "How are your legs and feet? Adam told me you walked miles in the dark. It's dangerous to do that when you don't know the land. Despite your self-defense skills, something could have happened to you."

Rosa didn't have to look at Adam to know that the episode with the three teenagers had been widely telegraphed.

"I wouldn't have walked if I'd known the keys were no longer in the car, and my cell phone was gone so I couldn't call anyone. My only choice was walking."

"Well, I'm glad you're all right. When Bailey comes home, you'll have to come by for dinner."

Rosa smiled. "I'd like that," she said, refusing

to glance at Adam as he got into the passenger's seat. She'd love to have dinner with Medea and Bailey, but Adam was bound to be there and she was unsure what to do with him around. Somehow the two of them had gotten off to a bad start and their relationship continued to go downhill.

"How is Bailey?" she asked.

"He's responding well to the medication, protesting about the food, and giving the nurses a hard time because he wants to come home." She smiled. "He's going to be all right. Thank you for helping him."

"I'm glad I was there."

"We're both glad you were there." Medea glanced at Adam. "No telling what would have happened if you hadn't found him."

Rosa looked at Adam. His eyes held an odd mixture of worry and love. And in that moment she was incapable of speech.

Juggling a huge bouquet of flowers, a box of chocolates, and several books, Rosa shouldered her way into the hospital. Bailey had been moved to a regular room. She found it easily. Letting out a slow breath, she was glad he was alone. She'd thought Adam might be there.

"Well, hello," Bailey said. A huge smile split his face. He opened his arms for her and Rosa went into them.

Pushing herself back, she said, "I hope you like flowers and candy. My brother is a doctor and these are the two things he says are always appropriate." Her voice fell as she looked about the room. It was full of flowers.

"Your smile is all I need," Bailey said.

"Even ill, you're still a charmer."

"Charmer," he said, mocking hurt. "I mean every word I say."

Rosa put the flowers in the vase she'd brought with her and filled it with water from the bathroom sink. When she turned back, Bailey had opened the candy and was popping a chocolate-covered coconut ball into his mouth.

"I have you to thank for getting me here," Bailey said. His tone was serious.

"No thanks necessary. From what I'm told, being neighborly is a requirement for living in the Valley."

"Sounds like my son."

Rosa nodded. She put the flowers on the windowsill. In addition to the flowers, there were many cards standing upright on every surface of the private room. Bailey had spent twenty-four hours in ICU, but now was in a regular room.

"I hope I'm not tiring you out?" Rosa said, thinking that if everyone who represented the flowers had come by, Bailey would be very tired. And she wanted to deflect the discussion away from Adam.

"You're a breath of fresh air," he said. "You make the Valley more beautiful than it already is."

Rosa blushed, even though she knew Bailey was charming her. "Everyone has been very friendly."

"Adam told me you had quite a night."

"Believe me, I have the aches and pains to show for that bit of bravado. I didn't think I'd parked so far away."

"Distances out here are deceptive."

"I know," Rosa said. "I'll be more careful." She had to get that in before she heard it again. Rosa had traveled the world and it was here that things were most foreign.

"You should hear Medea tell the story."

"What did she say?" Rosa asked.

The soft whoosh of the door opening had her turning. Adam strode in. He stopped when he saw her. She felt his glance roll over her, and her body warmed as if a blanket had been put around her. It was warm and sweet smelling and touched every sensual nerve in her body. Adam's expression was the same as it had been the day he'd kissed her. Her temperature rose several degrees. She had to get out of there. Bailey was already playing Cupid. She didn't want to give him any clues that she was attracted to Adam. And she didn't want Adam to know, either. Although how he couldn't know after their bodies had touched just short of the ultimate intimate act would surprise her.

Rosa picked up her purse. "It was good visiting with you, Bailey. Get well. I miss my riding partner."

"You're not leaving, are you?" Bailey asked.

She checked her watch and nodded. "I have some errands to run and I'm having lunch with a new friend."

"Oh. Who?" Adam asked. It was the first time he'd spoken in the short period he'd been in the room.

"Joy Stapleton-Jones. I met her at Vida's and recently in the grocery store. We were talking about me doing something more than riding horses and roaring down the roads in a red Corvette while I'm here."

"In the way of a job?" Adam asked.

"Not exactly." She looked at him. "In a lot of

the cities where I've had a lot of time, I used it to learn a little about their history. I thought I'd look into the history of Waymon Valley."

"Just don't let her talk to you about me."

"Why?" Rosa assumed talking about him would involve his appeal to the ladies.

"She's been after me for years."

Her suspicions confirmed, Rosa smiled. "I'm sure I know why."

Driving that red car around the Valley, Rosa could be spotted anywhere she went. Adam saw the car parked outside the library. The place had been closed for three hours. He knew sometimes Joy allowed people doing research to stay after hours and lock the door on their way out. But Rosa wouldn't be doing any research.

What was she doing in there? Since he was one of the people who often needed to do research, he was aware of the layout of the library. He knew how to get in through the back door. Walking around the building, he entered using an electronic code that hadn't been changed since it was installed ten years ago. Going up the steps, he found the place dark. No ambient light came from the main area. Was Rosa here or had she parked the car and *walked* somewhere else? The thought of her out alone made his heart speed up. She'd had lunch with Joy. Could the two of them still be out?

When he reached the central desk area, Adam noticed a small light coming from a corner. He knew there were private desks over there. People who needed to concentrate or wanted some privacy often commandeered them. He didn't want to scare Rosa if she was there. The place was quiet. His boots would echo on the marble floor if he crossed it.

He called her name. "Rosa?" There was no answer. But he heard a slight movement in the direction of the light. "Rosa, are you there?"

"I'm here," she answered, standing up. He could see her head over the top of the partition. Her eyes opened wide when she recognized him. "What are you doing here?"

"I could ask you the same question," he said. "I saw the car and the library closed hours ago."

"I thought the doors were locked. How'd you get in here?"

"Joy used to let me do research after hours. I still know the code to the back door."

"Well, as you can see, I'm fine. I'll close the door on my way out." She started to sit down, effectively dismissing him.

"What are you doing here?" he asked, refusing to accept her method of getting rid of him.

"Reading."

"Reading what?" He was surprised. He knew she was in Montana to rest and relax.

"I'm researching some . . . information."

Adam noticed she was choosing her words carefully. "On what?" he asked.

"On the Valley," she said.

"Why?"

"Interest. Joy told me some interesting facts at lunch. I wanted to read up on some of them. Besides, I'm here for a while. I can't sit around doing nothing."

"I see," he said. "Joy has enlisted you to get my father to write his memoirs."

He knew right away what was going on.

"Yes," she answered.

Her chin didn't jut out, nor did she raise it, but there was still the air of challenge that was part of her.

"I think it's a good idea. He knows so much about the area. Don't you think future generations will want to know how Waymon Valley came to be settled? How it's grown into a typical American town?"

He gestured but didn't commit himself.

"Look how much of black history has been lost. We lose more and more every day if people like your father won't pass along what they've lived through."

"My father isn't famous. Who would care what he had to say?"

"History isn't only written by the famous. And often the history that is written by them isn't completely true. It's public relations."

"Isn't this a reporter's job? Digging for the truth and sharing it with the public at large?"

"I suppose that's one definition, but it doesn't mean a layman like me can't get involved," Rosa defended. "Ordinary people experience things, too. Their perspective shouldn't be discounted. There are many oral histories left from the Depression Era and the Black Renaissance. They are invaluable in learning about that time period and what it meant to people. Waymon Valley, from what your father tells me, was a huge black community back in the 1800s. I didn't know that. I would never have thought it. Most of the history we learned concerns the South. There was a migration North, but very few times do we ever hear anything about people going West."

"Are you planning to write a book?" he asked.

Rosa shook her head. "Writing is a specialized field. I'm sure you know that. But I can at least record what he says. Maybe he'll write a book. You could edit it. You have the expertise. And it would give him something to do that's quiet and keeps him home, off that horse you don't want him riding. And give him something to occupy his time."

Adam thought about that. It *was* a good idea. Why hadn't he thought of it before? Often he was the one sitting at the computer producing stories for newspapers. He'd thought of writing a book himself. Editing one might be a way of getting his feet wet. Yes, it was a good idea. And having his father writing and him editing would give them a common goal.

"What are you thinking?" Rosa asked.

"I think it's a good idea."

She smiled. "So you'll help Joy and me get him to do it?"

"I'm not joining a conspiracy."

"It's a good one."

He changed the subject. "What are you reading?"

"A diary."

"Whose diary?"

"I think it's your great-grandmother's, Clara Winslow Evans. She came out from Virginia at the end of the 1800s."

He nodded. She was his father's grandmother. "I've read the diary," Adam said. "My father donated it to the library when they moved into this building. This was their house."

"Whose house?" Rosa asked.

"Clara and Luke Evans, my great-grandparents. When I was a boy I used to run through these rooms. I don't remember much of it, just that it was big and I used to slide down the banister."

Adam glanced over his shoulder. The staircase was still there. "And I always got a hug from my great-aunts."

"How long ago was that?"

"Ten years."

"I see you know a fair amount of the history of the Valley, too."

She was calling it the Valley now. Waymon Valley had been shortened to the Valley almost immediately after it was settled and after Waymon Evans died. Rosa must be feeling as if she belonged here.

"Where are you in the diary?"

"She's talking about her first winter. The snow. The people, miners, the Indians, her aunt Emily. How she met Luke. They have quite a love story."

"Risqué for their day."

"You should be very proud of your heritage."

"I am," Adam said. Then he remembered she was adopted. She didn't have this in her past. He could trace his family back to Clara coming to Montana. He could go back to her life in Virginia, her family living in Washington, D.C., and beyond that. Rosa knew nothing of herself. Adopted as a baby, she could remember nothing of her past. Adam wondered if this was why she was interested in the history of the Valley.

Adam had taken his heritage for granted until this moment. He had a wealth of knowledge to call on. He had his father, his aunts in Butte, and other relatives who had spread out across the West.

"I wish I had known my grandparents. I wish

I knew anything about my past, but I don't," she said.

Now he understood more about why she'd agreed to this scheme. "Didn't the parents who adopted you get a history from the adoption agency?"

She shook her head. "I told you I was abandoned. They found my mother, but she died without a word, and no one knew her. Not even DNA testing came up with a match for my father. The only conclusion we made is that I was probably not born in a hospital in Texas. I could have been brought there and then left."

Adam would guess there was some Hispanic blood in her ancestry. Her hair was jet-black and curly, although that could be done with a good curling iron. Her skin tone had an exotic look in the combination of yellow and brown. He could easily see why photographers loved to photograph her. She was made for the cameras, and the subdued lighting of the library was perfect to showcase her features. She was sexy even when she wasn't trying to be. All she needed to do was wet her lips and Adam was sure his body would stand at full arousal.

"I guess I should be getting home. I can finish this another day." She closed the books that were open in front of her and placed them on the side cart. Then, shutting down the library computer, she stood up to leave.

"Was there something else?"

"I thought I'd do the gentlemanly thing and see you to your car. I realize you can take care of yourself but I'm feeling chivalrous." He added the last to let her know he wasn't trying to patronize her. The truth was he was fascinated by her and wanted to spend a little more time with her. He knew he shouldn't be, but he'd indulge himself this once.

"Did you lock the door you came through?" she asked as they reached the front entrance.

He nodded. "As tight as possible."

Rosa pulled the front door closed all the way and tried it several times to make sure it was locked. She preceded him to her car. Adam opened the door and she slipped inside.

"Should I see you home?" he asked.

"That won't be necessary. I can find my way."

"You won't go walking again? If something happens, keep your phone with you."

"I could tell you the same thing. It appears that night we both had a lapse of protocol."

"I'm serious," he said. "We've told you it could be dangerous around here. It doesn't seem to have sunk in."

"So you're saying I shouldn't go out without an escort, someone who knows the dangers and how to handle them?"

"That's right."

"Well, since my usual escort is laid up, are you volunteering for the job?"

He hadn't been, but he was backed into a corner now. "I can fill in for my dad for a couple of days."

"Good, meet me tomorrow morning at six o'clock. I want to get to the hills before the mist burns off."

The following morning Rosa pressed the symbol on her key fob as she got out of the car, not waiting for Adam to come around and help her. The trunk popped open. Pulling it fully up, she lifted out a rifle and leaned it against the bumper.

"This is my rifle," Adam said. He lifted it, scanning it from handle to barrel. He held it as if he hadn't seen it in a while and needed to remember the feel of it in his hands.

"It was at the house," Rosa said.

"You just took this out of the trunk?"

She withstood his steady gaze. "Yes," she said. He'd seen her move it.

"You know carrying a concealed weapon in this state is against the law?" He replaced it against the bumper and folded his arms over the rifle he'd brought with him, carrying it in plain view as Rosa had driven into the naked hills.

"I believe it's against the law in every state." She reached for her camera case and at the same time pulled a piece of paper from the fanny pack on her hip and handed it to him.

"This is a permit issued by the state of Texas. It means nothing here." He handed it back.

Rosa said nothing. She pulled a second form out and without looking at it exchanged it for the one he held.

Adam was quiet as he read it. "I see you've thought of everything."

"A girl's gotta do what a girl's gotta do," she quoted.

The paper was a reciprocal and temporary permit allowing her to carry a weapon in the state of Montana.

"When did you get this?"

"A few days ago."

"Before or after the night you walked in the dark?"

She knew he already knew the answer. "After," she said. She caught the slight smile on his face. "You were so good to inform me of the dangers of living here. I thought I'd better be prepared to protect myself."

"Do you know how to use a gun?"

Rosa turned to him then. "I'm from Texas, Adam. We all know how to use guns."

"Dallas isn't the Old West. It's metropolitan. Much like New York. So, do you know how to use this rifle?"

"Would you like a demonstration?"

"A simple yes will do."

"Yes, I know how to use it."

Reaching beyond her, he lifted the tripod from the trunk while she shifted the camera bag to her shoulder.

"Where do you want this?"

"The best place is a little ways into the trees over there." She pointed toward the mountains.

They walked in silence to the place she indicated. Rosa was conflicted over spending time with Adam. When they were together she felt a connection to him. But at times she also wished she was alone. His mood said one thing, but his actions another. Since he'd kissed her that day in her living room, he'd mainly kept his distance.

Until last night.

She had the feeling that if they got too close, like magnets they'd be drawn to each other and unable to stop themselves. Yet while he kept his distance, he was always there when she needed him.

He set the tripod up and stepped away from it. Rosa fitted the camera into the screw mechanism. Adam walked several yards away. He had his back to her. He looked like a hunter reading the horizon, alert for any predator. Rosa looked through the viewfinder and snapped a photo of him.

Propping her rifle against the tripod, she took a deep breath, remembering her last trip to the mountains. The air was still thin, but she was getting used to it. She still felt a little weakness and knew it had more to do with the company than the air around her.

Framing the space in front of her, she got to work and took several photos. Turning, she saw Adam and quickly snapped another one of him. As much as he'd been in front of a camera while working as a reporter, she felt he shied away from her taking his picture. As she moved around to get better views, Adam moved, too, as if they were involved in a silent dance, one that kept him just out of sight. Still, she got him in several pictures.

The last one she took had him in profile, standing next to a natural rock wall and contemplating the distant mountain. Rosa envisioned it fully developed. An idea came to her then. She'd been thinking about Bailey's party. Watching Adam through the camera lens, she thought she'd put some photos together in a collection and give them to Bailey. His party was coming up and she hadn't bought him a gift yet.

"You can stop taking pictures of me now," Adam said without looking at her.

"So you knew I was photographing you." He didn't reply. "After being in front of the camera all those years, don't tell me you're camera shy."

"Not exactly. I was delivering a story, not posing for pictures."

"You're good looking enough to be a model." Rosa took a moment to appraise his many attributes. He still had a fine butt. And from what she could see, and the muscles she'd felt when he had her in his arms, she knew his image could sell clothes. "Want me to introduce you to someone? I have a wonderful agent," she teased.

"I'm a rancher, not a model," he said.

"It's not a working ranch," Rosa replied. "And you're not cut out to be the country gentleman. You can't tell me you're going to spend your life watching grass grow."

"When I do make a decision, I'll be sure to let you know."

"You don't have to get testy. I thought we were becoming friends . . . or at least being civil to each other."

Adam looked away from her. He stopped and listened in a posture that was much like a dog on point. Rosa followed Adam's gaze. She saw nothing.

"What is it?" she asked.

"Shhh," he said. He stayed in the same position for a long moment. Then he relaxed. "Nothing," he said. "I thought I heard something."

"A bear, maybe?" Rosa said it under her breath, but apparently Adam's ability to hear was keen.

"Yes, a bear."

She went back to her photos. Scanning the distance, she stopped several times to look from the camera lens to the mountains. The view was spectacular. Rosa took a deep breath and snapped. She thought about the diary she'd read. Montana was only a territory when Clara Winslow settled here. What must she have thought seeing this country in its virgin state, before there was a road and guardrails, before picnic tables and a visitor's bureau? Rosa took another picture.

"Thought any more about that book?" Rosa asked Adam.

"Yeah, I started making some notes."

Rosa swung the camera around to look at Adam. She opened her mouth to speak and froze. She went cold. Her arms and legs were numb and her voice closed off. In an instant, sweat poured over her and heat pumped through her system like an overloaded furnace. Her heart forgot to beat. Her body forgot to breathe.

Behind Adam was a bear.

She moved her head to the side. The image grew from an inch to life-size. It must have weighed a ton, she thought. She stared directly at it. She didn't want to call out to Adam. He might jerk and cause the animal to charge.

The bear was looking at Adam. Rosa moved quietly, stealthily, her heart resuming a thunderous beat. It was jumping in her chest like a drum, swollen large enough to lodge in her throat and cut her breaths to a mere fraction of normal, but her actions were slow and methodical.

She lifted her rifle and pointed it. The top had a viewfinder. She was grateful for it, even though she was a good shot. Adam was close in this one. This wasn't like target practice with Owen and Dean at the shooting range. This was the real thing. And Rosa *could* use the gun. She'd passed the Army Artillery test that one of Owen's friends had given her. But that was practice. Since then she'd never used a gun for anything but target shooting. And she'd never shot anything real, anything living.

Pointing it, she waited. If the bear turned and went away, she wouldn't fire. But if it took a step toward Adam, it was history. Time didn't move.

It didn't bend or warp; it seemed to cease. Rosa didn't know how long she remained in position, waiting and watching. She only knew that Adam stood to be killed and that she would not hesitate to choose which of them would have a bad day.

While she waited, Adam seemed lost in his own thoughts. He never moved. She didn't think he knew the animal was behind him. The wind blew away from them. He couldn't smell the bear, but the animal had found Adam's scent and come to investigate.

Suddenly it raised its head. It started running forward. Adam sensed something and turned. His rifle was lifting, but there wasn't enough time for him to get a shot before the bear reached him.

Rosa fired.

The bear went down, pounding the ground and writhing before going still.

Adam swung his gaze back and forth between her and bear.

"Are you all right?" she asked. The words came out, but they were too quiet for him to hear. Her arms dropped to her sides. The rifle's weight seemed to double after the discharge. Rosa held on to it, ready in an instant, to raise it and shoot again. She couldn't move. Her legs felt too weak to support her. Tears sprang to her eyes and rolled down her cheeks.

Adam came to her. "Rosa?"

She lifted her head and stared at him, but she didn't see him.

"You killed a bear."

"No," she said, finding strength in her knees to stand up straight.

Adam looked back. The bear lay where it had fallen.

"Tranquilizer," she whispered. "We should go."

He understood immediately. There weren't bullets in her gun, but tranquilizer darts. The bear would be out for an hour or so, but after that it would be alive and angry.

Regaining some of her energy, Rosa lifted the tripod, not bothering to remove the camera from it, and started for the car. Adam followed with her bag and the two guns.

"I'll drive," he said.

She handed him the keys without question. She was shaking. She knew she was in shock and driving wouldn't just be a bad idea; it would be dangerous. Storing the equipment in the trunk, Adam opened her door and helped her inside. He pushed her head back against the upholstery and closed the passenger-side door.

"I'm all right," she said as he took his seat and started the engine. She looked back as they drove away. She couldn't see the bear. It lay around a bend. She knew the tranquilizer would keep it down for a while, but it was first time she'd ever shot anything alive. It was an animal. And it was attacking, but she felt queasy even though she hadn't killed it.

"I guess you can now say you've saved the lives of both the Osbornes."

Rosa nodded. She was light-headed and working hard to remain conscious. "And I never want to do it again."

It didn't take long for the story to run through the Valley. Each retelling was embellished, until the story had her practically fighting the animal with her bare hands. It was necessary for Rosa to report the shooting to the park rangers, even if she hadn't killed the bear. From that report, word spread until the local news in Butte wanted to interview her. Rosa refused.

To get away from her ringing phone, she went to Vida's. Apparently everyone else decided to drop in that day, too. Rosa was obliged to repeat the story over and over.

"You understand how reporters work, don't you?" Vida said later that night after everyone was gone except Adam and Mike Holmes.

Rosa frowned. "What do you mean?"

"She means," Adam said, "if you don't grant the interview they will print other things about you. You're already a celebrity. The morgue must be full of photos of you. They can dig into your background and find your sister, your adoption, and incorporate that into the story."

"If you do the interview, it'll be over in one report," Vida continued.

"I hate interviews," Rosa said.

"Then let Adam do it," Mike suggested.

"No," Adam said quickly. "I'm no longer in the business."

"You were there, Adam," Vida said. "You'd be perfect. And since you know Rosa, you won't ask her questions she doesn't want asked."

Rosa looked at Adam. She wasn't sure she trusted him, either. She'd seen his interviews, and while his reports from war-torn areas of the world held a bit of compassion in the reporting, she had no doubt he could be ruthless. Yet if she compared him to someone she didn't know, he was the better choice. "If you'll do it, I'll accept the interview."

"Are you sure?" Adam asked.

"No," she said. "But I don't want a bunch of

strangers prying into my life and possibly upsetting my family. This will be a straight interview, right? A few questions. I'll tell what happened and it will be over."

Adam spread his hands. "Any way you want it."

And that's how it happened. Or how it was supposed to happen. Adam's report and footage, which were supposed to be a thirty-second filler on the evening news, were expanded into a full story. *Rosa Clayton, supermodel and the face of Arrow Cosmetics, saves reporter Adam Osborne from being mauled by a bear outside the little town of Waymon Valley, Montana,* the story began. On the screen were side-by-side photos of her and Adam.

Somehow the tape got sent to WNN and was shown on television stations all over the country, including those viewed by her family in Texas and Philadelphia.

Rosa hadn't even seen the segment when her cell phone started to ring. Luanne, her psychologist sister, was the first to call. As soon as Rosa assured her she was fine, Brad, Digger, and Dean in that order also needed promises from her that she would be careful and stay away from places where bears were known to inhabit.

Rosa promised even though that would include most of the state of Montana. She had to promise; otherwise she might open her door one day and find any number of the Claytons waiting there. They'd flown to places before to make sure one of their own was safe.

She would keep her promise, maybe not to the letter, but she would certainly never again leave home without the rifle.

* * *

The next morning, Rosa was back on her horse. She rode along the upper ridge beyond the Osborne Ranch but miles from the moutains. The air was crisp and fresh and she enjoyed this part of her day. She'd taken to meeting Bailey each morning and they rode together while he told her stories of his ancestors and the settling of the land. He spoke of his ranching, raising horses as if it were still the territory from the early part of the last century. After an enjoyable beginning to the day they'd separate, returning to their respective homes.

Since his heart attack, Rosa had ridden alone, keeping to the old trails and only exploring new areas when she was sure they were safe. She marveled at the wonder of the trees, lakes, and rivers that traversed the land. And she carried the rifle.

This morning she saw him. Frowning, she shaded her eyes and watched as Bailey rode up the hill. She thought it was too early for him to be on a horse, but she'd learned that Bailey never took anyone's advice over his own. She waved, her smile wide and welcoming. Turning her horse, she rode in his direction. A moment later she realized the man on the horse was not Bailey.

It was Adam.

Her frown turned to a scowl. She didn't want to see Adam. He'd interviewed her and brought out her family's wrath. Their last encounter hadn't added any affection between them. In fact, it had deepened the shaft of misunderstanding they couldn't seem to seal. And she'd promised not to ride alone. Anyone who'd come across a bear should know better. But she wasn't far from the house. Was she?

Swiftly she turned the horse around and

began riding away from him. She had no desire to begin her day with another argument. Why didn't he just leave her alone? If he didn't like her, why was he always in her path of view at every turn?

She urged the horse into a canter; then seeing Adam following her, she broke into a gallop. Adam was tenacious. Each time Rosa pushed her horse faster, he asked his for an equal or greater measure. Her filly was light, agile, and swift, but no match for the gelding that carried Adam ever closer to her.

Rosa pulled up. She didn't want to injure the horse by pushing her past the point of exhaustion. She couldn't ignore Adam. The community was too small. They were bound to run into each other. They might as well have their confrontation here and now.

He caught up with her in no time.

"What do you want?" Rosa asked.

"I want to apologize."

"Apology accepted. Now go away."

"That doesn't sound like an acceptance," he said. "I didn't know they were going to broadcast that story on WNN. I didn't file it there."

"But you knew the station would put it out there. And you didn't warn me. You're a reporter. They know you and your work. And what happened to the thirty-second spot?"

"That was my fault," he admitted.

"You couldn't resist, could you? You were back in a studio. You had film and a story and you couldn't resist turning it into the next Pulitzer nomination."

"Rosa, I never meant to cause you any strife. I expected the station to cut it."

She sighed, knowing he didn't know about the phone calls that had come from the people she loved, the cosmetics company, her modeling agency, her agent, and scores of friends.

"Apology accepted," she said in a lower voice.

"Friends?" he asked.

Rosa looked up. They had never been friends before. He was smiling and offering her his hand.

"Friends," Rosa said, and accepted it. The clasp was short, but seemed to seal the bond growing between them.

"I thought you were going to call before going riding alone," he said.

"I'm not going anywhere I haven't been before. And I have the rifle."

"I had a rifle, too, on that day. Anyway, I thought you liked company on these morning rides."

The right company, she thought, but held her tongue and said nothing. They'd just become friends. Rosa didn't want to spoil it.

"I even brought a peace offering." He reached behind him and placed a hand on a small wicker picnic basket. "Dad said you liked your coffee with a sweetener. I have some in my pocket."

Rosa narrowed her eyes. Was this real? Did he want something?

"No strings," he said, seeing her distrust of his motives. "If you're not hungry, I can go."

The smell of something delicious wafted toward her and her stomach spoke for her.

"There's a good place over there." Adam pointed toward a clearing that afforded a view with distant gold and orange mountains.

He hadn't waited for her to agree verbally, but nudged his horse toward a flat area under a tree.

The trees grew tall out here, too, as if they were trying to reach that huge sky.

Rosa got down from her horse. Adam did the same, pulling the basket and a blanket down with him. He'd brought a picnic, she thought. There he was again, acting like he liked her.

He spread the blanket out and sat on it. She joined him, keeping as far away as the space allowed. Unable to resist looking inside, she smelled delicious scents. He handed her a thermos and a cup. Rosa poured the coffee, finding it already included the cream and sweetener. It was perfect. She closed her eyes as she drank, thinking this was the best cup of coffee she'd had since the Kona brand she'd developed a taste for in Hawaii several years ago.

"I never got a chance to really thank you for saving my father's life," Adam said, his voice serious.

"Both Osbornes," she teased.

Adam smiled, but quickly the serious expression returned. "I am grateful," he stated.

"I won't go so far as to say I saved his life," Rosa said. "I was just there. I didn't do nearly as good a job as my sister-in-law."

"What did she do?"

"She saved my mother's life."

"How?"

"My brother Brad is a doctor—"

"Pediatrician, lives in Philadelphia, married to a doctor," he interrupted.

Rosa smiled. Adam had a good memory. She liked that. "During his wedding reception, my mother had a heart attack in the ladies' room. Owen's wife, although she wasn't my sister-in-law then, just one of the guests, found my mother and gave her some aspirin, then called for help. Later we discovered she was related to our mother and she wound up marrying my brother Owen."

Adam sat up straight. "What a story. I remember something about . . ." He stopped trying to remember.

"A kidnapped child who finds her birth mother after thirty years," Rosa supplied.

He snapped his fingers. "That's it. She was related to you?"

Rosa nodded. "At first we didn't get along." She looked at Adam. "It was all my fault. I didn't trust her. Owen was a ladies' man and I thought she had ulterior motives. Eventually I discovered she was trying to learn about us and Owen was the one falling in love with her. We're very good friends and family now."

Adam gave her a look but said nothing. She wondered if he was thinking of the way the two of them got along. That had not been all her fault, although she'd been talking to him so easily, she'd forgotten they were adversaries. It was only a short while ago they had agreed to be friends, but friendship was earned and Rosa was unsure if he was sincere in his offer.

"Seriously," he said. "I'm grateful you stopped and helped Dad."

Rosa felt a tug of embarrassment. She hadn't done anything special. Nothing a neighbor wouldn't do. "Isn't that what people do out here? It's one of the stories I read in your great-grandmother Clara's diary. The tradition continues to this day, your father says. How is he doing, by the way?"

"He's the same, cranky, wants to have his way. But Medea's keeping him in line."

Rosa laughed. "I'm sure she's capable." She could picture the woman taking charge and ordering Bailey around even if he didn't want to do what she said.

"Very capable. She's been with us since I was a boy. She knows all my father's tricks."

Rosa stared out at the mountains. They fascinated her. They had a calming effect on her and she liked seeing them, knowing they were there each day when she woke.

She looked back at Adam. He was staring at her, his expression confusing to her. It was open, seeking, intense, both asking and wanting something.

The air between them went from comfortable to awkward. Rosa didn't know why. Then Adam looked down. His index finger touched hers. It slid along her hand. Rosa felt goose bumps travel up her arm. But it felt good. These weren't the kind that she got when she was cold, dressed too scantily for the weather but posing for the perfect photo anyway. These were the chemistry kind. His touch was light, yet it caused a chain reaction in her. Localized for the moment, the swarm of warmth only covered her arm. Rosa knew it could burst into flame at any moment and encompass all of her.

"Adam." She spoke softly. Her voice wouldn't get any louder. "What are we doing?"

"Nothing yet," he said.

"Yet?" Anticipation jumped into her. She could almost hear it buzzing in her ears.

He lifted her hand. Rosa resisted, pulling slightly on it, but not hard enough to dislodge his grip. He brought it to his lips and kissed her knuckles.

"Adam, you don't want to start something we can't finish."

"We can finish this." The seduction in his voice was almost her undoing.

"No," she said a little stronger. "I'm only here for the summer."

Adam didn't hold her any tighter, but he kept her hand. "What are you afraid of?"

"Nothing," she denied.

He watched her a moment. Rosa wanted to drop her eyes, but she didn't. Wouldn't.

"You're afraid of me," he stated.

"Why would I be afraid of you?"

"Like you said, afraid of starting something you can't finish. I know what you're thinking."

"You do?"

"I've been there. Always moving, having no time to make lasting friendships, and relationships are out of the question. All you can think of is the next plane, the next city."

He was right. He read her as openly as if he were reading a tried-and-true plot.

"There comes a time when you have to stop," he said. "Miss that plane. Stop and be a part of what's going on around you." He tugged at her arm and she fell a little closer to him. "We won't say we're starting anything. We're just two people enjoying a morning on a Montana mountain."

His mouth was close to hers. Rosa could feel his breath on her lips. The airwaves between them transported the coffee he'd drunk to her taste buds. It was a fervent elixir and turned her blood to fire. Even though he held only her hand, he was carrying all her weight. His free hand went around her back and he pulled her close.

"Tell me to stop," he whispered.

Rosa could say nothing. The only thing she could do was lean into him. Her eyes focused on small portions of his face, his eyes, his cheeks, his lips, his chin. She looked up and down, as they moved closer and closer to each other. She wound her arms around his neck and let thoughts of resisting him fall away like discarded laundry.

Rosa wasn't sure what was happening to her. She should have been pushing herself up, or at least not letting herself get involved, but something was happening to her that had never happened before. She wanted Adam to kiss her. She wanted to feel his arms around her again.

She moved in, eliminating the millimeter of space that separated them. His mouth was sure, his lips soft and wet. Sensation streaked through her like lightning. She ran her tongue along the line of his mouth. It opened to admit her. Adam's arms tightened around her. The griplike vise felt good. She liked the feel of his chest against hers. While it was hard and solid, she felt safe and cared for. His arms caressed her as his hands smoothed over her skin. Fingers threaded through her hair, dislodging it from the confining band. He gathered the locks, using the band as a gentle rope to tie her hair.

The wind swirled around them, a vortex encapsulating them, bonding them together, and restricting the world to nonexistence. Adam's mouth tantalized hers. She never wanted it to end. She wanted this sensual assault to go on forever. Adam's hands had moved from the outside of her blouse to the bare skin of her back. She arched when he touched her naked skin. Fiery trails banked along the places where his hands explored.

Rosa's breath caught in her throat as his

thumbs came around her body and rubbed across her nipples. She wanted to get closer, remove the fabric of her bra, and feel the raw touch of his hands roaming over skin so sensitive she thought it would melt.

Finally, Rosa slipped her mouth from Adam's. She rested her head on his shoulder. Even from there, she could feel his heart beating against her cheek. Hers was beating fast, too. Adam's hands continued to caress her. Her eyes closed and she let the wonderment course through her. Then his hands stopped. He pulled them down her back and below the hem of her blouse.

Rosa lay for another moment lost in a dreamlike state. Then she pushed herself back. His legs were behind her and she couldn't move very far away.

"It's started now," Adam said.

For a moment she didn't understand what he meant. Then she remembered her own comment about starting something they couldn't finish.

"I suppose we're going to have to finish it," she said. "One way or another."

Chapter 6

It didn't take them long to decide which way. They rode the horses back to Rosa's as fast as they could. Adam slapped their tails as soon as they dismounted. The horses took off.

"They'll go back to the stables," he said. "The groom will rub them down."

"Won't he wonder where we are?"

"He might." Adam didn't explain any further, grabbing Rosa's hand. The two went inside and straight up the stairs to her bedroom.

He turned her into his arms, his mouth seeking hers like a homing device. He stopped just before their lips melded. Rosa wondered if there was something wrong. Had he changed his mind? He was looking at her as if he were memorizing her features, as if he wanted to capture this moment, burn it into his memory bank to pull out on some future night and relive.

She smiled at him, allowing him to divide her into features, to take in the sum of her. She did the same. He was beautiful, even more so in the preamble to love. His features were relaxed, unguarded, and open. Rosa quivered at the feelings that surged through her. She could feel her body making itself ready for him. The anticipation of them making love made her melt in his arms.

His mouth clamped down on hers as if he couldn't breathe the next moment without sharing it with her. Rosa felt the same. She tore at his clothes. He tore at hers, peeling her blouse down her arms. It fell to the floor. Her jeans took more time, but his hands working inside them, sliding them over her hips and down her legs had her clamping her teeth on her lip to keep from screaming at the pleasure of his touch. Waves of delight went through her. She couldn't step out of the pants because her boots held them on. Sitting down, she pulled them off.

When she looked up, Adam's boots were gone, too. His jeans joined hers on the floor. His shirt was completely unbuttoned and she could see his dark chest through the fabric. Reaching up, she pulled him down on the bed. His hand went behind her, into her hair. He pulled her head close and kissed her. A moment later Rosa felt the release on her bra give way and Adam's free hand replaced the fabric with the warmth of his palm. Her nipples grew hard.

"I hope you have a condom," she whispered.

Her body was hot, burning for him.

Rosa heard the crinkle of foil and looked at the packet Adam was holding. He removed his shirt and they quickly undressed the rest of the way. Rosa stared at him. He was gorgeous all over, not just in the places where the public could see. His muscles were hard and toned. His skin was an even color as if someone had painted it with a single brushstroke. His torso tapered to a waist and long legs, legs that swung over hers as Rosa anticipated their coupling.

He didn't enter her immediately. His hand traced her skin from shoulder to hip. Then he moved it between them, touching the core of her and watching her reaction as she sucked in air. She could taste the odor of sex in the room. It was pungent and guaranteed to get stronger the further they went with the primal dance.

Rosa tried to hang on to some control as Adam entered her, but it was a losing proposition. The pleasure curve rioted off the scale. Her arms went limp and she raised her legs to allow him greater entry. She took his body into hers full tilt. Biting her lip, she held the moan of pleasure inside.

As he began to move, she went with him, matching his pace. The room filled with grunts and moans. Their bodies writhed in unison. Rosa abandoned herself to the rapture. The pacing increased as Adam filled her time and again. Her body came alive with the heat of their lovemaking. He seemed to know her, understand her need, find the places on her body that would intensify her pleasure. She'd never known anyone like Adam. He was gentle with her, yet he was taking her on an ecstasy trip like she'd never known.

She felt her climax building. She held on, wanting to continue this feeling of being high on a mountain and knowing she would fall, but when she pitched off that mountain she would soar into the unknown with Adam. There was no fear in not knowing. She craved it, grabbed for each rung of the ladder that would take her higher and higher into an experience that she hadn't thought was possible.

She heard her voice calling Adam's name. With each hard thrust of his body, she wanted more and more of him. Then the explosion came. Together they burst, having reached a pleasure so high they couldn't move it a single step higher. Adam flopped down on her. Rosa let out a long breath. She hugged his shoulders, her heart hammering, her breath coming in short gasps. Her body was hot, liquid almost. But she was sated. She didn't move, never again wanted to move. Rosa wanted to stay where she was, her body still coupled with Adam's. She never wanted that connection broken.

The bedsheets under Rosa were tangled. It looked like the two of them had had wild sex, and that's exactly what had happened. Adam would be good in bed, but he never expected her to be perfect. He wanted to make love to her again and their first encounter wasn't over yet. Rosa's body was still humming with the aftermath of an erotic experience.

Rosa had never known anyone to make love like Adam. The two of them should be burning up, white hot and molten. She was amazed her skin could hold her body intact. Adam amazed her, but then he always had. Even when she saw him on the tiny screen and had never met him, he did things to her. She knew he was part of the reason she accepted Vida's invitation to visit. She and Vida were close friends, but Rosa had always gone home to Texas when she needed to rest. Her family helped revitalize her and if she only felt like lying around and reading, they didn't coax her or force her to get out and join the party.

When Vida had offered her a place to rest for the summer, Rosa found herself accepting because she wanted to meet the sexy reporter she'd seen so many times during her trips. Adam Osborne was a friendly face wherever she was. WNN was broadcast worldwide and she'd come to look at him as her anchor in unfamiliar territory. Then suddenly, two years go, he'd disappeared without a word. Vida was the one who'd told her Adam had returned to live in Waymon Valley. While Rosa told herself she was visiting a friend, she knew she wanted to find Adam.

And she had.

When Adam opened his eyes, he was alone. He sat up in the bed that used to be his. Today it had housed the two of them. At least for the last few hours. Yet Rosa was gone. Damn, he cursed to himself. What had gotten into him? Had his brain lost all touch with his body? He'd dreamed of having Rosa Clayton in his arms, but he never expected to act on that dream. She wasn't his kind of woman. He'd been with her kind and he never wanted to go there again.

But he had.

Maureen was the kind of woman he looked for. Pretty on any given day, beautiful when she dressed up. She was intelligent, caring, and knew what she wanted in life. Maureen had been his friend, not his lover. They never got to be lovers. But before Maureen, there had been Cassie. Cassandra Marteen, aspiring producer, and Corinthia

Gleason, Paris bureau chief, women who had torn his heart to shreds and walked away without a thought or care. Both of them had been beautiful. And both of them had used that beauty to get what they wanted. They thought he could help and he'd fallen into the trap like a gullible fourteen-year-old.

Pushing the covers back, he looked over the railing to the wide-open space below. She wasn't there. There was no sign of her, no presence that she was near. Adam was vaguely disappointed that she hadn't waited to wake up with him. Going into the bathroom, he showered. Lifting her shampoo, he read the printed label. *Violet Rain* was printed in script. Instantly he smelled her scent. He recognized the smell of her hair and remembered crushing that hair in his hands. It had been soft and springy and he liked the way it swung when she gathered it into a ponytail. He put the bottle back and turned the water to cold.

He hoped she wasn't back in the hills. She and her camera worried him. This wasn't the friendliest part of the country. Dangers lurked everywhere, especially for those who weren't familiar with the territory. And he didn't want any mishap to come to her. She'd already encountered one bear, yet he'd found her alone riding toward those hills.

Adam rubbed soap over himself, but he had to laugh. Why was he worried about Rosa Clayton? She wasn't just beautiful; she could handle three teenage boys, she rode like a champion, and she handled a rifle with cool efficiency. Maybe he was trying to protect the wrong woman.

After dressing, Adam walked back toward the stables. He'd borrow a horse and ride home. He expected to be interrogated by his father about being gone so long, but as he opened the door, he heard the familiar sound of his father's laughter coming from the back of the house. Adam went toward it. It was a room they rarely used. Mainly their movements involved the kitchen or the large room directly off the kitchen. The room in the back looked out on the property. There was a patio and garden Adam's mother had tended when she was alive. Medea took care of it now. She called it therapy for having to deal with two men in the house. There were large windows that made the room bright.

Adam stopped in his tracks when he saw Rosa sitting in one of the big leather chairs. His heart lurched. Of all the places he expected to find her, the back room of his house would be last on the list. A stronger sensation went through him when he noticed how she fit so well into the surroundings. She had on a western skirt and boots, her legs were crossed, but his mind saw her as she'd been right after they made love. She was radiant, beautiful in the light flooding through the windows. He shifted as he recognized the signs of arousal.

Bailey looked up. "Adam, I was wondering where you were. Medea said you went out riding."

"I did," he answered, unwilling to give any further information. "What's going on here?"

"Your father is telling me stories about the settling of this part of the country," Rosa explained.

Her eyes were radiant. Her skin had a glow to it he hadn't noticed before. She didn't have her hair in the ponytail. Curls framed her face and cascaded down to rest on her collarbones. Adam could spend the rest of the day staring at her.

"Memoirs," Bailey said.

His father's voice snapped him out of the daze he was in. Bailey Osborne's stare swung between Adam and Rosa, yet he said nothing about what he saw there. "I finally agreed to Joy's request."

It took Adam a moment to understand what he meant.

"Rosa is going to record and write down what I tell her. And she tells me you've agreed to edit it for a book." Bailey indicated the desk.

Adam saw a laptop computer sitting on top of it. "I guess you could say Rosa gets what she wants."

Her eyes flashed at him.

"We've been working about an hour," Bailey said. "We just stopped for something to drink. Want some lemonade?"

"Lemonade?" Adam hadn't moved from his position. His father never drank lemonade. He loved his coffee.

"I wanted coffee, but Rosa insisted that too much coffee is bad for my heart."

"I'm glad someone can get through to you." Adam moved into the room then. Rosa's eyes followed his steps.

He hadn't wanted their first encounter after making love to be with an audience. He didn't know that seeing her again would have him wanting to make love to her again. He needed time to think about how to handle the situation. Making love with her had been fantastic, but he knew life wasn't about sex. She was only here for the summer. She had a life, a career outside of the Valley. And he wasn't ready for a long-term relationship. The trauma of the past year had drained him of any desire to commit himself to a cause or a relationship.

Bailey handled him a glass of lemonade. Adam thought of the patio at Rosa's where they'd had lunch. She was a fan of lemonade. He accepted it and drank it in one long gulp. His throat was parched and once he started drinking, he kept going.

"Your father was telling me about his grandmother, Clara," Rosa said. "Things that weren't in the diary."

Adam nodded. He had heard the stories. His great-grandmother had come to Montana from Virginia in 1899. She was a teacher and apparently a lot about Waymon Valley changed with her direction.

She lived well into her nineties, but died when Adam was two years old. You couldn't grow up in the Valley and not know about Clara and Luke Evans. Adam had taken them for granted until he was twelve years old and a history class on the Civil War suddenly made the hardships she'd endured come alive. Later he wondered what it was like in the early days of the century.

Thankfully, Clara had left a diary. Adam had read it along with several other books on the territory. And thanks to Joy and Rosa, his father was also providing an oral history.

"I think Adam gets some of his strength from her, but he doesn't remember much about her when she was strong," Bailey said. "There are times I can see a lot of her in him."

"What a compliment," Rosa said. She glanced at Adam and it took all his resistance to remain where he was.

"I never knew my biological mother," Rosa

stated. "Or any relatives for that matter." Her gaze went back to Bailey.

"How so?" he asked.

"I was adopted by a doctor in the hospital where I was abandoned."

"Her entire family was adopted," Adam further explained. "Remember the story of that woman who found her birth parents after being kidnapped thirty years earlier?"

Bailey was nodding. He turned to Rosa. "That couldn't be you. You're not thirty years old."

"She's my sister-in-law now. She was the biological daughter of my adoptive parents. So you see why I find it so interesting that you know your history back to the 1800s."

"Have you ever tried to research your own history, to find who your parents were and what happened to them?"

"I thought of it, but I never did," she said. "Two of my brothers are biologically related. They found their birth mother several years ago. I thought of my mother then, trying to find out something about her. After my adoptive parents had both passed on, I thought of it again, but realized I was so lucky to have them as my parents. My family is my family. They're the only ones I've ever known. I love them all as if we were blood relatives. I don't want to know that there was another alternative, another road I could have taken."

"Alternative? It doesn't need to be that," Bailey said.

"It would plant the seed in my mind. My mother abandoned me and she died. There could have been aunts, uncles, even sisters and brothers. But no family could be more loving and supportive than the one I have."

"That's wonderful," Bailey said. Adam noticed he glanced at him when he said it. "And it's a good attitude. Although they couldn't help being proud of you and what you've accomplished."

"It's not a path I'm willing to pursue," she said. "The Claytons are enough."

She was decisive, Adam thought. His father pushed himself up out of the chair. "I'll be back in a moment. I have to go take a pill."

He left them alone. Adam took a seat in front of Rosa. She hadn't moved since he walked in, only uncrossed her legs and pushed herself up in the chair. He leaned forward, buying himself a moment to try to determine what he wanted to say.

"I didn't expect to find you here," he started.

"I had an appointment." She looked toward the door that Bailey had used.

Her voice was soft and quiet. Sexy, even, Adam thought. He remembered it against the pillow of her bedroom. "You could have told me."

"You were asleep. I didn't want to wake you," Rosa whispered conspiratorially.

Rosa lifted her lemonade and took a drink. She set it down on the table next to her and looked him directly in the eye. "What's wrong?" she asked.

"Wrong? There's nothing wrong."

"You have regrets," she stated. "I can see it in your eyes."

"You're blind, then," he replied. "I don't regret a single moment of today."

"But . . ." She led, trailing off, waiting for him to tell her what was on his mind. "You're not going for that way-you-look story again. It would be a little thin at this point."

"Rosa, today was . . ." He didn't know how to express it. He was used to reporting what other people thought and felt, not himself. "Today was unbelievable. But there was nothing behind it other than sex and lust."

Rosa stood up. "What makes you think it was more than sex and lust for me?"

She turned to leave.

"Rosa, don't." Adam stopped her. "We need to talk about this."

"What is *this*? You had a little fun today. But it's over now and you don't want me getting any ideas about the great Adam Osborne. You're a man who travels alone, and no woman with a pretty face is going to tie you down. Well, here's a news flash, you jerk, you're not the only man on the planet."

She left him, her steps sure as she crossed the carpeted room and passed through the door where generations of his ancestors had walked. She didn't look back, only held her shoulders level and moved as if there was a runway in front of her.

Adam felt as if his insides were being ripped out. She had gotten to him. She was in his blood and he knew it wasn't going to be easy to get her out.

Rosa took a horse and rode into the hills again. She didn't go to the usual place, the place where this day had begun, where Adam had found her and where they'd eaten and started making love. She didn't want to go to that place ever again. Yet her eyes insistently looked in that direction. Even the horse seemed to want to go that way. She had to steer the filly differently.

She walked the horse for several yards before she came to a clearing. She needed a place where the sky was open and the wind was calm. Dismounting, Rosa took her laptop from the backpack she carried and sat down on the ground. As it booted up, she wrapped her arms around her knees, rocking back and forth as if she were doing a routine from her daily workout. She wasn't. Her body was tight to the point of breaking a spring. She was trying to work Adam out of her mind and all the other places he'd infiltrated. Talking to her family would help with that. In all her travels she'd never met another person who stayed in touch with family the way she did with hers.

The computer beeped as it went through the last set of security checks. She looked down at the screen. Her customized wallpaper of the last family wedding, Dean and Theresa's, played over the screen. Everyone was smiling. They were a growing clan, looking out from the machine. The photo made her smile as it always did.

She plugged in the headset and fixed it over her ear. In seconds she had a signal and the screen changed.

"Hi," Dean said as his face filled the screen. "How's it going in Big Sky Country?"

"It's great," she lied for the first time that she could remember when talking to her family. "I came out here so you could see a little part of the sky." She angled the camera up at the sky.

"Looks pretty much like any sky," he said.

Rosa laughed. She put the camera back in

place. "I'll tell Robert Redford that next time I see him."

Dean winced as if hurt. As a filmmaker he admired Robert Redford and it was common knowledge that the actor/director loved Montana.

Moments later the rest of the group joined the chat. The normal round of hellos took up the first few seconds.

"Rosa, you look great," Erin, her sister-in-law, said. "Montana must agree with you."

"It's beautiful out here," she said, keeping the subject to the entire state.

"Any more bears?" Brad asked.

"None that I've seen." Rosa tried to keep her voice casual. The story had been distorted enough. "I'm keeping away from areas where they are likely to be found." She paused. "And I always carry a rifle." Picking it up, she held it in front of the small computer camera.

"I'm serious, Rosa. You be careful."

"Brad, I will. I don't go exploring anymore. And that story was greatly embellished. It wasn't as bad as the story sounded."

"Met anyone interesting yet?" This was a question she got whenever the family got together. This time she was grateful for a change in subject. In the last few years, there had been a wedding a year. She was the last remaining unmarried Clayton and her sisters-in-law were all paying matchmakers.

"Everyone out here is interesting."

"Forget the people," Digger said. "Tell me about the car. Does it . . ."

Rosa answered all their questions. They often got together for family meetings when there was an issue. There hadn't been any since Stephanie's

surprise revelation that she was actually the
biological daughter of their adoptive parents.
Dean's news that he'd been nominated for an
Academy Award for his first directorial effort had
them all flying to California for the event and
eventual party. And Luanne's announcement of
her pregnancy. Now they met to catch up.

"Rosa, are you getting any rest?" Brad asked.
Brad was a pediatrician. He was a quiet, moody
guy, but he saw deeper into all of them than they
sometimes felt comfortable with.

"Not much. I'm very busy."

"Doing what?" Owen, her architect brother,
asked. Owen still lived in the family home where
they gathered as a family whenever they were in
Dallas.

"I met a man named Bailey Osborne whose
family has lived here for generations. He's telling
me the history of the town and I'm writing it
down."

"Why?" Dean asked.

Rosa saw Theresa elbow him in the side.

"I mean, why you? You haven't decided to
become a writer and not told us, have you?"

Rosa smiled. "Nothing like that." She told
them the story of the librarian asking her to see
if she could influence Bailey to tell his stories of
the history of the area.

"He must have really taken to you to do something like this after knowing you for such a short
time," Stephanie said.

"Bailey is a character. He's charming and
funny and loves to talk."

"How old is Bailey?" Luanne asked.

Rosa knew where they were going with that
question. "He's old enough to be my father.

Don't get any ideas. There are enough women vying for his charms. I'm not one of them."

"How's he related to *Adam* Osborne?" Mallory spoke for the first time since saying hello.

"Father and son," Rosa said.

"And is Adam just as charming?" Erin asked.

Rosa stiffened, hoping no one would notice her reaction on the small screen. Memories of them making love rushed into her mind. On its heels was the argument she and Adam had had at his house only a couple of hours ago.

"Help me out here, guys," she appealed to her brothers. "This isn't a get-Rosa-a-man call."

"Rosa, I might be coming out that way," Dean said.

"Why?" Rosa's back went up. Dean's statement was news to her. She hoped he wasn't the family designate selected to check up on her. Being the baby of the family had its drawbacks, and an overprotecting family was something Rosa had to live with.

"It's still up in the air, but we're looking for a movie location and one of the scouts thinks Montana is best."

"When would you be here?"

"Not sure. These things change from moment to moment."

"Maybe you can get Adam to show you around, Dean," Erin suggested. When all eyes seemed to focus on her, she said, "I've seen him. He's gorgeous." Digger looked at his wife as if he was surprised she'd looked at another man. They laughed and kissed.

"Is he as good looking in person as he is on television?" Stephanie asked.

Rosa thought of many ways to answer that

question, but discarded them all for honesty. "Yes," she said simply.

"Hi, Aunt Rosa," Samantha said. She was nine now. Her entrance saved Rosa from answering any more questions about Adam. She was grateful to the niece and made a mental note to send her a present. For the next few minutes they talked about the kids—Samantha, Digger's adopted daughter, and Chelsea, Dean's adopted daughter. It seemed the adoptees were adopting. As far as she knew, no one was pregnant. Her sister Luanne had delivered an eight-pound baby boy last year, but her sisters-in-law were still as thin as they ever were.

"Rosa, now that you've met Adam Osborne, I suppose we'll never break you of your addiction to the news," Erin said.

Rosa hoped her smile wasn't too off center. "You'll be glad to hear, I don't even listen to the news."

"What? Why?" Brad asked.

"The house I rented doesn't have good reception. The Internet is better, so I get a little, but I don't watch it like before."

"So in a way, Montana is weaning your addiction," Dean said.

"Maybe you can get Adam to read it to you," Stephanie teased. Everyone laughed except Rosa.

She blushed. She could feel the blood under her skin. Memories she'd been trying to banish rushed into her mind. She saw Adam's head on her pillow, remembered the feel of his body inside hers.

Shaking her head, she tried to remove the image. "I'll think about it," she told Stephanie.

They rang off and Rosa closed the computer top. She remained sitting in front of it, looking at the sky, the trees, the mountains. The place was serene, as beautiful as any location she'd been in, yet Adam was back in her head. She had to do something to clear him out.

Getting up, she replaced the laptop in her backpack and mounted her horse. Later she'd drive into Butte and buy Samantha the most popular video game they had. She'd also get something for Chelsea and Luanne's baby. But right now there were other things on her mind.

Namely rejection. Adam Osborne's rejection.

Rosa hadn't fooled them. The moment she came in the door the phone was ringing. It was Stephanie asking if she was all right. As soon as she hung up, Brad called with the same question. And then Digger was on the phone. She told them it was just that she was tired from so much work, but that things were going well here.

That wasn't totally a lie. Things were going well with everyone except Adam. She was sure they believed her story of being tired. But to avoid any further calls, she grabbed her camera and left the house. This time she headed for Butte. She had enough scenery photos of the mountains. Her collection could do with some buildings and faces if the people would agree.

Rosa didn't make it that far. Going through the Valley, she saw the library and thought of Joy Stapleton-Jones. She turned and parked in the small lot.

"Rosa, good to see you again," the sixtyish

woman greeted her warmly when she opened the door. "How are things going with Bailey?"

"Very well," Rosa said.

Joy nodded.

"Bailey's telling me a lot of stories. I'm recording them, so you'll have an oral history along with the written one. He's a very good storyteller."

"I know," Joy said. "That's one of the reasons I wanted him to write them down."

"Adam has also joined the project. He and Bailey are going to turn the stories into a book."

"That's more than I hoped for," Joy said. "You must be a miracle worker to get father and son to collaborate."

"I think it'll be a bonding experience and they both want that."

Joy nodded, but she wasn't totally convinced. Rosa thought it would work out well and the two men would be closer for it. It was the way it had worked in her family.

"From what I hear, you have a large collection of information on the area already," Rosa said.

"We do, but it always helps to get firsthand accounts."

"I'd like to read some of the works. Bailey and Adam mentioned there were other books besides Clara's diary."

Joy checked her watch. "We'll be closing in an hour and I have an appointment in Butte, but you've locked the door before, so if I leave you alone everything will be all right."

Rosa smiled. "I promise."

"I'll get the books."

Rosa settled into one of the private booths and

Joy came back with a cart of books and odd-shaped files.

"These are some of Lucas Evans's plans for buildings he constructed in the Valley. There are also several other accounts of the mining that went on here and a rather humorous account of a baseball game that one of Clara Evans's students wrote."

By the time Joy closed up and left, Rosa was engrossed in the early part of the 1900s. Clara Evans's diary was a copy of the original. Rosa imagined the original was in the personal library at Bailey's house. In addition to the books Joy had left her, Rosa had a box of letters and some personal papers with a tag that read *donated by Emily Hale.*

Rosa didn't know what she expected to find in the dog-eared pages, but like Bailey had said, Rosa could see a lot of Adam in the tenacity of the woman whose handwriting was scrawled across the paper. She wondered if she'd unconsciously turned in to the library because she wanted something of Adam. Sitting back, she stared at the ceiling a moment. The room was quiet with a silence that told her she was the only living soul among the thousands of volumes of stories. Among the lives these books held.

What had she expected, coming here? Why hadn't she just stayed away from Adam the moment she realized he didn't like her? But she felt drawn to him for that reason. Men buzzed around her the way women flocked around him. They should be opposite poles of a magnet, repelled by each other, all wanting the spotlight for themselves and unwilling to share it. Yet that wasn't proving true for them.

Stopping any thoughts that might pull Adam further into her mind, Rosa went back to reading. Unfortunately, the section she was reading was a retelling by Clara's aunt of Clara caring for Luke after a dynamite explosion. Luke had saved Clara's life and been hurt in the process.

While Adam hadn't saved Rosa's life, he'd shown her the promise of what life could be like. And then he'd taken the hope of it away.

"Crawford, you're not listening to me."

Rosa pulled into the drugstore parking lot and cut the engine. She didn't immediately get out of the car, but pulled the cell phone from its cradle and spoke into it. "I am not interested. This is my vacation. You remember, we agreed that I was taking the summer off. That means no contracts. No shooting schedule. No emergencies."

"I know, Rosa. And I understand." Maxwell Crawford was her agent. They'd worked together for years and held a mutual respect for each other. But he always called her in a pinch. And she always caved. But not this time. "This really is an emergency. They're willing to pay you triple your rate. For just a few hours of work."

"Crawford, we both know it's more than a few hours. These things can take days."

"I promise it won't. It was one of the points I stressed. If you do it, you were only available for one day."

So he had committed her for a day, not a few hours.

"Why can't they get someone else? There must be a hundred models dying for this chance."

"They want you."

It was a simple answer and it fed right into Rosa's ego. She was highly sought after, which was what had prompted this vacation. She worked hard and had been doing it for years with little relief. Her face graced many products, many magazines had her standing in the most expensive fashions in the world. Television commercials had her selling everything from soap to jewels. This was her chance to be without deadlines.

"Say you'll do it, Rosa. It's a chance to increase your worth. After this you can work less time for more money."

"You can't entice me with money, Crawford. I don't need the money."

"Then do it for me," he said. "I have children in college and a wife who lives high."

Rosa laughed. Ingela Crawford had come from a poor background and she never got it out of her blood. While she didn't spend her days clipping coupons, and her closet sported several designer labels, she assessed the worth of everything before buying it. She and Crawford were well off. He did well as her agent and he handled several other high-profile and highly paid clients.

"Rosa, it's one day. Don't you have a day you can take to wear beautiful gowns and enjoy the sun and sand on a beautiful island?"

"The answer to that is no," she said. She heard his frustration through the bouncing signals that brought his voice from New York through several outer-space satellites to the phone she held. "The sun is harsh and hot and the sand blasts against my skin with enough force to remove a dermal layer. But . . ."

"But what?" He jumped on the word, his voice raising in anticipation. "You'll do it?"

"I'll do it," she said.

Crawford shouted in her ear.

"Hold it," she stopped him. "There's a condition."

"What is it?" he asked cautiously.

She didn't ask for favors often. She wasn't like many models who became prima donnas the moment they got a little success.

"We don't do the shoot on some beach on an island."

"Where do you want to do it?"

"Here," she said. "In Waymon Valley. The place is gorgeous. The mountains will make a great backdrop. Imagine me all dressed up in a gown in an area that's juxtaposed to what I'm wearing. It's like those photos of people sitting on sofas in the middle of a forest."

"I don't know if they'll go for it. They're all set to fly to Bermuda."

"If we don't do it here, they can get someone else. Even at triple the rate," she added.

Crawford sighed. "I'll call you back."

The photo counter of the drugstore was in the far corner at the front of the store. Rosa heard the small chime that indicated someone had broken the signal when she crossed it, heading straight for that area. Bailey's party was approaching fast and she needed to get everything in place if her present was to be ready in time.

The store wasn't one of the chain types that look the same no matter which one you stop in. This was an old-fashioned store that still had a soda fountain in the back and a candy counter opposite it. The pharmacy was along a side wall and aisles held everything from hair products and cosmetics to diapers and pregnancy kits. The place was well lighted, the gaslights having given way to electricity during the early twentieth century.

Rosa smiled at a man in line as she passed him.

"Good *morning*," he said.

She smiled wider, and nodded, but did not alter her step. A commotion in the back of the store had her looking in that direction.

"It's her." Rosa heard the whispered remark from a young woman who was pulling on Adam's arm. Rosa's eyes locked with his. The young woman turned around as if she didn't want Rosa to see her or she wanted to say something that she didn't want Rosa to hear. There were three other women the same age as the one talking to Adam sitting on stools with ice-cream sodas in front of them. Rosa acknowledged Adam with a nod and continued toward the photo lab.

It appeared she couldn't go anywhere in the Valley without running into him. After their discussion and lovemaking, she tried avoiding him. She'd told herself she didn't want to see him, but each time she heard a deep voice, she turned her head expecting to find him nearby. He'd been there more times than not. He seemed to be inside her head and knew exactly where she was going before she got there.

"Hi." A young woman smiled widely at her. "I'll get your photos," she said without asking for her claim ticket. She turned to find the bag in a large bin of unclaimed packages. It didn't take her long. Rosa was aware that Adam was in the store and she was nervous and jumpy just knowing that. She wanted to get out and return to the task she needed to complete. The one thing she didn't want was to stand and make small talk with him. He'd made his feelings known to her. There was no need for them to pretend friendship. He'd offered it, but his actions proved different.

Unfortunately, this was not her lucky day. As she paid for the developed film and turned with her package, Adam and one of the young women were coming forward. She couldn't get to the door without running into them. Rosa stopped.

The young woman with him looked to be about eighteen. She hung back a step as if she didn't want to speak to Rosa. Adam took her arm and brought her forward.

"Hi," she said.

"Hello," Rosa answered.

"Rosa, this is my cousin, Tommie," Adam said.

"Tomasina," she corrected in a stage whisper. "Thomasina Evans," she said louder and directly to Rosa.

"Tommie wants to be a model. She thought you might be able to give her pointers on how to get started."

It was a question Rosa got more often than anything else. She'd been asked to speak at her old high school in Dallas one year and the first question was the same as Thomasina's. The girl was tall and slender. She had good bone structure and beautiful hair. She had all the qualities needed to make a model except her posture. Modeling would fix that.

"It takes a lot of work," Rosa said.

"I know," she said a little too fast. "But I'm willing to work hard."

"Why don't you and I have lunch tomorrow and I'll answer your questions?"

"Really?" she asked, her smile as wide as the Grand Canyon.

"Really," Rosa said. "I live at—"

"I know where you live," Tommie cut in. "What time should I be there?"

"I was going to suggest we meet at the Angus. I haven't have a good steak since I've been here."

"The Angus?"

Surprise showed again on her face. The Angus was the best restaurant in the Valley.

"I'll ask Vida to come, too. Davida King. Between the two of us, we should be able to tell you a few secrets."

"Thank you so much," she breathed, clasping Rosa's free hand and squeezing it. Her voice filled with awe. "I'll see you tomorrow."

"Noon," Rosa said. "Do you need me to pick you up?"

She shook her head. "I have a car."

She rocked back on her feet and hunched her shoulders before turning to return to her friends in the back of the store. A moment later Rosa heard one of them say, "*You are kidding me*" in a quick staccato.

Adam turned back to Rosa. "Thanks, you've made her day."

"She seems like a nice kid."

"She is and she really does want to be a model."

"Vida and I will tell her the good parts and only a few of the bad. We don't want to discourage her."

Adam looked back again. Tommie waved and smiled at him.

"Can I buy you a coffee? Or a lemonade?" Adam was smiling at her. "I told them you like it with fresh lemons."

For her own preservation, Rosa knew she should refuse. She needed to get home with the photos and begin working, but she heard herself saying, "Then I suppose I'll have to order it."

The two of them moved to a booth along the wall. Adam signaled the guy behind the counter and moments later he dropped a lemonade and a coffee on the table. They were far enough away from his cousin and her friends to not be heard.

"I've missed seeing you," Adam said, his hand hugging his cup.

"You've seen me."

"Only from a distance. And then you run away quickly."

"I thought that's how you wanted it."

"I did, too, but I found not seeing you is harder than having you close by."

"Does this mean you don't dislike me anymore?"

He looked into his cup, then back at her. "I never really disliked you."

Rosa heard a catch in his voice and it caused her heart to skip a beat. She didn't state the obvious, only lifted her glass and toasted him. "Then tell me about the other woman."

He didn't pretend to misunderstand her. "We need to get out of here for that."

Chapter 7

"Where are we going?" Rosa asked the moment they were outside. She didn't think it was a good idea to go to her house. They would be alone and she didn't know if she could trust herself. She'd longed to see him for the last week, talk to him as a friend if nothing more. When she did see him, her heart raced as it was doing now.

"For a ride. I'll drive."

They got in his truck and he drove out of town, away from both their homes and toward the imposing mountains. Mainly they were silent. Rosa couldn't think of anything to say. And Adam's stoic presence kept her quiet. He finally pulled the truck into the parking lot of a movie theater. Rosa was confused, but she didn't say anything. The theater was closed. No letters lingered, hanging askew on an aged marquee. No posters remained, curled and faded in the glass cases outside the building.

Adam got out and came around the truck. When he pulled her door open, she turned and faced him. She didn't immediately slip off the seat. Adam was looking at her, staring, his eyes piercing her.

"Why are we here?"

Adam looked at the old building. Many of these vintage theaters had closed down in the wake of multiplexes and enclosed malls. Rosa had the feeling he wasn't seeing the same building she was.

"I had my first job in there," he said.

"What did you do?"

"I started out sweeping the floor after a showing. By the time I left for college, I was running the projector. This was before everything went computer digital. Technology closed this place down. That and the high price of electricity."

Adam went to the door. Selecting a key from the chain in his hand, he opened the door.

"You have a key to this place like you knew the code for the library entrance."

"Nothing so secretive," he said. "I own this building."

He opened the door. Rosa entered the cool dark cavern.

"What are you planning to do with it?"

"I was going to renovate it. Spend time doing some of the work myself. Open it during the day for children's movies, those rated G and PG. At night for other ratings, private parties, that sort of thing."

"You're speaking in past tense. What made you change your mind?" Rosa didn't think it could be Bailey and his health concerns. If Bailey took his medicine as directed, he was perfectly capable of taking care of himself. And he had Medea there to see that he did.

"A court order," he said.

"The court won't let you open the theater? Why?"

Adam had led her into the main viewing room. The place should have smelled musty and old, but it didn't. There was a strange quietness to being in a theater with no sound and very little lighting. Unconsciously, Rosa reached for and found Adam's hand. She grasped it and held on as he moved toward a distant wall. With a penlight he opened a panel and flipped several switches.

"Wanna watch a movie?" he asked.

"Not as much as I want an explanation."

Adam pressed a button and Rosa heard the whirr of a motor beginning. Music began to play and she turned as the screen came to life. He lowered the sound and took her hand again. The two of them walked to the center aisle and down a few rows before taking seats.

"Sorry, the popcorn maker isn't on right now."

Rosa said nothing. She glanced at the screen as the title came up. A train rode across the western frontier. *Bad Day at Black Rock* disappeared as the credits changed from one to the other.

Adam's face jumped from bright to dark as the film changed scenes. "I had a camerawoman in D.C. Her name was Maureen Carter. She was with me before I became a regular weekend anchor."

Rosa listened intently. She turned sideways in the seat and folded one leg under her. Her legs were too long for her to sit Indian-style.

"We went everywhere together. She was really good at what she did. She had all kinds of awards for her photographs."

Rosa was slightly jealous of the other woman. She'd known Adam. And Adam had liked her. Unlike what he felt about Rosa. There was an attraction between them. One he fought at every turn. Rosa wondered if Maureen was the reason he put up barriers against her.

"Was she very beautiful?"

His face changed. Rosa didn't know if she should call what he did a smile, but it was a pleasant movement, as if he got a visual image that he remembered fondly.

"She was beautiful, but we weren't lovers if that's what you're thinking. Maureen isn't the reason I distrust beautiful women."

Rosa couldn't help wondering who was.

She felt Adam was in love with her even if they weren't lovers. And who was the beautiful one?

"A couple of years ago she was out on a job. I wasn't there. It was a Saturday night, full moon in the sky. People go a little crazy during a full moon. I was doing the anchor job. Maureen was working with someone else, covering a suspected drug house. It was routine. They weren't trying to enter the house, only doing some footage for a story the reporter was working on. Nothing was supposed to go wrong."

"But it did." Rosa finished Adam's thought. He was looking at her, but he wasn't talking to her. She could tell he wished he'd been there, that he could somehow change the outcome.

"It did," he conceded. "There was a drug bust going on they didn't know about. People came rushing out of the house as the police converged on the place. Maureen kept her camera running until one of the bullets hit her. She died at the scene."

A lump rose in Rosa's throat.

"She left behind a son. Left his custody to me."

"Where is he?" Rosa asked. She hadn't seen

any children at his house and no one had mentioned a child. Maybe he was a teenager and away somewhere.

"He had a distant aunt. She came forward and petitioned the court for custody. I challenged it, but the judge ruled in her favor." He paused a second. Rosa knew there was more to it than the simplified version he'd given her. "That's when I chucked it and came out here. It was my plan to bring him out here. The theater would give us something to do to get to know each other. You know, learn to trust each other. Learn about each other and get over our grief. But all that went down the drain."

"So you never restored the place?" Rosa asked.

"Not fully." Adam looked around the place. "I had some work done, the seats repaired, the projection room redone. I refinished the floors."

"You have a pattern of that," Rosa said.

"A pattern of what?"

"Running away, not finishing things."

He frowned. "What are you talking about? What have I run away from?"

"To start with, there's your house. A lot of loving work went into that house and you left it as if it meant nothing. Even when you came home, you left it sitting idle."

"I got a job. I needed to move. That wasn't running away."

"Then there's the job in D.C. and the custody."

"I didn't have a choice in that."

"You *always* have a choice."

"You know nothing about it."

"I know more than you think."

His head whipped around and he stared at her. "No, no one's said anything to me." She answered his unasked question. "You're the only one I've talked to about you. But I've learned a few things from what you've said."

"I didn't bring you here for a reading."

"Shall I stop?"

He sighed, expelling a long breath. "I didn't run away. I was so bruised after all that was going on. Maureen's death, the custody hearing, I needed to get away. Starting over seemed like a good idea."

"What about the child?"

"What about him? He's with his aunt."

"When was the last time you called him?"

He hesitated. "I haven't, not since last Christmas."

"Is he doing all right?"

"He seems to be settling in."

"You miss him, don't you?"

Rosa knew she'd struck a nerve by the way he answered. His simple yes was tight and hard.

"You say you and Maureen weren't lovers, but you were in love with her." It was a statement.

Adam contemplated her question. The film's light painted across his features. Rosa's gaze was direct.

"I suppose I was," he said. "I never thought of it before. We were so like each other, each so in tune with what the other would say or do. I felt like I'd lost an arm when she died. And when the court ruled against me . . ."

Rosa wanted to ask if he was still in love with her, but she didn't. "Have you thought of going back?"

"No." He said it quickly. Too quickly. "You heard me on the phone with Ben Masterson."

"I did and I saw your face when you hung up the phone. And when you looked at me for coming to the Valley. You smelled a story and you tried to find out the reason." She waited for a reply. When none came, she went on. "At least until the day of the picnic."

At the mention of that he turned away, giving his attention to the screen. The shot was of the sky and distant hills. It was bright and lit Adam's face up as if it were high noon.

Rosa felt he was uncomfortable. She kept to herself the smile that threatened to break. "What about the other woman?"

"There are no other women."

"The beautiful one, the too beautiful woman."

"That's an attitude, not a person."

"And you think I have it?"

"Thought," he said, turning his gaze back to her and away from Spencer Tracy on the screen.

"Wasn't there someone named Cassandra?"

"How'd you find out about her?"

"I looked you up on the Internet. For a while your name was linked with hers. I only found a few photos. She's very pretty."

"She is that, but that's all she is and she uses her looks like a badge."

"We all use our looks. I use mine and they've done very well for me."

"But you're not selfish, conniving, and untrustworthy. Cassie would never have done for Tommie what you did. She'd have brushed her away like an annoying fly."

"Is that what she did to you?"

His head snapped to face her. "For the most part. She used me. And when someone better came along, she took off with the speed of a jetliner."

"So you swore off beautiful women because of that."

"She wasn't the only one. And I thought you were one of them."

"What changed your mind?"

"The picnic."

The two words, although spoken quietly, had enough force to knock the wind out of her. Rosa was sure if she hadn't been seated, she wouldn't have been able to support herself. Then, like a vacuum, she sucked air into her lungs.

"You don't really mean that?" Rosa asked, her voice so low she could only be speaking to herself.

"I mean it," Adam answered.

For the length of eternity emotions warred within her. Elation bubbled up and threatened to overwhelm her. It was damped down by cold reality. What was she thinking? She and Adam weren't a couple. They weren't committed to each other or even intending to be. She'd let her imagination fly away with thoughts of them that weren't to be. He was a loner and she . . . she was too.

Rosa got up. Adam followed her movements. They stared at each other. The screen burst with gunfire.

"Take me back to my car," Rosa said, anger evident in every line of her body.

Turning away, she walked along the folded seats and out onto the carpet.

"Rosa," Adam called.

Her steps didn't falter. She reached the carpeted runners and walked up the short aisle to the back of the theater.

Adam got to the door before her. "What's wrong?"

"You're playing with my head," she said. "And

I'm not willing to join your game." She moved past him and opened another door. It led to the anteroom that housed the ticket booth and candy counters.

"Rosa, this is no game."

"You're right." She stopped and turned to face him. "To play a game you need as least two players for anything but solitaire. So game over."

Proceeding to his truck, she got in. She hated that he'd brought her here and she needed to ride back with him to get her car. They were still in town, but the drugstore was miles away, and she'd had her day walking in nothing but a strappy pair of sandals.

Adam got in the truck. "I don't understand. What did I say?"

"You said it all at your house a week ago, Adam. You said you were sorry. You said this couldn't go any further. Well, I agree with you. And I'm not willing to participate in a . . . a summer fling." She didn't know what else to call it.

"Rosa—"

"Please," she cut him off. "Take me back."

Adam started the engine. The drive back was short. He pulled into a parking space next to the Corvette. Rosa reached for the doorknob as soon as the truck stopped. Sliding down from the seat, she fished for her keys in her purse and got in the car. Since the car was low to the ground and Adam's truck sat high, she didn't see him when she backed out of the space.

It was only after she'd driven to her house and was safely inside that her knees gave way. She leaned against the door for support. Taking deep breaths, she tried to quiet her heart. She'd wanted to jump out of the theater chair and into

Adam's arms when he mentioned the picnic.
Both of them knew they weren't talking about
eating. They were talking about the result of the
picnic, their time in bed together.

Rosa lifted her head and looked at the loft.
Visual images of the two of them poured into her
memory. Her body suffused with heat as if some
internal furnace had suddenly come to life.

Forcing her eyes away, she told herself Adam
was playing with her head. She wasn't going to
let that happen. She hoped she'd never see him
again. But she knew that wasn't going to happen.
She was invited to Bailey's party.

The party! Thoughts of the photos suddenly
struck her. In her haste to get away from Adam,
she'd left them in his truck.

"Damn," she cursed, stamping her foot. She
needed those to complete the photo book she
planned to give to Bailey for his birthday. And
she was running out of time to get it done.

She was going to have to go and get them. And
that meant seeing Adam again.

Today had proven to Adam that initial in-
stincts were the best judge of a person's character. He should have trusted his first impression
and steered clear of Rosa Clayton. But he'd felt
drawn to her. Adam hadn't had to go riding after
her on the ridge that day. He could have made
sure she was safe from a discreet distance. He
didn't need to pack a picnic breakfast and take it
with him.

There were so many things he didn't have to
do, but it was too late. He couldn't undo what
was done. Just as he couldn't go back and keep

Maureen from going on that assignment. He couldn't undo the judge's decision regarding custody. He had to live with the consequences. Just as he had to live with knowing that Rosa Clayton had claimed his heart.

He'd also captured part of hers. He'd seen it in the photos she left on the seat of his truck. The truth was visual. As was her attempt to keep him from seeing them. Adam drove up her driveway, not even letting himself think why he didn't allow her scheme to work.

She'd called Medea and asked her to retrieve the envelope and leave it on the back porch. Rosa planned to come and get it after dark. Medea had to go into town and volunteered to drop it off. However, Adam had seen Medea taking it from the cab and wondered what she was doing. It didn't take much for the housekeeper to tell him the story. Anger initially spurred his action. He refused to let Rosa skirt around him. She wasn't going to stay in the Valley and avoid him. This last week had been miserable. Seeing her at the drugstore had jolted his heart. As he turned into her driveway, he realized he wanted to see her again. He wanted to wake up next to her in the morning.

Rosa opened the door when she saw the lights. She would be expecting Medea. The smile on her face evaporated when Adam stepped down from the truck. She took a step back inside the door, then stood her ground.

"Where's Medea?" she asked.

"I'm filling in for her," he told her. "But don't think she volunteered your call without a lot of coaxing."

He sucked in a breath. God, Rosa was beautiful. Her hair hung past her shoulders. She'd changed clothes and wore a T-shirt that hung past her knees. Adam wondered if she was wearing anything under it.

"You brought my photos?" Rosa reached for the package.

Adam had every intention of handing it to her and leaving. He lifted the envelope, then remembered what was inside. As her hand closed around it, his tightened and she tugged. She looked up at him. Adam's free arm went around her waist and he pulled her into contact with his body. Instantly he was hot.

Hot for her.

Dropping his grasp on the envelope, he circled her waist and took her mouth. He felt her surprise, which lasted an instant before he heard the package fall to the floor and felt her hands slowly moving up his arms.

"You're driving me crazy," he said, lifting his mouth. He kissed her again. "I can't go through this summer with you walking away each time you see me."

He kept kissing her. Between each word he repositioned his mouth. He couldn't get enough of her. He wanted to consume her, kiss every inch of her.

"You don't like me," she whispered against his mouth.

"I know," he groaned.

"I'm beautiful."

"Too beautiful," he whispered.

He went on pressing his mouth to hers. She *was* too beautiful, but her beauty penetrated beyond her skin. It was on the inside, too, deep down in places where no one could see. He knew that from the way she worked with his father. Bailey couldn't hold a conversation in which her name didn't come up.

Adam didn't wake on any day without thinking of her, remembering her sitting in the big chair in the great room. His heart hammered whenever he came across her or saw that red car parked somewhere in town.

His arms tightened around her, his mouth devouring hers. He wanted her, all of her. He wanted to be inside her, feeling the wild sensations that rioted through him each time he saw her. He wanted her legs wrapped around him, the feel of smooth skin rocking against his own. He wanted to listen to her soft sighs as he ravished her body. And hear the final climax as their mutual satisfaction echoed about the room.

He was very close to doing that. His hands roamed freely over her and he now knew there was nothing under the T-shirt but more of Rosa. Not a bump, a snap, or a panty line marred the smooth exploration of his hands. The knowledge aroused him more than he already was. His body grew tighter, harder, his emotions drawing hot blood from his toes and pouring it into his loins.

He couldn't wait to slip his hands under Rosa's shirt, smoothly lift it up her body and over her head. He wanted to see that body again, the even color tone that ran from her ankles to her hairline. The sexy way she moved. He wanted to taste her, kiss her, explore her region by region. And take his time doing it.

Rosa turned in his arms. Her body aligned with his and it nearly undid him. He moaned against her mouth, a sound of pure pleasure as she brushed against his hardness. As tall as she was, Adam lifted her feet off the floor. Her arms tightened around his neck as he carried her to the sofa.

"Upstairs," she whispered as her feet touched the floor. "I need a bed."

Adam heard the need in her voice and nearly ran them up the steps. The moment they reached the bedroom he pulled her into his arms. They hadn't switched on the lights upstairs. Light from below filtered up, shadowing her features as if she were the female lead in a movie-set love scene. Her eyes were dreamy, lids half closed. Adam kissed her mouth, drawing her close to him, feeling the two of them merge shoulders to knees.

Instantly, he removed her clothes. The T-shirt slipped with ease up her torso, leaving her naked. For a moment he watched her heaving breasts, moons that begged him to touch them. Lowering his mouth, he obliged. He felt her head fall back as if she were giving him both room and permission to continue.

Adam's mouth covered the dark circle of her nipple and Rosa arched in his arms, her body instinctively yearning for his touch. Adam's body strained against his clothing. He wanted them naked. He wanted to feel her skin next to his.

Her hands found his waist and undid his belt. He felt her slender fingers at his waist. Slipping her splayed hands inside his waistband, he felt the soft scratch of her nails over sensitive skin. Her hands went lower, pushing the pants down slowly until her palms cupped his buttocks. He thought he'd come right then and there.

Grabbing for her hands, he pulled them away from him, but kept them trapped in his grasp. He pulled back a second. They looked at each other, breathing but not speaking. Guiding her hands, he let her remove his pants. Then he sat on the bed, pulling her into his arms and removing the remainder of her clothes.

She was beautiful, more so than he remembered. He understood how her image jumped off the pages of a magazine. She was sexy, sensual, and moved with an elegance that was every man's sexual fantasy, including his. He kissed her belly, his tongue jutting out and tasting the warmth of her scented skin.

Lying back, he pulled her with him. She laughed as the two of them became entwined in each other. He flipped her over and parted her legs. Entering her was like nothing he could compare. The experience was totally and unexpectedly new. And something he wanted to do over and over again.

His rhythm changed at that moment. Intensity spurred him on. Rosa's legs encircled him, drawing him into her. She met his thrusts with those of her own. For Adam in that instant, something changed within him. He more than wanted this woman. He needed her. He needed her for more than sex. He needed her humor, her anger, her love.

Their bodies merged, released, connected. Pleasure coursed through him, heated with the chroma of volcanic lava. Then he felt the wave, the coming of his climax. He warded it off, straining, holding, continuing, wanting to make sure Rosa understood the pleasure she was giving him and in kind returning it. The strength built within him. He heard her sounds, mingled with his own. Animalistic grunts filled the room as their bodies seemed to catch fire, light the room, and work toward an inevitable explosion.

Then it happened. He heard her name, shouted as if it were torn from a dying animal, and realized the sound had come from him. Moments later he heard her scream and together they fell spent on the coverlet. Adam didn't want to break the connection between them. For the first time in his life he thought he'd found the one person who completed him.

He held her, falling to his side and pulling her with him. His heart pounded in his chest and he knew nothing would ever satisfy him like she did. And he wanted her with him, forever.

The Angus was no surprise to Rosa. As its name indicated, it was a beef restaurant. The decor was rustic, log walls, huge paintings of Angus cattle gracing them. The chandeliers were reproductions of longhorns with bulbs positioned in them. There were a few booths along the back, remnants of a long ago time before the place was updated to include white tablecloths and bud roses. There was no doubt that the food had always been superb.

Rosa smiled and acknowledged strangers as she was led to the table where Thomasina and Vida sat waiting. She was used to both the silence her appearance often caused and the low whispers and covert stares she sometimes received. Today it was the whispers first, then silence when she stopped to say hello to someone she'd met earlier. After a brief exchange, she went on to her waiting party sitting near the center of the room.

Tommie looked in awe of her entrance. Her mouth nearly hung open. Rosa could see the young girl wished she'd get the same kind of reception. Little did she know what a burden it could be. Rosa often wanted to be anonymous, part of the group, not set apart by some status. She had to be strong enough to ignore the way people looked at her. It was a learned trait and it did separate her. So she adapted, walking a line between being thought arrogant and stuck-up if she ignored the stares and friendly and approachable if she didn't. She'd learned the hard way that getting too close to the public could mean someone harmed her.

"We ordered," Vida said when Rosa was seated. "I got a salad for you." A waiter seemed to have followed the maitre d'. Immediately he set a glass of lemonade in front of her.

"No steak?" She laid her sunglasses on the table and adjusted her purse strap over the back of her chair.

"And a steak," Vida conceded. "Medium well."

Rosa smiled. She was watching her weight. It was ingrained in her after so many years of refusing pizza, sugared drinks, mashed potatoes, and anything fried.

"Well, Thomasina, has Vida told you anything about becoming a model?"

"She told me how she got to be one."

Vida had gone the traditional route. She'd sent a letter and photo to several agencies. When she got no response, she attended an open call and got a job and an agent. From then on she worked. Not always at the best jobs, but eventually she made it to the top.

"My method was different," Rosa began. "I fell into modeling."

"Fell?" Tommie asked. "How?"

"I'd just graduated from college. I was an engineering major and planned to get a job as soon as the summer ended."

"Really?" Tommie said on a long breath, obviously impressed. "Engineering. You must be really smart."

"Roads, bridges, concrete structures," Vida supplied. "Our Rosa has a lot of talents. She used to explain things to us about the structures where we were photographed. Of course, we didn't understand a word she said."

"Anyway," Rosa went on, "that summer I went to Italy. It was a graduation present from my family. I'd studied the language and they knew I longed to go. While coming out from under a bridge that was very well constructed and looked as if it had been there for centuries, I happened upon a designer who wanted to know what I was doing under his bridge."

"He owned the bridge?"

"It was on his property. I didn't realize I'd strayed onto an estate. There was no gate. I was driving along and stopped when I saw it. Instead of throwing me off the place, he invited me to lunch and afterward asked if he could take a few pictures of me."

"And you let him?"

Rosa nodded. "We took them on the bridge. A day later he called me and asked me to model for him. I didn't believe him."

"Why not?"

Rosa looked at the two women from Waymon Valley. "It's a vastly different world in some places," she said.

"No, it's not," Vida objected. "Men are the same all over."

"You thought he was on the make," Tommie stated.

Rosa nodded. "This was Italy and while he was handsome, older, with that worldly air that is so appealing, and had an accent to die for, I was from Dallas and knew a pass when I heard one. At least I thought so, but he was serious. And my career was launched."

"She's a Cinderella story," Vida said. "Most people go the route I went or they register with several agencies and hope for the best. It's probably what you should do. I'll write you a letter of introduction. That'll get you past the crowd."

"I have a better idea," Rosa said.

Both women looked at her in anticipation. "You can start immediately. Well, almost immediately."

"What do you mean?" Tommie asked.

Rosa didn't get to answer. At that moment she heard a familiar voice and her throat closed off. Vida and Tommie turned to see what Rosa was looking at. Adam Osborne had come in, smiling and shaking hands as he passed by table after table. Rosa could see he was heading for them. Rosa wondered if each time she saw him or heard his name, she'd have the same reaction. She wondered if this was how her brothers felt when they met the women they fell in love with. And what did Adam feel when he saw her?

Rosa thought about last night. Her body grew hot and she was sure she'd spontaneously combust within seconds. Vida and Tommie sat next to each other, leaving the only free seat next to Rosa.

Without asking, Adam slid into the chair, his leg grazing hers as surely as if it were a hot poker. Rosa had no doubt that it was intentional.

"What are you doing here?" Tommie asked. Her smile was wide. She was obviously glad to see him.

"I don't mean to interrupt. I was just over at the cable station. They need news. I thought I'd do a story for them."

"On what?" Vida asked.

"You three," he said.

"Us?" Tommie said, sitting up straighter in her chair.

"Human interest," he said, glancing at Rosa. "Two veteran models helping a novice get started. People love that sort of thing."

"I thought you were finished with broadcast news," Rosa said. She remembered her past encounter with his reporting.

"This isn't broadcast. It's cable. And they need something at the station. It seems there isn't much to report and few people to do it. I'm helping out. It'll be nothing like the last time," he told her.

Rosa stared at him. News was in his blood and as much as he said he wasn't interested in it, she knew differently.

"So, what's been going on?"

Without asking permission, he placed a small digital tape recorder on the table.

"Rosa and Vida have told me how they got in the business," Tommie said, and went on to recap the stories for him. "Rosa was about to say something more when you came."

Three pairs of eyes swung toward her.

She was suddenly tongue-tied. Images of herself and Adam flooded her mind and she couldn't think coherently.

"Don't mind me," Adam said. "Pretend I'm not here."

She could do that as well as she could pretend he hadn't rocked her world.

Clearing her throat, she took a sip of her lemonade before trying to go on. "I was about to say that I have a photo shoot coming up."

"You do?" Vida's eyes opened wide. "When?"

"In a week."

"I thought you were here for the summer," Adam said. "No work."

Rosa wondered if she heard something else in his voice. Regret? Concern? Disappointment? "I am here for the summer."

"But you just said—"

"I know." Rosa cut Vida off. "I'm not leaving." She wasn't sure why she added the last. She wanted Adam to understand that there was something between them and she wanted to pursue it to its natural conclusion. Or the end of the summer when she'd have to return to work. "I got a call from Crawford. He wants me to do one shoot."

"That could take days," Vida said. She remembered well the delays that could happen at a shoot: equipment failure, late deliveries, differences of opinion on how the setup should be, temperamental models or photographers, the weather. "And once he's got you some place exotic there'll be another job and another one."

"I only accepted one day. I told Crawford it had to be done here and after one day, finished or not, it's over."

"And you think they went for that?"

Rosa watched both Adam's and Tommie's heads swing from Vida to her.

"I might be willing to let it roll over another day," Rosa said. "Because Tommie here is a novice."

"What?" Tommie said. "What does that mean? Who's Crawford?"

A smile slowly spread over Vida's face. "That's a wonderful idea."

"What?" Tommie asked again, looking confused.

"This will make a very good story," Adam said.

"What?" Tommie asked for the third time, exasperation showing on her face.

"Crawford is my agent. And you're going to be a model in a shoot," Rosa told her.

"What?" she said, but this time her voice held breathless wonder. After a moment, questions poured from her like a waterfall. "What do I have to do? I'll need to get my hair done. What are we to wear? Where are they taking the photos? What magazines will the pictures be in? When is it? Adrian is going to be so jealous."

"Slow down," Rosa told her, making the connection that Adrian must be her best friend. "All you need to do is show up on the day. Your hair will be done by professionals. Your makeup will be done. Clothes will be provided for you. And there will be someone there to fit you."

Rosa glanced at Vida. "I thought she could wear some of your designs."

Vida reached for Rosa's hand and squeezed it. "Don't worry about any of the details. I'll take care of them."

"Another supermodel in the making," Adam said.

"What about the model walk?" Tommie asked. "Don't I have to practice that?"

Rosa and Vida laughed. "You won't be on a runway, Tommie," Rosa said. "You're going to be positioned by the photographer and stand still while a photo is taken. You can move in some cases, but in most instances it'll be a still photo."

"I can hardly wait to tell everyone."

"Not yet," Adam said. "I have some background questions."

The waiter brought their food and while Adam hadn't ordered anything, a T-bone steak was set in front of him. Rosa was reminded how well he was known in this town. Dallas was much larger. She could go places where people only recognized her from her modeling jobs. Few of them would know how she liked her steak. And even fewer of them would know her order without her giving it.

Tommie was a very interesting person. While Adam was supposed to interview her, Rosa asked more questions than either Vida or Adam. She was the only one who didn't know Tommie as well as the others. She discovered Tommie had appeared in several local productions. She would be comfortable with being onstage so to speak. Cameras, lights, and people barking instructions could be nerve-racking. Rosa felt she was going to be fine when she had to sit for the photos.

Of course, she still had to tell Crawford there was a new development to his plan. He was going to just love that. Rosa smiled at the explosion she knew was imminent. But eventually he'd see the merit in it. If Rosa was right, Tommie was going to be good. And Crawford would have the first crack at a new client.

Adam walked her to her car after they all left the restaurant. Tommie was practically floating. She couldn't wait to run and tell her friend. Rosa remembered that enthusiasm. It was good to see it hadn't been lost.

Adam took her hand and then put his arm around her waist. At the car, he turned her toward him and kissed her lightly on the mouth.

"You know this is a small town," Rosa said. "Not only does everyone know your name, they know what you eat."

From the look on his face and the way he stared down at her, she realized the double meaning of her words. "If you keep holding me like this, we're going to be the talk of the town."

"Don't tell me you think we're not already?"

Surprised, Rosa stepped back but came up against the car. The heat of the metal against her back was a weak rival to the internal furnace generating inside her. Adam's gaze was like fire. Rosa felt herself burning in it. After a moment, he released her from his stare, somehow knowing the two of them were in a public place and what was on their minds required the privacy of a closed bedroom door.

"That was a wonderful thing you did in there." Adam gestured toward the restaurant. Rosa heard the tremor in his voice. "If the shoot doesn't go well, she'll know she had a chance."

"Don't worry about the shoot. She's going to be fine."

"You're that confident?"

Rosa looked beyond his shoulder, at the place where Tommie had left them. "I'm that confident."

Chapter 8

Rosa hadn't been this happy in years. And she felt as free as the clouds high in the Montana sky. She'd always had a schedule to maintain, places to be at specific times of the day or night, dresses to wear, makeup to be done, fittings to be had. It was unnerving to have none of that to do, even though Crawford and a crew would be coming in a week. Rosa knew their presence would be temporary.

She drove without a destination. The land was simply too beautiful to ignore. She could understand why Robert Redford loved Montana so much, why he put it in his films and showed it to the world. She could see the huge expanse of emerald green carpeting flowing for miles and miles before it reached a tree line or butted up against an outcropping of hills. Hills that became mountains. Mountains that became sky and sky that added an enormous roof to the landscape.

As she passed a road she hadn't gone down before, a bridge caught her attention in the distance. It was beautiful. Slowing the car, she turned and stopped as she approached it. Taking her camera, she pushed herself up over the windshield and took a few shots. Only when she got out of the car did she see the truck parked under some trees a few yards away. Looking around, she saw no one.

Going toward it, she peered inside to see if anyone was there. It was empty. After her encounter with the teenagers in town, she wasn't taking any unnecessary chances. Adam had told her it was relatively safe in Waymon Valley. The crime rate was low and mainly limited to teenage pranks. The truck reminded her of the day she had found Bailey along the road. She couldn't drive away without checking to see if someone needed help.

She wondered where the owner of the truck was. She should just get back in the car and leave. Seeing no one, she headed back for her car. Just as she reached it, she heard a voice.

"I knew I didn't leave a red car up here. Especially not a Corvette." Then a man looked at her. "Rosa, what are you doing here?" he asked.

She opened her eyes wider. "Mike," she said. "It's your truck. Her voice held relief in it. She hoped he didn't hear it.

He offered a hand and Rosa shook it. "I didn't expect to find you coming from under the bridge," she said.

"I'm the local engineer, remember?" he asked. "Once a year we come out and inspect all the bridges in Waymon Valley."

"When I was in school I studied engineering."

"Vida told me. Did you ever work in the field?" he asked.

"Unfortunately no. Right after school I began

modeling. I suppose I have a little bit of regret about that."

"Regret? Why?"

"I won't be a model forever. Unfortunately looks fade. Younger models come along. It's a very fickle business."

He laughed. "From where I'm sitting you have years to go. And then some."

"What were you doing down there?" she asked.

"Inspecting the bridge, looking at the struts, making sure nothing's corroded, rotting away, making sure the bridge is safe."

"How long has it been here? When was it built?"

"Sometime in the 1930s," he guessed. "It was built pretty solidly back then. Even though engineering has changed, materials have changed, we know a lot more about stress, wind, and water, pressure, and movement of the earth than then, we can't keep things from deteriorating. So those built prior to our modern times need as much attention to make sure they are as structurally sound as those built today. Not only do cars go across this bridge, but at least one truck for every man, woman, and child in the county crosses it, too. And then we have some heavy-duty equipment that needs to come out here and reach some of the outlying communities. Not to mention the occasional Corvette." He gave her a friendly wink.

"Are there many ranches around here? I've actually only seen parts of the Osborne place."

"Most of them are gone. A lot of land was sold off to corporations. Nobody wants to run a ranch these days. They're more interested in running computers."

"I run a computer myself," Rosa said. "But

mainly to reach my family, get on the Internet, do e-mail, read the news. That kind of thing. Nothing heavy-duty. I'm not a novice at it, but I'm certainly not an expert."

Rosa lifted the camera and took a photo of the bridge.

"I heard you were working with Bailey Osborne on his memoirs."

She nodded.

"You could probably enhance them with some good pictures."

Rosa lowered the camera and looked at him.

"It's pretty country. And there are plenty of buildings in town that his ancestors built or re-stored."

Rosa thought about it. "I'm not writing a book. Bailey is doing all the talking. I'm just writing down what he says."

"How's the car driving?" Mike asked, changing the subject. His attention was totally absorbed by the car. It seemed no one was able to resist the beauty of the machine, including her.

"It drives like a dream."

"Most people out here drive trucks or SUVs. This car is pretty low to the ground. It could get torn up along some of the roads."

"I'm trying to stay off those," she said. "Mainly my travel routes will be in and out of the Valley. Maybe I'll go to Butte once in a while. I'm sure a Corvette won't be a problem."

"When you have a car like this," Mike said, "you don't want that kind of driving. You want open roads."

She smiled. He'd gotten her number right away.

"It's a luxury. I don't often get to drive, be-cause I'm always working. When I'm home in

New York, public transportation is the fastest route to anywhere. But now that I need to drive to get anywhere, I figured it's worth doing it."

Mike smiled. "It certainly is," he said.

"It does command a certain amount of attention," Rosa said. "People know me everywhere I go."

"That has nothing to do with the car."

Whoever said once newsprint is in your blood, it's there for life, was a liar. Adam stared at the Delete key on his computer keyboard. The print on the screen was junk. Worthless drivel. He understood the love of people who grew up using typewriters. They could rip the paper from the roll, crumple it into a ball, and pitch it toward a wastebasket strategically set across the room. That's what he wanted to do, but the physical satisfaction of expressing his frustration was denied to him with a little key.

He'd been working on the story about Rosa's interview with Tommie for nearly an hour. And he had nothing. He punched the key and a message appeared seeking his confirmation. This time he tried to murder the ENTER key. The screen went blank. He'd written news, hard news. For years he'd covered presidents, dictators, rock stars, disasters, and coronations. So why was this simple human-interest piece eluding him?

Adam began typing again. The letters slid across the screen, forming words, then sentences. But when he looked at the paragraph he'd written, it was all about Rosa, not Tommie. Highlighting the screen, he deleted the text again. The

cursor blinked at him. He remembered his first
official job as a reporter. When he went to write
the story, his hands were clammy and he continued deleting it and starting over. Maybe he'd
been out of the business too long. Maybe he
didn't have it anymore.

"What's going on?"

Adam swung around in the office chair and
looked at his father. Bailey held a book and
walked into the room. He dropped down in a
chair opposite Adam. "What are you writing?"

"Nothing, I'm watching a blinking cursor. I
think I've been away from it too long. Nothing is
coming."

"What's it about?"

"Something for the cable news. I interviewed
Tommie, Rosa, and Vida. They're helping Tommie
with her dream of becoming a model."

"I heard. Rosa's including her in a photo shoot
she's doing here."

"I guess I don't have to write the story if everyone already knows the details."

"No, it'll do you good to keep your skills honed."

"What are you doing?" Adam asked his father.

"I'm expecting Rosa. We're going to go over
some notes I made."

At the sound of her name, Adam couldn't
help remembering their last time together. He
forced himself to remain relaxed.

"I see you two have gotten past your differences."

"What does that mean?"

"You were seen kissing her on Main Street. You
know nothing is ever a secret in the Valley. Like
your truck being parked outside her house
overnight."

"Technically, that's my house."

Bailey raised his eyebrows. "You think anyone's going to make that distinction?"

"I don't really care."

He didn't know what to expect from his father, but he didn't expect what happened.

Bailey smiled. And then he laughed, a deep belly laugh, like Adam hadn't heard in years.

After a moment, he smiled, finding it contagious.

"What's so funny?"

"You. Her. You're right for each other." Bailey stood up. "She's bringing you back to life."

"Back to life?"

"Yeah, and don't pretend you don't know what I'm talking about."

The doorbell rang at that moment. Something inside Adam jerked. He heard Medea's footsteps as she headed for the door.

His father referred to Maureen Carter, her death, her son, and Adam's subsequent return to the Valley. Adam had been thinking about going back to some form of the news. It's why he went to the cable station that morning and why he jumped at the chance to write a story. He knew it would give him more time with Rosa and he was fresh for a new experience with a woman who completely captivated him.

"Don't blow it," Bailey said. He gave Adam a piercing look and pointed his index finger at him before leaving to go and meet Rosa.

Adam heard her voice in the hall. He was unable to move. Although he wanted to rush to her side, he was too afraid of what he might do. He'd kissed her on Main Street, an action that hadn't gone unnoticed. He'd known at the time that the street was full of people he knew. Stares had followed them out of the restaurant and undoubtedly people sitting near windows looked out to see them in the parking lot.

Relaxing his shoulders, Adam knew he really didn't care. He wanted Rosa to know how he felt, even though he knew she was only here for the summer and the days were running fast toward fall. She wouldn't be here the rest of her life. She had commitments waiting for her return. And once the photo shoot was done, she might be ready to leave. She was a complication in his life. One he'd tried to avoid and couldn't. His dad was right about one thing. She had made him live again.

He heard footsteps again. She was following his father. As she passed the door to the office, she stopped. Leaning into the door, he watched her hair swing past her shoulder. He remembered running his hands through that hair. In an instant, he relived them coming together. If she felt even a tenth of what he had, she couldn't leave.

He didn't think he could live without her.

"Go on in," Bailey prompted Rosa. "I have some papers to get together. Talk to Adam while I find them."

Bailey gave her back a little push and Rosa stepped across the threshold. She saw the understanding gleam in the old man's eyes. He was playing Cupid. Rosa didn't mind it. She looked forward to a moment alone with Adam.

"Hi," she said, standing in front of him.

Adam didn't answer unless she could read it in his eyes, in the way he looked at her, in the way she saw his demeanor change. He started for her, his stride removing the distance between them. His arms went around her waist and his mouth sought hers. Rosa went up on her toes to meet his kiss. The camera around her neck pressed into her belly. Adam deftly pushed it aside and their bodies joined.

Hunger climbed through Rosa's system like she'd never known. Pressing herself closer to Adam, she accepted the invasion of his tongue. Together their heads danced and bobbed until they were forced to breathe. She lay in his arms for a moment after he broke contact, trying to get her temperature down and her heart back to a normal beat.

Bailey was due back at any moment and while he condoned the feelings she had for his son, Rosa didn't want him to find them embracing each other.

"I've thought about you all day," Adam said. Rosa noticed his voice was deeper than usual.

"My thoughts have been on you, too."

He stepped back, his hands running down her arms to her fingers. Then he pulled her across the room and they sat down.

"You've been out taking photos again. I'd think you had the entire valley photographed by now."

Rosa looked down at the camera and back at him. "I was following one of Mike Holmes's suggestions."

"Mike Holmes?"

Rosa nodded. "I met him under a bridge."

"You meet a lot of people under bridges." Adam smiled. He relaxed in the chair, crossing one leg over the other.

"He was coming out from inspecting the bridge. I was taking pictures."

Adam looked interested.

"He suggested something for you, too."

"What?"

"That I add photos to your father's stories. Only I'm not writing a story. I'm just writing down what your father says. You could include them in the book."

Adam walked to a credenza and put his hand on top of a large worn wooden box. "That's not a bad idea."

Rosa went to him and ran her hands up his back. She looked down at the box.

"What's this?"

"A present. For you."

"Me!" She smiled, struggling to look over his shoulder. "I like presents. What is it?"

He pushed it toward her. Releasing her hold on him, she moved around and opened the box. Inside were cameras. They weren't new, but they had been lovingly maintained. There were three of them, a collection of lenses, filters, a light meter, flashes, and rolls of film.

"I don't know if the film's any good," Adam said. "I've had them for two years."

Rosa stared at the contents. She rubbed her hands on the cameras, lightly touched the filters standing up in a tray.

"Adam, I can't take Maureen's cameras." She spoke softly as if she had entered a graveyard.

"She would want them used."

He hadn't denied who had owned the cameras.

"I'm sure she would have liked you," Adam said.

Rosa looked up. "Are you sure?" She wasn't sure which question she was asking. Would Maureen really have liked her or would she really want her cameras used? "I'm not a professional. Photography was her life."

Rosa looked through the viewfinder of one of the cameras. She lifted a lens out and snapped it in place. She liked the feel of the instrument. There was no film loaded in it, but Rosa snapped a few shots anyway. Lowering the camera, she looked from it to Adam.

"She couldn't have used these on assignment," she said.

Adam shook his head. "They were what she used when she wanted to do things for herself. She had a huge collection of photographs that she said she was going to turn into books."

Rosa knew she never got the chance. "What happened to them?"

"They belong to her son. When we packed up her apartment, I had them put in storage. When he's old enough I'll make sure he understands what they are."

Rosa turned and faced him. "Are you sure you want me to have these?" she asked. "I mean, I can't take them, but I wouldn't mind borrowing them."

"Use them as long as you like."

Rosa looked up at him. "I'll take very good care of them." Then she lifted her face and kissed him.

"What is this?" Ben Masterson shouted into Adam's ear when he answered his cell. "You've sunk to doing nonsensical human interest stories."

"I love you, too, Ben. How's it going in the newsroom?"

"I can't believe this." Ben ignored his question. Adam heard paper rustling and Ben began quoting his article. "Thomasina Evans, an aspiring local model, will get the chance at a national magazine layout because of the efforts of visiting model Rosa Clayton. Ms. Clayton—"

"You don't need to read it to me, Ben. I wrote it."

Adam stood at the window of his bedroom. He looked toward Rosa's house, although he couldn't see it from where he stood. It was nearly midnight, but to Ben time only meant something if it was 6:00 PM or 11:00 PM when the cameras had to roll. Other than that he assumed if he was awake so was the rest of the world.

"Adam, this is not you," he continued. "You do hard news. You investigate, expose, you don't write fluff." His voice grew louder with each action. Adam could imagine his face getting redder and redder.

"Ben, this is not the way to convince me to return," Adam told him.

"What should I say?" Immediately, Ben changed his voice level and his tone. He was serious and all business.

"Nothing, I'm not coming back."

"I don't believe you. You wrote this story. That shows you're still interested in the news."

"How did you get that, anyway? I gave it to a local cable station."

"They thought it was good enough to send out on the wire."

"Wire? Cable stations don't have wires."

"Apparently, yours does. Your highly recognizable name popped up and someone brought the story to me. So how about it? I'm holding a chair for you."

"No dice."

"I can hear the wall cracking, Adam. Give it some

thought. You could be permanently stationed here, work regular hours instead of the chaotic ones you're tired of doing."

"What about the unknown world events?"

"We can't predict those, but you'd have your choice. If you want to be on the scene, we'd write it in your contract that you get to choose."

Adam hesitated. Then he remembered the reasons he'd left the newsroom. "Ben, give it to someone else. I'm staying here."

"And working for a cable company? Adam, you're better than that. You think about it. I'll call you in a week."

Ben rang off before Adam could tell him not to call. He knew his former boss did it on purpose. He didn't want to hear what Adam had to say. Ben had to notice that Adam hadn't hung up on him the way he'd done in the past. Adam had enjoyed writing the article on Tommie and Rosa. Despite his frustration in getting started, when he'd gotten into it, it flowed like water. All the training from years in the field, from filing a story over the phone came back to him in a flash.

The cable station had even asked him to sit in as a guest reporter and read it on camera. Adam had refused that, but the pulse in his blood to get in front of the camera was there.

Then his phone rang again.

Rosa had been checking the cameras Adam had loaned her since she got home. One was an antique. She took it out of the box and displayed it on a shelf. The other two had been used regularly, she thought. Rosa opened them. No film. Looking at the canisters, she found them, expired. She didn't expect they were any good, but she loaded one anyway. Looking around the room, she quickly used the film, taking pictures of the cabin. It was too dark to try anything outside.

As she lifted the camera to take the last shot, she heard something hit the door. Rosa looked at it, expecting the knock to come again. She hadn't heard a car drive up. She wasn't expecting anyone, but Adam was unpredictable. Her heart beat faster. He might have seen her lights and decided to come by.

Curiosity got the better of her. She went to the door and peered through the small glass at the top. Darkness was the only thing that greeted her.

"Is anyone there?" she called. No response.

Rosa looked through the peephole again. Still she saw nothing. She wondered if someone had thrown something against the door. With the safety chain on, she opened it a crack. The slit of light that painted the darkness on the ground showed her nothing. Then she heard something.

"Adam," someone said. The voice was low and tired sounding, barely more than a whisper. But it came again. "Adam."

Rosa closed the door and removed the chain. She pulled it inward and looked outside. A body fell on her. She stepped back to keep her balance. The male was short, thin, not much heavier than she was. She couldn't remain upright. The two of them went down. She pushed herself free of him, and he remained prone on her floor. Rosa scrambled away. Approaching him, she gently turned him over. His eyes opened. He tried to sit up, but fell back. He was thin, hardly more than skin and bones.

"Who are you?" she asked.

His eyes rolled and he closed them. Rosa got up and rushed to the kitchen. She got a glass of water and another of orange juice. He was exhausted, but he wasn't bleeding and she didn't see any scars on him. He'd called for Adam. Rosa had a sneaking suspicion she knew who this was.

Going back, she raised his head and coaxed him into drinking a few sips of water.

"Adam," she said, hoping the name would spark conversation.

"Walked . . ." He trailed off.

Rosa took the orange juice and helped him sip it. He couldn't be more than twelve years old. His clothes were dirty and he needed a bath. She looked at his shoes. They were worn, the heels practically walked away.

Taking the water, she poured a little in her hand and patted it on his face. "Wake up," she said. "Wake up."

He opened his eyes.

"What's your name?"

"Joel," he said.

"Joel? Joel Carter? Maureen Carter's son?" Rosa already knew the answer to her question.

The boy nodded. He reached for the glass of water in her hand. She helped him drink it.

"Is Adam here?"

Rosa shook her head. "He doesn't live here."

She saw the child's face fall.

"He lives nearby," she told him. "Can you sit up?"

He nodded again. Rosa helped him to a sitting position. She'd never seen anyone who looked as if they were starving to death.

"Are you hungry?"

"Yes, ma'am," he said.

"I'm going to help you to the sofa and then I'll get you something to eat."

"Could you call Adam for me?"

"I will. It's after midnight. He may be asleep. And we should get you cleaned up before we let him know you're here."

Rosa knew how Adam felt about Maureen. He'd been devastated when the judge denied him custody. Rosa was sure Adam shouldn't see Joel in this condition after an absence of two years.

Again she saw his face fall, the desperation in his eyes.

Putting her arm around him, she felt through his clothes to the skeletal bones that supported him.

He stood up. Most of his weight was on her as he limped to the sofa. "Do you think I could use the bathroom?"

"Of course," she said. She took him to the small bathroom and opened the door. "Will you be all right?"

"I think so."

Rosa eased him down on the toilet seat, not wanting to drop him for fear he'd break. She thought of Vida and her osteoporosis. This kid felt as if his bones would snap at the slightest movement, but she could tell he still wanted his privacy.

Leaving him alone, she went to the kitchen and looked to see what she had to feed a kid who probably hadn't eaten in days. Her refrigerator had mainly salad fixings, diet drinks, and fresh vegetables. She found a container of leftover spaghetti that Medea had sent her home with two nights ago.

Popping it in the microwave, she went to the bathroom door. "Joel, are you all right?"

After a moment, he said, "I'm all right."

Rosa didn't think he sounded all right. "Do you have any other clothes?"

"Not with me." He opened the door. "I had a suitcase, but I left it in a locker in St. Louis. It was too heavy to carry."

Rosa wanted to pull him into her arms, but she had enough brothers to know he wouldn't like that.

"I made you some spaghetti. After you eat it, you can take a bath. I'll find something for you to sleep in."

"What about Adam?"

"I'll call him."

Draped in a soft Mexican blanket, Rosa waited outside for Adam to arrive. He stopped his truck when its lights hit her, and she raised her hand to shade her eyes.

"What are you doing out here?" he asked after he parked and jumped down from the cab.

"Joel is inside. I didn't want you to wake him."

"Joel?" He glanced toward the front door and back at her. "Joel Carter? What's he doing here?"

"He walked most of the way trying to get to you. He thought you lived here."

"Why didn't he call?"

"Apparently, his aunt tore up the paper with your phone number on it and confiscated his cell phone. He didn't remember the number. Only that you lived in the Valley. He set out for you ten days ago."

"He's been on the road for ten days? He's only

twelve years old. Something could have happened to him." Adam started toward the door.

Rosa grabbed his arm and stopped him. "But it didn't. He's asleep. He's exhausted and very thin. I fed him. He took a bath, but he's so weak I had to help him in and out of the tub. I also examined him for any cuts or sores on his body."

Adam looked at her. She shook her head. "He doesn't have any. I didn't think of beatings, Adam. I thought of the road, sleeping outside, eating out of trash cans."

"What? He did that?"

"I don't know. My brothers did it when they were homeless. Before they came to live with the family. I don't remember it, but they told me stories after a while."

She looked at the door to the house. Joel slept inside. "Only his feet have sores. They're swollen and cut from walking so far. The soles of his shoes were nearly walked away. After I got him out of the tub, he fell instantly asleep. I think sleep is what he needs most, but it would be good if a doctor examines him."

"I'll make sure he sees one."

Rosa saw the hurt on Adam's face. Without thinking, she opened her arms and enfolded him inside the blanket with her.

"He's all right," she said. "He's here. He just needs some sleep and food."

Adam's arms went around her. She felt his weight sag against her body. He trembled with fear for the child only a few yards away from where they stood. For a long moment they held each other. She knew he felt helpless and guilty that Joel had gone to such lengths to reach him, that the child had put his life in danger by traveling so far alone.

"You're here now," she said, understanding that part of him felt he'd let Joel down by not being there when he needed him.

Rosa imagined the thoughts that were going through Adam's head as she held him. She shared his pain and she'd be there to let him know that Joel was safe and everything was all right.

"He'll be fine," she said softly. "He knows you're his haven."

"I should have called him."

"Shh," she said, quieting him. She kissed his cheek and then his mouth. "You're here now. And that counts."

Chapter 9

Sunrise spread light across the bed, waking Rosa. The rustic cabin had some modern features. A skylight was one of them. And Rosa woke each day with the dawning of light. Opening her eyes, she reached for Adam. Her hands closed around nothing. Flipping the hair from her face, she turned over. The opposite side of the bed was empty. It hadn't been slept in. Rosa sat up. Adam had told her he'd be right up when she finally climbed the stairs in the early morning hours.

Pushing the covers back, she slipped her arms into her robe and got out of bed. Looking over the railing, she saw him sitting in the same position where she'd left him a few hours earlier, his chin resting on his hands. Joel slept quietly on the sofa unaware of the vigil Adam was keeping.

Rosa descended the steps quietly. She went to the kitchen and started a pot of coffee. She fixed two cups and silently joined Adam. With one hand he took the cup she offered and captured hers with the other, holding it against his shoulder.

"Come with me," she whispered.

Taking the blanket she'd been wearing when he arrived last night, they went outside. The cabin had no porch, but there was an arrangement of garden chairs near the front shrubs. Rosa sat down and curled the blanket around them. "Have you decided what to do?"

"Not yet."

Rosa could feel the leashed anger in him. "You should let his aunt know he's all right."

Adam sipped more of his coffee before answering. "I need to talk to Joel first." He reached for her, sliding his arm around her waist and pulling her warmth against him. "I'm so angry with her now that if I called, I'd probably pull her through the phone line. He's been gone ten days and she never called me. Wouldn't it make sense that I'd be the one he'd come to?"

"Adam, it's been two years. He could have gone to any number of places. A friend's house. Somewhere near his home. Maybe even to someone you don't know. His traveling across half the country would be an unlikely choice."

His head dropped in defeat. "I didn't think of that. It's not like I lived across the street. But that doesn't excuse her. In ten days she could have taken it as a long shot that he might try to at least contact me."

"True," she conceded. Rosa wondered how people could be so neglectful of children. She came from a family of neglected children, at least until they had settled with the Claytons. Her brother Brad continued to try and save children he found on the street. "You're going to have to alert someone in authority."

Adam didn't respond.

"My sister is a child psychologist. She works with child welfare."

"He's not going to child welfare." Adam's voice was adamant. "And he's not going back to her, either."

"Don't jump to conclusions. You haven't talked to either Joel or his aunt. There could be a perfectly good explanation."

"Like what?"

"I don't know. Maybe she's ill, incapacitated in some way and Joel was with someone else when he ran away."

He obviously hadn't thought of that.

"I know the two of you don't see eye to eye where Joel is concerned, but you need to think clearly when he wakes up." Rosa spoke softly as if she were treading over scabs that hadn't healed. "He's going to need you."

Adam looked at her then. His eyes were darkly circled and worry lines edged the corners. He needed sleep.

"Thank you for being here," he said. "I don't know what he would have done if you hadn't been here when he came. He couldn't have asked for me in town. If he had, someone would have pointed him to the ranch."

"How did he know about the cabin?"

"I told him about it long ago." Adam leaned his head back. He laughed, although the sound that came from him was more of a grunt than of humor. "I'm surprised he remembered. We were talking about things to do. You know, city versus country. He couldn't imagine living in a place where there was no subway, shopping malls, movie theaters, and video arcades. I told him about horseback riding and swimming in water holes. He said it wasn't the same, and he could ride horses in Virginia and then go home."

"He's a kid. What did you expect?"

"About that." The shadow of a smile lifted his mouth. "Until you've been here, most people can't comprehend the beauty."

For a moment they were silent. "He's going to be asleep for a while. Why don't you get some rest? I'll watch over him."

"You are a very wise woman," Adam said, and leaned over and kissed her.

"You won't send me back, will you?" Joel asked at noon as they were having lunch. He'd finally awakened and immediately called for Adam. Rosa knew Adam needed more sleep, but he was by her side the moment the child called his name. Joel bolted up, unmindful of his feet, and bear-hugged Adam. Rosa had to step back to prevent herself from being knocked down again.

"I need to hear what happened," Adam said. He gave his full attention to Joel.

The boy sat at the table on the patio, facing the majestic mountains in the distance.

"I ran away," he said.

Adam waited a moment before asking, "Why?"

"They didn't want me there."

"They?"

"Aunt Lillian and her husband."

"Husband? She got married?"

Joel nodded. "A year ago. All they ever did was holler at me, order me around and criticize everything I did. The only reason she kept me around was for the money."

Adam glanced at Rosa. She sat silently eating.

"Joel's mother had a trust fund set up for him. She also had a large insurance policy. The executor is a lawyer friend of Maureen's."

"Yeah, and he wouldn't give Aunt Lillian any money. She was really mad about that."

"There had to be some kind of an allowance for your support," Rosa said.

"According to her, it isn't enough." Joel bit into his sandwich and drank some of his cola. "She always wanted more, but he wouldn't give it to her. So she took it out on me."

"She beat you?" Adam said, his anger close to the surface.

"No, she never hit me. She just talked all the time, saying the same thing over and over about how she wished I'd never come to live with her. So a few days ago I left."

"Have you called her at all?" Rosa asked.

Joel shook his head. "I never want to see her again."

Rosa could see some of Adam in the boy. She knew he wasn't Adam's son, but the two were like personalities. By the time Joel was a teenager, he and Adam would clash hard.

"Why didn't you ever call me?" Joel asked. Rosa could hear the mixture of hurt and censure in the twelve-year-old's voice.

"I did," Adam replied. "In the beginning. Your aunt told me I would confuse you, hinder your ability to settle into your new life. I saw the wisdom in that."

"I don't."

"There are some things you're too young to understand."

"Like being abandoned by the only person I wanted to be with."

Adam shifted in his chair. "I didn't abandon you, Joel. The court awarded custody to your aunt. She was right that you needed time to get used to the idea."

"She hated me. I told you she only wanted the money. Once she found out she couldn't get it, she didn't want me there, either. And I'm not going back."

"We'll table that for right now," Adam said.

"I won't," he said, defiantly, staring at the man he'd traveled two thousand miles to see.

"It's not that easy, Joel," Adam shouted.

"Guys," Rosa interjected, knowing things were about to get out of control. "None of this has to be addressed now." She looked at Joel. "It's going to have to be done sometime," she said. He started to speak, but Rosa raised her hand to stop him. Then she looked at Adam. "The first thing we need to do is get him checked out by a doctor."

"I don't need a doctor," Joel protested.

"It's not your call," Adam told him. "You practically walked across the country. Your feet are swollen and cut. You've lost so much weight I'm not sure your body isn't eating itself. The best thing to do is to make sure you're healthy."

"Well, I do have my insurance card."

Rosa and Adam looked at each other. She fought the smile that threatened to spread across her face, but lost after a moment. Adam was trying to fight his own. Soon they burst into laughter.

"What?" Joel asked.

"You have no clothes, shoes that we threw out, and no money but you have an insurance card."

"It's in my wallet. Mom told me to always carry it."

"At least he has priorities," Rosa commented

as she pushed her chair back and got up to clear the table.

Adam was relieved when the doctor only prescribed megadoses of vitamins, a diet to help Joel gain his weight back, and a topical antibiotic for the boy's feet. Other than that, Joel would be all right in a couple of weeks.

Rosa had gone to pick up some things Joel would need and Adam studied the street for her as they left the medical building. She waved to them as she crossed the street. Adam and Joel, sporting crutches, turned to meet her.

"Clean bill of health?" she addressed Joel when she reached them.

"Other than these walking sticks"—he indicated the crutches—"I'm fine."

"We have a couple of prescriptions to be filled," Adam added, overriding Joel's statement that everything was all right. He supposed it was youthful invulnerability. Adam had done some pretty risky things in his own youth, but nothing as crazy as hitchhiking more than halfway across the country with no money and only the clothes on his back at twelve years old.

He had to admit Joel was resourceful. Despite his weight and his feet, he'd come through the experience virtually unscarred. In later life, being resourceful was an admired trait. But Adam was scared to death when Rosa had explained that he was there and how he got there. Afraid for what could have happened to him.

"What's in the bag?" Joel asked.

Rosa pulled a pair of soft slippers from the bag.

"Is this all?" Adam asked, seeing only the small bag in her hand.

"I knew better than to get anything else until he could choose it himself," she said, looking at Joel. "I know you need clothes, but your tastes are probably different than mine. And now that you have *legs*"—she indicated his crutches—"you can hobble over to the store with me."

Rosa leaned over and put the slippers on the ground. Joel wore only socks. She helped him into them.

"I look like a dork." He stared at the brown slippers and then at the two of them.

"Yeah," she agreed. "You do."

Joel's mouth opened in surprise. Adam smiled.

"But you're our dork." Rosa reached for his neck and hugged him.

"Let go." He wiggled free of her.

"Sorry, I forgot that twelve-year-olds can't be hugged. So let's go and get you something to wear."

The three of them began walking.

"Joel, when you left home, didn't you think to take any clothes?" Adam asked.

"Sure I did," he said. "I left them in a locker at a post office in Missouri. The suitcase was heavy and I couldn't carry it anymore. I have the key." He stopped and rooted around in his pocket. The key wasn't there.

"I emptied your pockets when I washed your clothes," Rosa said. "The key is on the shelf in the laundry room."

"What were you doing in Missouri?" Adam asked. It wasn't exactly on a direct route to Montana.

Joel hesitated. Adam assumed the story wouldn't be a pretty one.

"I hitched a ride on a truck and it went to Oklahoma."

"Didn't you ask the driver where he was headed?"

Joel dropped his head, staring at his new slippers as if they were acceptable footwear.

"No, he didn't," Rosa answered.

Adam turned to her.

"He hitched a ride, but the driver didn't know he was there." She paused. "Isn't that right, Joel?"

After a moment of hesitation, the boy nodded. "I had enough money to buy a bus ticket to Kansas City. I stowed in the back of a truck. It was a furniture truck and there was a sofa all wrapped in plastic. I didn't think it would hurt if I lay on it. I was tired and I fell asleep. When I woke up the truck had stopped. I jumped off it. I was in a town, and the truck had stopped at a red light. I didn't know where I was so when I saw the bus station, I went in there."

Adam didn't know whether he should be angry or laugh at the situation. Joel had been through an ordeal to get to Adam, and he was obviously afraid of what Adam thought. Adam chose laughter. Joel stared at him unsure what to do. Slowly a smile lifted the corners of his mouth.

Adam reached for him and pulled Joel into a hug. The boy let go of the crutches and his small arms went around Adam. Through his mind the years of separation melted. He remembered playing video games that Joel always won. They'd gone camping and to ball games together. When Maureen was away, Adam had been there to care for Joel. He'd been the boy's surrogate father, a role he'd been willing to continue, but for the court.

And he knew he'd have to go through the courts again.

And soon.

Rosa was silent on the trip back. Joel fell asleep. Even though he'd slept for hours, the short trip to the doctor's office and shopping had tired him out. Adam knew the ordeal took a greater toll on his young body than he understood. He drove straight to the ranch. As the truck came to a stop in front of the house, Bailey rode up on his horse and dismounted.

Adam got out of the truck as his father opened the door for Rosa.

"Bailey, you're riding," she said.

He gave her a tight smile, then glanced at Adam, knowing his son wouldn't approve. "I didn't go far," he explained, getting down. "Only around the building a couple of times. Medea has already lectured me."

Joel chose that moment to sit up and look through the window.

"Ah, this must be the boy," Bailey said. "Word has it he was asking how to get to the cabin."

When Adam opened his door Joel scrambled out, awkward as he tried to get all four of his land legs in a balancing position.

"I'm Joel," he volunteered.

"I see. I'm Bailey, Adam's dad."

Adam knew his father was aware of who Joel was. Adam had told him the circumstances involving the custody battle and its outcome.

Joel looked between the two men. Adam wondered if he was trying to find a resemblance. Adam favored his father more than his mother.

"Looks like you have a problem with your feet," Bailey said.

"Oh, I'll be all right," he said. "Is that your horse?" Joel's eyes were as big as saucers.

Bailey glanced at the horse. "Yep, this ole guy and I have spent many years together."

"Wow! It must be great. I've never been on a horse." He looked at Adam for confirmation.

"Well," Bailey, said, "we'll just have to get you up there."

Rosa nudged Adam's arm. "Put him on the horse," she whispered.

"His feet. He can't put them in the stirrups."

"*Put* him on the horse," she insisted. "Lift him up."

Adam stepped forward. "How about right now, buddy?" He put his hands under Joel's arms and hoisted him into the air. Joel swung his legs over the animal and settled into the saddle. Rosa grabbed the falling crutches.

"Wow, this is really high up."

The stirrups were set for Bailey, a man with much longer legs than Joel's. There was no way the boy could slip his feet in them and hurt his soles.

"Do you think I could ride him?" Joel was already moving back and forth the way he'd probably seen people on television ride. Bailey's hold on the reins kept the horse steady.

"In time," Adam said.

"How much time?" Medea asked as she joined the small gathering. "Who is this child?"

"This is Joel," Adam answered.

"You the one," she stated. "I expected you two years ago. Where have you been?" Her smile took out of her words any sting Joel might think was there. "I see you had a hard time getting here. Well, come on in. You can tell me all about it."

"I'll bring him in a moment," Bailey said. "We'll let him ride back to the stable." He reached for the crutches Rosa held and took them from her.

They all went into the house. Joel and Bailey came in moments later. Without discussion Medea took over the care of Joel. Bailey, Rosa, and Adam went into the great room, where the two of them quickly recounted Joel's story for Bailey.

"What now?" Bailey asked when they finished.

"Now I call his aunt and get her part of the story."

Adam left them and went to his office. He dialed the number in his Rolodex for Lillian Reynolds. The recording said it had been disconnected. He dialed it again, sure he'd pressed the right keys, but there was the chance he'd dialed incorrectly. The same recording advised him the number was disconnected.

Returning to the kitchen where Joel sat talking to Medea and eating cookies and milk, Adam asked him for the phone number of his aunt.

"I'm not going back there," he said.

"I still have to talk to her, Joel. What's the phone number?"

Reluctantly, the boy gave him the number. It was different from the phone number Adam had. He tried it when he was alone again and it rang. On the second ring a man answered.

"This is Adam Osborne. Is Lillian Reynolds there?"

"You mean Lillian Clegg. This is her husband."

"I'm calling about Joel."

"He's not here."

Adam heard a second voice in the background and then Lillian came on the line.

"Hello, this is Lillian."

"Lillian, Adam Osborne here."

"Adam, it's been a long time."

"Over two years," he said. "I hear congratulations are in order." Adam hated small talk. He wanted to get right to the point, but like any good reporter, he wanted to give her the chance to tell him the story.

"Yes, I've married since the last time I saw you."

"Congratulations again."

"I suppose you're calling to talk to Joel. He's not here at the moment."

"I know that. He's here."

"There? What's he doing there?"

"Apparently, he doesn't want to live with you any longer. He's been gone for ten days and you're telling me he simply isn't there. Have you reported him missing?" Adam forced himself to keep control of his voice.

She stammered. "I sent him to camp."

"What camp?"

"It's a summer camp in . . . in Virginia. He's supposed to be there. I drove him myself."

"Well, he's here."

"Is he all right?"

At least she was concerned about him. Adam gave her credit for that. "Only a little worse for wear. He hitchhiked across the country."

"Oh my God," she said. "Send him back."

"He doesn't want to come back. He's very adamant about that. He says you and your new husband don't want him around."

"That's not true. We love Joel."

Adam didn't hear the sincerity in her voice that he wanted to know was there. "Then why is he saying he doesn't want to return?"

"Adam, you know how boys are at his age."

"How are they, Lillian?"

Ignoring his question, she tried a different tactic. "Adam, I have a court order. You put him on the fastest plane back here."

"I don't think so. You might have a court order, but he's twelve now and I'm sure the court will be interested in what he has to say about what his life has been like for the past two years."

Silence followed his statement. Then Lillian said, "Adam, we don't need to bring courts into this. I'm sure we can work this out ourselves."

"I don't think so, Lillian. Joel is going to stay here until we work things out. I suggest you get a lawyer because I'm taking you back to court."

"Adam—" she started.

"I don't think we should discuss this anymore." He cut her off. "I'll have my lawyer contact you later this week."

Adam said good-bye and broke the connection. He wasn't a compulsive man, but seeing Joel so thin and worn angered him. Maureen had not intended for her son to be unhappy. Adam had made her a promise and no court was going to keep him from honoring it.

Rosa's life changed in the space of time it took Adam to make a single phone call. She'd known what he was going through, the moment she found him sitting vigil over the sleeping child. And now she was back where she'd begun the day, yet it was a different Rosa who entered her house from the one who'd left it seven hours earlier. When Adam returned to the kitchen after making his phone call to Joel's aunt, he only asked Joel one question. What was the name of his camp?

The boy clearly looked guilty. He confessed that Lillian *had* sent him to camp. It was from there that he left to find Adam. And it was possibly why Lillian didn't know he'd been missing for ten days.

"Do you think his aunt knew he was gone?" Rosa asked Adam when he closed the door. She needed to fill the air with conversation. The house felt hollow and she was sure their budding relationship had taken a gunshot wound in the last twenty-four hours.

"I do." Adam walked to the refrigerator and got a bottle of water. He twisted the top off and drained the bottle as if he hadn't had anything to drink in days. Tossing the empty container in the recyclables bin, he absently took a second bottle and handed it to Rosa. "After Joel gave me the name of the camp, I called them. I spoke to the director and told them Joel had run away and he was here. He told me Joel was no longer registered at the camp, that his aunt had been notified when he ran away from there the second time."

"He'd done it before?"

"Yes, they found him and returned him to the camp. They'd notified Lillian and she'd told them he would return there."

"He'd returned home as far as they knew. The man on the phone suggested I call Lillian and let her know Joel had run away again."

"So she knew. How could she not report him missing? Anything could have happened to him. There has to be another explanation."

"I'm sure there is."

The finality with which he spoke the words told Rosa he'd made a decision. She knew without asking what it was, but she asked anyway.

"You're going to go back to court and fight for custody again," she stated, holding the unopened bottle of water.

Adam stared at her for a long moment before nodding.

"Before you jump to conclusions, why don't you hire an investigator to check out what's really going on in Joel's household? You already know he didn't tell the whole truth. Maybe there's some explanation that needs a clearer head and less emotion behind the decision."

Adam sat down. "You're right," he sighed.

Rosa went to him. "Stop thinking of what could have happened to him. He's here. He's all right."

Adam put his arms around her waist and pulled her to him. The day had been tiring. Rosa felt a surge of love for him that she'd never felt before. Her arms went around his neck and she kissed the top of his head.

Rosa knew Adam was doing the right thing. It was what Maureen had asked him to do. He was honoring her final wish. And she could tell he was attached to Joel more than he wanted anyone to know. She had fallen in love with Adam and now his priorities had changed. He wasn't in love with her, but she thought he could be—in time. But they didn't have much of that. She had to return to jobs that took her around the world.

And Adam now had Joel.

Chapter 10

The day was perfect, clear sky, comfortable temperatures. There would be no delay. The camera crew, makeup artists, hair designers, sweepers, and a miscellaneous group of other people were all assembled. Rosa looked at Tommie, who was awed by all the activity. Rosa, Tommie, and Vida sat in director's chairs—waiting. It was normal for Vida and her, but new for Tommie.

"Ready," the photographer called. "Let's try you first." Tommie pointed a finger at herself and he nodded. She looked at Vida and Rosa.

"You'll be fine," Rosa said. "He'll tell you what to do."

Vida and Rosa watched Tommie for a moment. She was awkward and scared at first, but the photographer was first-rate and after a while she relaxed.

"I didn't realize how much I miss this," Vida said. "The smell of hair spray, clothes rustling, the sound of cameras being loaded with film, or shutters opening and closing, the slap of equipment falling, sitting still in a chair while someone pampers me, doing my hair and makeup, and bringing me bottles of cold water."

"I thought you said you didn't miss it."

"I lied." Vida smiled. "I can't do it any longer, and I suppose it's true that we miss what we used to do when we can no longer do it."

Vida's condition prevented her from vigorous activities. Her rare form of osteoporosis meant she could break a leg running through an airport. When she fell off the runway, it was the final straw for her career. She had to quit the road. She tried doing small jobs that required little in the way of movement, but they weren't satisfying. Luckily, she discovered designing. She'd thrown her heart into it.

"Vida, I'm sorry."

"Don't be." She looked directly at Rosa. "It's only because this is going on here. I probably wouldn't have thought about it if I weren't here to see it. And there are other compensations."

Rosa watched her closely. Vida looked as if she had a secret.

"What?" Rosa asked.

"Mike asked me to marry him last night."

Rosa jumped up and turned to her friend. "Vida, that's wonderful." A strange array of feelings went through Rosa as she bent down and hugged her friend. "I can't believe this."

"It's hard for me to believe, too. I've been in love with him since puberty. I suppose he finally figured out he was in love with me, too."

"Have you made any plans? Set a date?"

Vida shook her head. "We both want a short engagement, so I suppose we'll be doing something fairly soon."

"You have to let me know. No matter where I am I'll come back for the wedding."

"You bet your boots you will," she agreed. "You're going to be my maid of honor."

"Great," Rosa said. "I'd be hurt if you hadn't asked me."

"After all the time we've spent together, who else could I choose?"

"Rosa, I'm ready for you now." The photographer interrupted them.

Both women turned to face the photographer. Rosa gave Vida a smile and moved to the spot where she was to stand. She wore a white gown made of an elasticized material. It clung to every curve of her body. Over it was a red lace coat that billowed out as she walked. The photographer took note of the way the material moved and snapped several frames as she walked.

Rosa raised her arms and let the breeze flow freely through the fabric. When she reached the center where Tommie stood, she turned the girl around and the two stood back to back. Photo after photo was taken.

"All right, let's have Rosa alone," he said.

The gallery of people around the shoot watched as she moved forward, backward, lifted her arms, sat down, stood up, twirled around. As she moved, the photographer moved, too. Like a fencing match, they parlayed about each other, stepping in and out of sword range, as he angled his camera at her and she performed her routine in front of him.

"She is so good," Tommie said to Vida, who had left her chair and was standing on the edge of the photographer's space.

"These two have worked together a long time. Don't worry. It will come to you."

"I feel good in the dress." She turned all the way around as if she were modeling for Vida.

Tommie wore a royal blue ball gown made of satin. The lines were simple, a fitted bodice with small straps that crisscrossed in the back and continued down the wide skirt to the hem. It was one of Vida's designs for her new fledgling company. The only adornment to the dress was a row of semiprecious stones that followed the shoulder straps and the path to the floor of the gown. It retailed for a small fortune.

"You look wonderful," Vida told Tommie. At the same time, the makeup artist came over and repaired a little of Tommie's makeup.

"You're doing fine," Vida assured Tommie. "But you better go and change. They'll be ready for you again soon."

Rosa watched what was going on beyond the photo area. She saw Tommie and Vida smiling at her before Tommie turned and went into the small trailer that was brought in as a changing room. Rosa wondered where Adam was. When Vida told her she was engaged, Rosa's thoughts immediately flew to him. She envied her friend. For the outside world, Rosa's life looked glamorous. And it was, but lately she hadn't felt fulfilled by her work.

Vida basked in her design work. Rosa loved her camera. They were both growing older. It was time for people like Tommie to take over. Rosa's contracts were still the highest, but she had enough money to last a lifetime. And then there was Adam. He changed her life, too. When she left the Valley, she'd take regrets with her. Regrets that she wasn't able to pursue their relationship to its natural end. She admitted that end was somewhere around fifty or sixty years in the future.

"Rosa, what are you doing?"

She snapped back to the present. She hadn't been paying attention to instructions. "Sorry, I was thinking of the mountains." It wasn't a total lie. Adam was a metaphorical mountain. There was so much about him she didn't understand, yet so much she knew.

"It's time for the next outfit. And I need Tommie now."

Rosa moved toward the trailer. Tommie came out as if on cue. She'd changed into a casual pair of tan safari shorts that came to her knees, where they were met by a long pair of sheer white stockings. Her top was sleeveless, an over-the-head concoction of ruffled material. The contrast worked and looked great on the young girl. Her youthful exuberance would surely be captured on the film.

Rosa had just pulled the door of the trailer open when she saw the truck coming up the road. Immediately she recognized it as Adam's. Instead of doing what she should, changing clothes for the next segment, she went running off toward the approaching vehicle.

The truck led a dust trail. Adam stopped and got out as she made her way to him. He opened his arms and Rosa flew into them. Her mouth found his and he kissed her as if he were a man returning from war. He'd been away, speaking to a private investigator and setting in motion his plan to verify Joel's story.

"I missed you," Rosa said, unguarded.

"I missed you, too." He pushed her back but

didn't release her. He looked her up and down. "You look good enough to eat," he said with a leering smile on his face.

"Well, don't. It would be a three-thousand-dollar meal."

"Ouch," he laughed.

"How did you like Simon?"

"I think he's competent. I gather your family has used his services several times."

Rosa nodded. "He found the birth mother of two of my brothers and our adoptive mother's biological daughter."

"That's a mouthful. Want to run that by me again?"

They started walking toward the changing trailer. Adam kept his arm around Rosa. She liked the way she felt with him holding her.

"Two of my brothers are really brothers."

He looked at her with a frown.

"That means they are biological brothers. Same parents. One of them never gave up on finding his birth mother. He searched for her for over thirty years. Then he hired Simon Thalberg and several months later Simon found her in a nursing home."

"That's wonderful. What a story."

"That wasn't the story. Finding Stephanie made the news, but you know about her."

"Simon found her, too?"

She nodded. "In a very short time. She'd registered at the center for missing children and he found her. She's now married to one of my brothers."

"One of the two biologicals?"

Rosa laughed. "I know it's weird language. Most people who are not adopted never use the terms biological or adoptive, but we need to somehow distinguish between them when we're talking."

They had reached the trailer.

"I have to change now."

"How's Tommie doing?"

Rosa had one foot on the bottom step of the trailer. She turned and looked at Tommie in the limelight of the camera. "Just look at her. She's having fun. And from the way the photographer is continually snapping pictures without giving instruction, he likes what she's doing."

Tommie had a big smile on her face. She was running and jumping, acting like a playful teenager. The pictures were going to look great and Rosa was sure Crawford would get them into a high-end teen magazine. After that Tommie would be on her way. And it wouldn't hurt Vida's design company, either.

Rosa kissed Adam and disappeared into the trailer. Ten people must have grabbed her, dressed her, repaired her makeup, found her shoes, and got her back onto the spot where the cameras would snap picture after picture of her in a new outfit.

Rosa couldn't wait for the day to be over. Adam watched from the director's chair. Her thoughts were on him. She smiled at the camera, but her happiness was due to the man watching her. Temporarily Rosa had put leaving out of her mind. The morning after Joel's arrival, when Adam had brought her home, she'd been depressed at the change in their circumstances. Yet his lovemaking that morning had told her he wanted her around for a long time. The words

didn't come from his mouth and Rosa refused to
think further than one day at a time.

She turned around, glancing over her shoulder as the camera snapped. She wasn't looking at
it, however. Her eyes had just captured Adam's.
She read the look on his face and wondered if it
matched her own. The shutter clicked and her
image was recorded for posterity.

No modeling job Rosa had ever worked on
went as smoothly as the one today. Even when
everyone was a professional, there were screwups,
people who weren't in the mood that day, people
who didn't like the way they looked or were
dressed, or even personality clashes between crew
members. And of course there were the prima
donna models. Rosa was glad Tommie's initiation
into what she thought would be her career was an
easy one.

"All done," Vida called, standing up as Tommie
came running over and hugged her.

"This was great," she said. "I had a wonderful
time. Is it always this much fun?"

"Not always," Vida answered honestly. "But you
can always make it fun for yourself." Tommie was
too enamored from her first day to hear the underlying warning in Vida's words.

While every job had its drawbacks, Rosa wouldn't
have made another choice of a career if she could
go back. She would still be an engineering major
in school. She'd thought she might be able to do
something with it when she finished modeling,
but she didn't think that way any longer. She had
enough money to last her if she never worked

again. So modeling had freed her to do whatever she wanted to do in the future.

"Rosa, I can't thank you enough for letting me do this." Tommie hugged Rosa, too. "If nothing happens with the pictures, I appreciate what you did for me."

"I don't think you need to worry about continuing," Rosa told her. "Crawford thinks you're going to be a good model." They both glanced at Rosa's agent, who didn't often attend her shoots, but had come to this one.

"I better change clothes," Tommie said. "These are beautiful." She looked down at herself. "But I have to give them back."

"Don't worry, Tommie." Adam spoke for the first time since the end of the session. "One day soon you'll be able to afford to keep them."

"I hope so," she said, and waved as she headed for the trailer.

"She's probably going to call her girlfriends and tell them everything that happened before she can get out of those clothes," Adam said.

Rosa nodded.

"We've created a monster," Vida said. The two women laughed.

"But she's an awfully good monster," Rosa pointed out.

Rosa slipped her arm around Adam's waist. She liked being anchored to him.

Adam drove Rosa home. The low-sitting car wouldn't have made it up the mountain to the shoot. Mike, Vida, and Tommie had picked her up. Adam stopped the truck in front of her house. He came around and opened the door. Rosa slipped from her seat into his arms.

"I don't know why you went to the trouble of putting your clothes on," Adam said, pinning her between him and the truck's open door. He pulled her into his arms and spoke against her mouth. "I'm only going to take them off you."

"I couldn't very well get past all those people without them," Rosa moaned. "But think how much fun it will be getting me out of them."

"You are a wicked woman."

"Only when I'm with you."

"Aren't you tired?"

She shook her head. She should have been dead on her feet. A day like today would usually leave her wanting a long bath and an early night, but she felt energized.

"Good," he said.

"Why?" she asked. "What have you got planned?"

"You'll see."

Pulling her arm through his, he led her to the door. Rosa smelled buttercream the moment she walked inside. The smell took her back years, to her ninth birthday. Her brothers baked the cake and the smell was delicious. The icing was delicious, but the cake was raw inside and burned on the outside.

"You baked a cake?" she asked.

"Candles," he corrected.

For a moment, she didn't understand. "Oh, you bought candles." She looked at the several lighted jars around the room.

"Now you're going to go upstairs and take a bubble bath while I fix us something to eat."

She smiled as he walked her to the steps. "I could get used to this pampering."

He kissed her lightly on the lips. "You ain't

seen nothing yet." Then he patted her on the
behind and sent her up the stairs.

Rosa walked slowly, keeping her eyes on
Adam. He watched her, too, until she reached
the bathroom door and disappeared inside. One
of her dresses hung from the shower rack. "I
guess I'm supposed to wear this," she said to herself. It was the dress she'd bought in Butte the
day Adam had taken her there.

Rosa smiled at the memory of that day. They
had disliked each other then. He was only trying
to help Vida, keeping her from driving. But the
truth was, they were both putting up barriers,
hiding their feelings even from themselves.

Turning on the taps and pouring bath salts into
the tub, Rosa found several candles had been left
on the shelf of the tub. She lit the candles. Their
scent immediately mixed with the bath salts and a
pleasing fragrance filled the room.

Stripping, Rosa pulled her hair up and anchored it on top of her head. Then she lowered
herself into the hot water. Tension she wasn't
even aware of eased from her muscles. She let
the water wash over her, making her weightless
as her arms floated freely to the surface.

A soft knock had her looking at the door. It
opened and Adam came in carrying a glass of
wine. He smiled and set it on the tub's lip. No
words were exchanged. None were necessary.
Rosa spoke with her eyes and her heart. She
picked up the glass and tasted the sweet wine.

"You look beautiful there," Adam said.

"Join me," she offered.

"How I would love to," he said. "But if I did
we'd never get to dinner."

"I can wait," she told him, her voice several

notes lower than normal. Her eyes were steady, and she didn't hide their meaning. She wanted him here and now.

"Hold that thought," he said as if he could read her mind. "We *will* get to it."

He left with a smile. Rosa had never been so bold. She knew her time was short and she wanted Adam, but the summer would be ending soon. Taking a drink of her wine, she relaxed in the hot water, and when it cooled, she got out and dried herself. Taking the dress into the bedroom, she spent several minutes lotioning and perfuming her body. Then she slipped into the fundamentals of underwear and covered herself with the dress. It was red, scarlet actually, and it still fit as if it were made for her.

Rosa thought she'd never have an occasion to wear the gown in the Valley. And while she didn't expect to go anywhere other than downstairs, this was an occasion. She opened the bedroom door and started a slow walk along the catwalk. Her heels clicked on the wooden flooring. Adam looked up at her. He'd changed from the khakis and polo shirt into a dark suit and white shirt. The lights had been lowered and only the candles posed any illumination. He was gorgeous.

The expression on his face told her he appreciated her, too.

He met her as she descended the stairs. He kissed her lightly on the mouth, a promise of more to come. Rosa submitted her own promise.

"I thought I could picture what you'd look like in that dress, but I was *wrong*," he said. He pushed her back a little and admired every bit of her. "My imagination is not that good. You look like a queen."

"I could get used to compliments like that."

"You will," he promised.

"The food smells great," Rosa said, hiding her confusion over his comment. "What are we having?"

"Mademoiselle, to start we have champagne framboise garnished with fresh raspberries. This will be followed with a fresh lobster bisque on an island of lobster mousse and continued with bouchée of escargots and morel mushrooms in a cognac-roasted garlic cream sauce and chives. Then—"

"Then? There's more?" Rosa asked.

"Ah, mademoiselle, a meal is to be enjoyed."

Rosa laughed at his mock French accent.

"We will go on with the salad course, a chiffonade of Boston lettuce with Belgium endive and hearts of palm. This is enhanced with an arugula balsamic vinaigrette. To clear your palate for the main course, an interlude of passion fruit sorbet with a splash of passion fruit liqueur."

"I get it. If food doesn't work, use liqueur," she teased.

Adam smiled, but continued with the menu. "The main dish, maigret of duck Martiniquaise with caramelized leg confit and banana tempura in a Caribbean rum sauce. I trust you will love it."

"Absolutely," Rosa agreed.

"To conclude this wondrous occasion, we have *profiterolles au chocolat.*"

"That sounds wonderful. What is it?"

"A cream puff filled with crème patisserie, topped with warm chocolate sauce, flavored with Grand Marnier and cognac, and garnished with fresh whipped cream and toasted almonds."

"I can hardly wait."

"Be seated and we can begin making love to our palates."

He held her chair and Rosa sat down. "When did you have time to do all this?"

"Didn't I tell you I was a magician?"

"No, I mean, I know you have a certain paranormal attraction for the opposite sex. There must be something magical about that. However, a master chef is not on the list."

Rosa tasted her meal. "This is delicious," she said. "We look like we're celebrating something. Are we?"

"It's Tuesday. We're here. That's enough to celebrate." He poured wine into her glass, his eyes fixed on hers and not the wineglass. Yet not a drop was spilled.

"I'll take that," she said, raising her glass to her lips. She, too, didn't take her eyes off Adam. Throughout the meal they seemed to play the sex game, both of them looking at each other as if the food on their plates wasn't as delicious as each other would be.

"I saw you writing today. Are you filing a story on the shoot?"

"I thought I might."

"You didn't think it was boring?"

"Boring?"

"I mean compared to stories you're used to covering, world events, presidential inaugurations, wars."

"You think your work is boring?"

"No, but I don't expect to see it on the front page, either."

"It won't make the front page unless someone dies. It will make the fashion pages where it will mean something.

Light dawned in Rosa's brain. "You're doing this for Vida? Her collection?"

He winked instead of nodding.

"That's wonderful. I take it she doesn't know about it?"

"I didn't mention it, but when I saw Tommie and the clothes, I got the idea."

"And since you always have your pen and paper at hand . . ." She left the sentence hanging. Adam didn't use paper and pencil. He had a small electronic device that he typed into. "Does she know?"

He nodded. "While Tommie was modeling her creations, I interviewed her."

"Adam, this is wonderful. It'll help her so much."

"So that's what we're celebrating . . . Vida's new company."

"Then why are we celebrating for her? Shouldn't she be here?"

Adam cut a piece of his duck and ate it. "I believe she and Mike are having their own celebration."

Rosa's ears suddenly went white hot as she pictured them having their own private dinner with dessert to come. "You know Mike proposed to her?"

"She told me. All I can say is, it's about time."

"I suppose it is."

"What's the matter?" Adam asked.

"Nothing." Rosa put her chin in her hand and stared across the short table into his eyes.

"If you keep that up, this dinner is going to be ruined."

"I know," she said, holding on to the last syllable.

Adam moved first. Soft music played in the background, but Rosa only just heard it when he got up. Everything seemed to move in slow motion. Him leaving his chair, the few steps it took to get to her. Adam offered his hands. Rosa put hers in them and stood up. Without thinking about it, she leaned into him, her arms following the curve of his shoulders and closing around his neck.

They began swaying to the music. Adam danced her about the room. Rosa lay her head on his shoulder and let herself be lost in the feel of him. They danced well together. She anticipated his steps, following him flawlessly, matching his movements one by one. Adam's hands caressed her back, sliding upward to her neck and down to her waist, each time going slightly lower than the time before. Rosa's eyes closed at the delirium of the moment. Her breath came in small, controlled puffs. Adam's arms were strong and tender at the same time. She felt loved, her entire body sensitive to his touch.

His lips touched her temple, then her forehead. His mouth lingered over her brow. Rosa felt spirals of sensation radiating within her. Need bubbled up and gripped her. She'd anticipated this moment all evening and now that it was here, she wanted it to go on a little longer. She wanted to hold on to the memory of each touch, the feel of Adam's fingers against her sensitive skin, the smell of his aftershave, the silkiness of the fabric of his jacket. She wanted to capture the moment as if she were snapping a photograph that she could pull out and revisit at will. Only this one would be placed in the vault of her heart.

Rosa lost count of the times they circled the room or they could have stood in one spot; she was unaware of time passing, of the music moving from one note to the next. Her total being was consumed by the man holding her in his arms.

She looked up at him. His eyes were dark with need. His head descended. Rosa went up on her toes to meet his mouth. Their touch was like the spark that started the universe, exciting, bright, explosive. Adam didn't try to deepen the kiss. He teased her lips, lifting his mouth and joining it with hers again and again. The kiss was more tender than anything Rosa had ever felt. Yet their joining was no less flammable.

She could feel the burn, the need to have him, the arousal of her body as it craved his touch, his invasion, the sweet surrender of intimacy. Her arms went higher on his shoulders, her body curved into his as if a well had been created in her exact shape. Adam crushed her to him and his mouth devoured hers. His tongue pushed past her teeth and swept inside her mouth. Rosa moaned at the whirring sound in her ears, like holding a seashell up and listening to the ocean. Only this tide was of her own creation.

Without her realizing it, her feet left the floor. Adam lifted her. Like a ballet dancer, her legs came up and he cradled her body while his mouth continued to work magic over hers. They broke the kiss and Rosa took in a huge breath. She hugged Adam as he walked to the stairs and carried her up to the loft.

She slid down him. For a moment they looked at each other. Rosa reached up and pushed his suit jacket from his shoulders. It fell to the floor. In the distance the music still played, but she could barely hear it. Her fingers opened the buttons on his shirt and her hands flattened against his moist skin. Heat generated inside him, too. Rosa rubbed her fingers across his nipples, feeling them rise into hard nubs. Adam lowered his head and kissed her naked shoulders. His mouth seemed to sizzle on her skin and it felt so good. Her knees threatened to buckle as his tongue wet her heated skin.

Then Rosa felt the zipper on her dress opening. Adam slowly pulled it down. She could hardly breathe. Her fingers fumbled with his belt. She got it open, then lowered his zipper. As each article of clothing was removed, their bodies entwined, skin touched skin, heat connected with heat, mouths burned.

By the time Adam lowered her to the bed, her body was ready for his, but he wasn't about to satisfy her yet. He kissed her shoulders and traveled down her body. Tiny moans issued from her of their own volition, the outward expression of the pleasure that seemed to spawn in every cell of her body.

Briefly he stopped at her breasts. As he'd done with her lips, he teased her nipples. Rosa sucked in air as waves of rapture gripped her. Grabbing handfuls of bedding, she held on, letting Adam bring her live body to white-hot sensation. At her belly, his tongue dipped into her navel. Rosa never thought there was any sensation in her navel, but when his tongue circled it, she felt a pull, a huge craving, all the way through her body.

"Adam, now." Rosa heard a strangled voice call Adam's name. It was her voice, but she barely recognized it. She was vaguely aware of him tearing open a condom and covering himself before his warmth returned to her, covering her.

In a flash, he parted her legs and joined with her. Rosa cried out at the waves of delirium that bargained with her senses. Together they danced the primal dance. Adam filled her completely. She matched his rhythm, joining and unjoining in a cycle so sweet, so essential to her survival that she'd wouldn't be able to breathe without completing the circle. Adam rode her, wildly increasing the pace.

His hands stretched with hers, raising them over her head as every inch of their bodies intimately touched each other. Rosa writhed beneath him, working without thought, only intent on giving, giving back to him the immense sense of wonder that he gave to her with each filling. His body seemed to pump life into her, complete her, show her in the most personal way that this was what she was made for, that this was the meaning of life. The language was loud and clear and Rosa didn't doubt it for a moment.

And then she felt it, felt the waves pounding inside her and their imminent need to reach satisfaction. She could feel their rawness, their hunger, their strength gathering and building, climbing higher and higher until they exploded. Rosa shattered into a million pieces—each infinitesimal segment its own erogenous zone, a hedonistic incision that writhed with pleasure.

Adam shouted and together they passed through the portal to absolute rapture. Rosa clawed at the air, grasping it and dragging it into her lungs. Her heart pounded in her ears, cutting out any other sound. No on had ever made love to her like that before. She knew the experience was unique, that no one could have replaced Adam. She loved him. She wanted to shout it, to tell him that she didn't think she could exist without him. She never wanted him to make love with anyone else, never wanted to leave this room, this bed, this moment. She wanted him completely, his body joined to hers, for always.

Chapter 11

Rosa opened her eyes. She reached for Adam. The bed was still warm where his body had lain. Rosa stretched, lounging in the light of morning. Her body hummed with the aftermath of their lovemaking. Adam had held her, stroking her breasts as if the action somehow added to his satisfaction. She could still feel his hands. Her body was suddenly drenched in heat.

Pushing the covers back, Rosa got out of bed and headed for the shower. She'd better get moving before she was so aroused she'd have to go and find Adam. He'd left before daybreak to get home before Joel woke up.

Hot water sluiced over her, running through her hair and down her back. Quickly Rosa washed herself, deciding to go for a ride. It had been a while since she'd been out in the morning. It would be good to take her camera and go into the hills again. Each time she saw the landscape it seemed different, like some secret was being unveiled before her. In minutes she was dressed and on horseback. She hadn't forgotten to take the rifle that Adam and

Bailey insisted she carry. Since Rosa had had to use it once for real, she felt safer with it.

She hadn't gone more than a hundred yards before she saw another rider on horseback. Instantly she knew it wasn't Bailey. He was too small. She recognized Joel. Turning, she rode toward him.

"What are you doing here alone?" she asked.

"I'm all right. I was just practicing."

"Let me see. Ride over there." She pointed toward a clearing.

Joel pulled on the reins and the horse turned left. Clicking his tongue the way Rosa had heard Bailey do, Joel began to move at odds with the horse. It was a common mistake. He looked back at her after a moment. She rode next to him and stopped.

"You need to move with the horse. You're moving against it. Watch me." She demonstrated what she meant, then came back to him. "Each time you moved, the horse went one way and you went the other. After a short while you'd be in pain."

He nodded, taking direction well. "Let me try it." He rode again, this time working with the horse. Rosa smiled.

"That's it," she called, and caught up with him. "Keep doing it that way and soon it'll be natural."

"Where are you going?" he asked. "Can I come?"

"I was just going to go up in the hills and take some pictures. You can come. I won't go that far." She adjusted her plans for him. With only a few lessons under his wing, he needed to take short rides.

They rode for about twenty minutes and Rosa stopped to rest. She wasn't as close to the mountains as she'd like to be, but this was a good spot to stop.

"Mind if I take some pictures?" she asked.

He shook his head. Rosa began snapping.

"Do you want me to do anything special?"

"Not yet," she called. "Just relax and do what you want."

She took several of him mounted on the horse. Then he slid to the ground and she snapped more.

"Are you just going to take my picture all day?" he asked as she was changing the film in the camera.

"Don't you like having your picture taken?" She glanced up at him with a smile.

"Sometimes, but you must have used up ten rolls of film already. Only my mom used to take that many pictures."

It hit Rosa with the suddenness of an avalanche. Maureen had been a photographer. Of course she'd take pictures of her son.

"Joel, I'm sorry. I didn't mean to bring back bad memories."

"It's all right. I think about her a lot. I never talk about her because Aunt Lillian wouldn't."

Rosa sat down on a huge rock. Joel took a seat beside her. "Do you want to tell me about her? I promise I'll listen and if you don't want me to say anything I won't."

He waited awhile. Rosa stopped pointing the camera at him, although the look on his face was so poignant she really wanted to capture it on film. But that's when he began to talk.

"She laughed a lot. It was only the two of us . . . and sometimes Adam would come by. But mainly we did everything together. She liked to take pictures and she taught me how to compose them in the viewfinder and develop them in the darkroom."

"That's wonderful," Rosa said. "Maybe you'll be a photographer, too."

He didn't react and Rosa thought it still hurt him to think of her and her cameras. She looked down at the Leica she held. It had belonged to Maureen.

"She would tell me everything. We used to visit all the monuments in D.C. and she'd explain why all those people were important. I really liked the FBI building. They have a whole room-ful of guns. You should see some of them."

Rosa smiled at his enthusiasm. She had been to the FBI building and she knew the room he talked about. "Maybe we can both go one day, and you can explain it to me."

She got a smile for that.

"Course there were things she made me do that I didn't like. She said it was good for me."

"Was that like doing homework and eating your vegetables?"

"How did you know?"

"I had the same thing when I was twelve. And you know what?"

"What?"

"She was right."

He frowned. "I'll do it. But I don't like it."

Rosa laughed. Joel did, too. She was glad the moment of sadness in his voice was gone.

Joel didn't say anything for a while. Then he spoke. "Mom was a good cook. She loved to make desserts. And I loved to eat them. She got on this kick once of making muffins. She bought a lot of muffin pans. And something she called a muffin top pan. It would only bake the top of the muffin.

Every night she'd make a different type of muffin, lemon ones, bran ones, raisin muffins, blueberry. I liked the blueberry ones best."

"She sounds like a wonderful woman," Rosa said. "You're very lucky to have had a mother who loved you so much."

"I'm lucky to have Adam, too," he said.

A tiny trickle of jealousy snaked through Rosa. Maureen must have been very special to Adam for her to trust her son to him. And for Joel to love Adam so much. Rosa knew that kind of love didn't come from a casual relationship, but from years of being there, from attending the high points of a child's life, from both the giving and the receiving of love. Her own family had that kind of love. She was the youngest of the group, and she'd never experienced the hardship that her brothers had. She was the recipient of all the love they could shower on her, but she also knew how that wasn't true for every child. Joel was indeed lucky to have Adam.

"Adam came to tell me," Joel began. He glanced up at Rosa and down again at the ground. "I knew right away that something had happened. I knew she was dead. The look on Adam's face told me that before he said a word. I was at camp in Virginia, not the one Aunt Lillian sent me to. Another one. We were going to learn a new diving move that day. Then I saw Adam coming and I knew."

Rosa felt helpless. Joel's voice was steady, but she could feel the emotion underlying it. All she could do was sit with him. She couldn't touch him, cradle him, or even offer him a supporting hand. He wouldn't welcome it. He'd been surviving with his pain too long. But he needed understanding. He needed someone to listen, and for the time being, she was that person.

"I didn't cry," Joel said. "I didn't feel anything, only this weird numbness like I'd suddenly been stung all over by bees."

"Joel, have you never cried?"

He looked at her and slowly shook his head. "We left that day. I stayed with Adam. He took care of everything, I think. The station may have done something, even Aunt Lillian, no one ever told me. Then we went back to the apartment. I wanted to go there and Adam took me."

Rosa wasn't sure if that was a good thing or not. After her mother died, they all went back to the house where she'd been such a live person. Memories lurked in every corner, behind every shadow, but they were all adults. Joel had been ten years old.

"Then the custody fight began and I had to go live with Aunt Lillian. I didn't want to, but Adam explained the reasons."

"You understood them?"

He nodded. Rosa wanted to make sure that if the courts forced him to return to his aunt, Joel would understand. Although at twelve, he was old enough to make the decision for himself. Yet she knew you could never be sure what a judge would do.

"We'd better get back now," Rosa said. "I'm sure you didn't tell anyone you were going riding and they might be wondering where you are." She and Joel stood up.

"I left a note."

"Did you tell them which way you were going?"

He looked at the ground. "I didn't think of it."

"It's a big country out here," Rosa said. "You shouldn't ride alone. If you want to go again, don't do it alone. It's dangerous." She felt like she was repeating phrases that Bailey and Adam had said to her.

They walked to where their horses were standing. "Did you really kill a bear?" he asked.

"Where did you hear that?"

"My grandfather told me."

"Grandfather?"

"Adam's dad. He told me I could call him that. He doesn't have a grandson and he said he doesn't know when, if ever, he'll get one."

"Adam isn't that old. He could still marry and have children."

"Are you going to marry him?"

The question hit her like the sudden stop of a fall. All the wind left her lungs. "I don't think so," Rosa said. It wasn't like she hadn't thought of marrying Adam before, fantasized about what it would be like to come home every night and meet him, what it would be like to sleep in his arms and wake to his embrace every day.

"He likes you. I can tell. Not the way he liked my mom. I think he's in love with you."

It's a good thing Rosa wasn't eating or drinking because she would have choked on the food. "Did he tell you that?"

Joel shook his head. "It's the way he looks at you. I've seen people look like that before. You know, in movies and old people on the street."

By old people, Rosa thought he meant young twenty-somethings. They were the ones on the street who often showed their love for each other.

"Adam hasn't said anything like that to me," she said.

"He might. In the movies, it always takes time, but it happens."

Life is not a movie, Rosa thought. She didn't say

it. She helped Joel mount his horse and then she mounted hers.

"So, did you really kill a bear?" Joel asked again as if the change in subject was natural and expected.

"I didn't kill a bear," Rosa answered.

Joel's face fell. They started walking the horses back toward the ranch.

"I shot a bear, but I didn't kill it. The gun had tranquilizer darts in it. So the bear went to sleep and Adam and I left it in its natural environment."

"Oh," he said.

"You don't have to sound so disappointed."

"I'm not disappointed. I wish I could have seen it."

"Joel," she called, a warning note in her voice. "The bears own this land. We are the trespassers. But they are dangerous. Don't underestimate them. And don't glorify them, either."

"I won't."

"Do I have your promise that you won't do this again? You'll always ride with someone else?"

This time he studied his hands holding the reins. "I promise," he finally said.

As they came across the rise, Rosa saw Adam astride his horse. Bailey stood on the ground next to him. She could see Adam's body sag in relief when he recognized them.

"I think they were about to send out a search party to find you," Rosa warned Joel.

"Do you think he's mad?"

"Angry, yes, but he's probably relieved, too."

Adam got down from his horse and waited for them to reach him. Rosa tried to read his face. Joel's words came back to her. Did he really love her?

Her heart was hopeful. More than anything she'd ever thought of or wanted, she wanted Adam to love her.

The morning sun was warm on her face. Adam's expression was dark and drawn. They watched as Bailey and Joel disappeared into the house.

"Don't be so hard on him, Adam. He's a very lonely little boy."

Adam looked at her. "Is he all right?"

"He told me about his mother. He loved her immensely, like any child would. They were very close."

"I know. They did a lot together. Maureen was widowed when Joel was four. He barely remembers his dad. She's all he's known."

"He's known you, too," Rosa said.

She glanced at the door where Joel and Bailey had gone in to breakfast. "Apparently his aunt didn't talk about Maureen. I got the impression she didn't allow any talk of her sister. Joel needed to do that." She looked up at Adam, who had a strange expression on his face. She touched his arm. "Joel's going to be fine, but give him some space and some understanding."

"I'll bear that in mind," he said. "And speaking of understanding, is there something wrong with your brain?"

"Not that I'm aware of." She didn't know where he was going with this, but he was obviously angry.

"The two of you are the greenest people in the Valley. I asked you not to go out riding in the hills alone."

"I hear and obey." She bowed lavishly as if he

were her master. "As a matter of fact, we weren't in the hills. We never even made it to the base. Satisfied?"

Rosa didn't wait for an answer. She turned on her heel and walked back to her horse. Grabbing the reins, she swung herself into the saddle. Before she could turn the horse and head for the stables, Adam had his hand on the pommel.

"Rosa, I worry about you." The words seemed to be torn from him.

"Adam, I—" She didn't know what she wanted to say. He reached for her and like a child, Rosa accepted his arms. He pulled her off the horse and stood with her in his embrace. Rosa's head lay on his shoulder. She'd never felt so loved, so protected.

Pushing herself back, she looked at him. "Adam, I wasn't going into the hills. After this morning—" She stopped, thoughts coursing through her of lying in his arms. "I wanted to create something. And I have no skills for drawing like Vida. I took the camera and left the house. I met Joel on the trail. I would never put myself in danger intentionally."

"It's my fault. When we couldn't find Joel, I was . . . worried. Anything can happen to him without supervision. Neither of you understands the danger." He hugged her close, kissed her hair. "I can't take the chance of anything happening."

He came short of saying anything happening to her or to them. Rosa wondered if that was how he would have continued the sentence. It was how she would have ended it.

* * *

The Waymon Valley Post Office was a modern redbrick building sitting on a quiet street not far from Vida's house. Many of the buildings Rosa had researched and photographed had initially been designed by Luke Evans. The post office was not one of them. The interior had rows of gold-colored post office boxes and three windows for patrons. There was a short line and Rosa waited her turn.

Reluctantly she'd left Adam's arms and returned home. Waiting for her was a post office slip saying she had a package. Rosa was expecting one from New York and it looked like this was it. She called Vida and told her she was coming by after she picked it up.

The clerk gave her a huge smile and went to retrieve the package. Rosa had the usual conversation with the other clerk about being a model. It was short as the package was found immediately and given to her. She left with a smile and several new friends.

Rosa wanted to open it as soon as she reached the car, but decided to wait until she got home. It was a surprise for Bailey's birthday and she didn't want to tell anyone about it before he opened it. She put it in the trunk and drove to Vida's.

"Come in," Vida said as soon as Rosa rang the doorbell.

"What's wrong?"

"Nothing. Everything. I need your help."

Rosa rushed inside. "What can I do? Is it your leg?"

"No, I'm fine. Healthwise. It's the wedding."

"Vida, you're scaring me. You and Mike haven't decided to call it off, have you?"

Vida stopped in her quest to get some place.

Rosa didn't know where they were going. Only that her friend was pulling her along as if they were tied together.

"Heavens, no."

Then they started moving again. Rosa went into Vida's office, the room she had designated for designing and running her one-woman business. The room was littered with papers. Some were balled up, others were crumpled and lying on the floor.

"Other than this needing a good cleaning, I don't understand what's going on."

"Look at these." Vida spread her arms. "I think I've lost it. Why did I think I could be a designer anyway?"

Rosa bent down and picked up a piece of paper. She unfolded it. The drawing was at least the partial design for a wedding gown. Rosa relaxed. "You're designing a wedding gown?"

"I'm trying and coming up short."

"Relax, Vida. You don't have to design a dress today. You don't have to design it at all."

"But I want to. Imagine what this will do for my business. But it's got to be the most sensational dress in the world. And I've got to lose some weight. I want to model it myself in the catalog."

"Catalog? You're doing a catalog?"

"Yeah, why? Don't you think it's a good idea?"

"Sit down." The two of them sat among the room's debris. "I think that you're doing too much. You're getting married and you have a fledgling company. You can't do it all. Hire someone else to handle something. Free yourself to focus on a few things, not *everything*."

"That makes sense. I could focus on the wedding and some designs. I could hire someone to handle the paperwork, correspondence, maybe put off the catalog until next year."

"See how it goes. Adam's done some press for you. Maybe it will turn into some contracts."

Vida smiled. "I hope so. He asked me a lot of questions about the clothes Tommie was wearing. About me as a former model turning designer."

"I'm sure things will work out. I love your designs," Rosa said. At that moment she noticed the sketch on the designer table. Getting up, she went to it. "What's this?"

Vida joined her. "That was something I was playing with."

"What do you mean?" Rosa stared at the page. It was a design for two gowns. "These are beautiful. Which one are you leaning toward?"

"I thought you would choose."

"Me? Why?"

"I had the idea of a double wedding."

Double wedding. Wedding. The words kept running through Rosa's mind. It wasn't even lunchtime and already Rosa had discovered that Adam might be in love with her. *Might* being a very big word. And that her best friend was designing a wedding gown for her, and the groom hadn't declared his intentions. In fact, the intended groom was unaware of the entire situation.

This had to be the most bizarre day Rosa had spent in a long time. Yet as she turned the car along the road and headed back for her summer house, the thought of being married to Adam was taking root in her mind.

She scanned the road just before the turn. She'd hoped to see his truck turning toward her, but the road was clear. She turned, remembering Joel's arrival a few days ago. He would probably be staying, yet Rosa was going to leave. She had only a few more weeks and then it was back to reality.

As Rosa got to the end of the driveway, she saw a strange vehicle. This one was a Jeep. The only person she knew with a Jeep was Mike Holmes and this wasn't his. She pulled alongside it and as she got out of the Corvette two tall men got out of the Jeep. Rosa recognized her brothers, Dean and Owen. She screamed in delight and rushed to hug one, then the other.

"What are you doing here?" she asked. "I'm so glad to see you. How's Theresa and Stephanie? Have you seen Luanne?"

"Stop. Stop," Owen said, holding up his hands. "We'll answer all your questions, just take a breath."

Rosa stopped, but launched herself into their arms again. "I've missed you so. It is so good to see you."

"It's good to see you, too. Now, if you'll release your choke hold on my neck, I'll be able to talk."

Rosa laughed and let go.

"We were in the area and decided to stop by," Owen said.

"Nobody is in the neighborhood of Montana," Rosa contradicted.

"The truth is, I'm scouting a film location." Dean had mentioned that during their family call. "I needed some advice from an architect, so I asked Owen to meet me." Dean was quickly developing a name for himself in Hollywood and was much sought after since he'd won an Oscar a year ago for his first major undertaking.

"I thought you had scouts who look for locations," Rosa said.

"I do, and they've been here. I'm here to approve the choice."

Rosa nodded.

"And I wanted to see you," Dean said.

"We thought we'd make sure your summer was going all right," Owen continued.

"And one or both of your wives insisted you come," Rosa finished for them.

The two men looked at each other. "Both," they said in unison. The three of them laughed. "We'd have come anyway."

"Well, you can report that things are going well. I'm doing fine."

She headed for the door, then heard another car coming up the driveway. It was Adam's truck. Her heart skipped a beat. She'd wanted to see Adam, wanted him to come down the road as she entered her driveway. Now she wished she could turn back time. Her brothers, undoubtedly, would ply him with questions. She'd seen them do it before when she was much younger. They were always the protectors.

"Adam," she called as he stepped down from the truck. "What are you doing here?"

Adam strode over and slipped his arm around her waist. He kissed her lightly on the mouth and looked up at the two men watching them.

"I'm on my way to Butte. Dad said you wanted something in particular and I should come and get a sample of it."

Rosa couldn't think what that was. She wondered if it was just an excuse for Adam to appear at the same time her brothers did. "Adam, these are two of my brothers, Dean and Owen."

Adam offered his free hand. The one around her waist remained in place. "I know your work."

He shook hands with Dean. "Congratulations on that Oscar."

Dean nodded.

"I'm an architect in Dallas. My work doesn't get on the silver screen," Owen said as they shook hands.

The small group went inside.

"You used to be on the news in Washington, D.C.," Dean stated as if the fact were known worldwide.

"I'm just a rancher now," Adam said.

"Not according to our wives," Dean said. "Or our sister." The three of them looked at Rosa. "They watched you all the time. Of course, Rosa is the news junkie."

"I left the station a while ago," Adam said.

"No plans to return?" Dean asked.

"None," Adam said.

"Have a seat," Rosa said. Then she looked at Adam. "I'll get the picture." She remembered what she wanted. She hadn't told Bailey everything about it, just enough to get something that he liked. It was a frame for his birthday present, which she remembered was in the trunk of the car. Running up to her office, she quickly located the photo and ran back down the steps. She didn't want to give her brothers too much time alone with Adam. Knowing them, they might ask him what his intentions were.

"Tell me about this scouting trip," Adam was saying when Rosa rejoined them.

"It's not far from here, outside Missoula. We're thinking of making another epic-style picture, like *The Horse Whisperer.*"

"I thought a lot of movies were made in Canada or places that aren't in the States."

"That's true," Dean said. "Costs tend to be cheaper outside our borders, and the budget is always the key to any large production. But Montana seems more in line with our thinking this time."

"This is the photo," Rosa interrupted. She showed it to Adam. Proximity to him with her brothers looking on made her nervous. "I ordered it from Hollenders. You only need to pick it up."

"I will." Adam stood up. "Good meeting you," he said. Rosa walked him to the door. He kissed her again as he left. She knew when she turned around her brothers would be smirking as if Adam were the first man she'd ever gone out with.

"Want something to drink?" she asked when she did return to them.

"I'll have a beer, if you have any," Owen said. "And you can tell us all about Adam."

Rosa got the beers and handed them to her brothers. "So the story of just being in the neighborhood was an ambush, right?"

"Oh no, we are on a scouting trip, but the fact that you were here made the decision of coming easy."

"I'm not a little girl, guys. You can trust me to make my own decisions."

"Involving him?"

"Him and anything else I decide to do."

Then Dean asked in a serious voice, "Are you all right, Rosa?"

Her brothers were all special to her. Brad was the one she seemed to have some incredible connection with, but Dean would be second on the list. He could read her feelings even when she tried to hide them.

She gave him her best smile, not the one she

reserved for photo shoots, but the genuine one. "I'm fine."

For a long moment they only looked at each other. Then Dean nodded. It was his way of giving his assent.

"So, are you guys spending the night?"

"We wouldn't dream of it," Owen said. "I'm sure Adam will be back."

Rosa's cheeks warmed.

"We reserved a room in town. It's an old boardinghouse. Apparently, it's been there since the 1890s," Owen said.

"Aunt Emily's boardinghouse?"

"You know the place?" Owen said. "The architecture of the building is authentic early western America."

Rosa nodded. "I've been recording the history of the town with Adam's dad. He has a direct bloodline to the town's founders."

"We'll be leaving early in the morning, but we hoped you'd have dinner with us."

"I'd love to," she said.

"And bring Adam," Owen said. "You two are a couple."

Chapter 12

The long robe that covered Rosa's naked body rippled through Adam's fingers like running water. He loved the feel of her warm body beneath it, and while they had just made love, he wanted her again. Pulling her onto his lap, Adam kissed her. No matter how often they made love, he found it hard to believe he could ever have enough of her. They had come down from the bedroom only a short time ago, both in need of drinks to assuage the thirst their lovemaking had created. Yet as he held her, kissing her aroused him and he wanted her a second time.

"What did you think of dinner?" she asked when he slid his mouth from hers.

He drank thirstily from the bottle of water he'd retrieved from the refrigerator. He'd just endured dinner with her family. He'd never had to do that before, never had to gain the approval of a parent or relative of anyone he was seeing. Yet in Rosa's case it was important to him that her brothers sanctioned their relationship.

"The food was excellent," he said. "I could have

done without dessert. I had something much more tasty in mind."

She swung at him, but he dodged the punch. "You know what I mean."

"What do you think? Did I pass muster?"

Rosa sat up, pulling her robe closer together. "You think that's what my brothers were doing?"

"Absolutely. There could be no doubt about it. So, did I pass?"

"I didn't ask them. Their opinion doesn't matter."

"Well, have I passed with you?"

She sat back, her expression indignant. "You have to ask?"

"I wanted to know," Adam said.

The sky was big and clear on the morning of Bailey's seventieth birthday. Rosa began the day with a short ride. She met Bailey and Joel at the stables. They only walked the horses, as Bailey told them more stories of his youth. Rosa enjoyed them and Joel asked a lot of questions.

"You know, you should teach history," Joel told Bailey.

"What?"

"Well, if my history teachers were as interesting as you are, I wouldn't be so bored in class."

Bailey let out a huge belly laugh.

The ride was short and they returned to the house quickly.

"Coming in for breakfast?" Bailey asked as they left the horses behind.

Rosa nodded. "I can already smell Medea's bacon." She rarely stayed for the meal. The temptation of Medea's cooking was too much for her to resist, but this was his birthday and she wanted to give him his present early. She expected that everywhere she would go that day people would be talking about the party. It appeared the entire Valley planned to turn out for the celebration. Medea had been busy getting ready for days.

Joel looked so much better than the thin child with dark circles under his eyes he'd been when he arrived. They went to the kitchen and took seats at the table.

"Morning," Medea said.

"Good morning," they all said choirlike.

"Where's Adam?" Bailey asked Medea.

"He went out early this morning. I suppose he's picking up your gift."

She set plates in front of each of them and put food on the table.

"Yep, it's my birthday. I never thought I'd live this long."

"How old are you?" Joel asked, digging into his eggs.

"Seventy," Bailey said quickly. "Born at ten o'clock in the morning. So we have another couple of hours before the blessed event."

"Not quite," Rosa said. "I want you to open my present now."

She got up and left the room. She retrieved the wrapped gift from the car and returned to the kitchen.

"Happy birthday," she said, and slid it in front of him.

"Gee, such pretty wrapping paper," Medea said. She'd stopped what she was doing and looked at Bailey and the present. "Well, go on," Medea prompted. "Open it. Don't keep us waiting all day."

Bailey pulled the paper free, opened the box, and removed the framed book. The cover was etched glass and had his name and photo engraved on the surface. "What is this?" he laughed. "I can't believe it."

"Open it," Rosa said.

He removed the frame and lifted the hardcover coffee-table-size book out. The cover held the same photo of Bailey as the frame had. He was on horseback, looking directly at the camera.

"Handsome guy, don't you think?" he said to Joel.

Joel laughed.

"Thank you, Rosa. This is absolutely beautiful." He opened it and looked at some of the pictures that Rosa had taken. He read a few of the captions and chuckled. "I wish my grandmother could have seen some of these. They are beautiful."

He got up and came around to her. "Thank you, dear." He kissed her on the cheek. "This makes me very happy."

Rosa smiled. She was moved, too. She could see that Bailey really liked what she had done. The book had turned out better than she imagined it would.

"Look at this, Medea. She's got one of you in here." He showed the book to Medea.

She flipped through a few pages. "They are really good pictures, Rosa."

"Any of me?" Joel asked as if they had forgotten he was in the room.

"Sorry, Joel, when I sent them off to be bound you hadn't arrived yet."

"It's all right," Joel conceded. "You did take a lot of pictures of me, too."

"I'm going to have to ask you all to leave my

kitchen," Medea said. "With the party tonight, I have a lot of work to do."

"Evicted from my own kitchen," Bailey teased. "And on my birthday, too."

They laughed and left the room. While the party wasn't at the ranch, Medea was preparing food there. Joel went upstairs to brush his teeth and play video games. He'd made himself at home, seemingly settling in and ready to stay.

Rosa and Bailey went into the great room. She took the chair she liked so much and together they looked at each of the pictures in the book. When they came to the one she took of Adam the day Rosa shot the bear, Bailey stopped.

"You're in love with him, aren't you?"

Rosa coughed, not knowing what to say. Adam had never said he loved her, no matter what Joel had told her. Or how she interpreted his words.

"There's no use denying it," Bailey continued. "I can see it in the way you look at him. And if I didn't know it by that, this would convince me." He looked down at the picture. Adam stood on the mountain, looking in the distance. Rosa had captured the essence of him. She'd found the one second when he was vulnerable, when emotion instead of logic ruled him, and she'd opened the shutter.

"I know Adam wants to return to Washington. I know I'm the obstacle that's keeping him from returning to a life he loves. He may even love you and I'm keeping him from letting your relationship move ahead."

"I'm sure you're wrong," Rosa said.

"Nope," Bailey said. "I'm seventy today and I tell no lies."

"How could your presence keep Adam and me apart?"

"You'll be leaving. Adam is torn between wanting to go with you and leaving me here."

"Adam loves you," Rosa told him.

"I know that. I love him, too. But he can't keep me alive. When it's my time, there'll be nothing he can do about it."

"He can spend time with you."

"At the expense of his own life. That is not the natural order of things. Not how it's supposed to be."

"Have you told him this?"

"Yes, but he's pigheaded and won't listen."

"Gee, I wonder where he gets that trait?" They both laughed. Rosa didn't want to get between Bailey and Adam. Their relationship was unique to them and she was an outsider who didn't know both sides of the story. She wanted Adam, but she couldn't make him change his mind, either. And she couldn't stay past the summer.

She knew she'd come back, however. While Adam and his father had a special relationship, so did she and Adam. And she'd passed the point where she wanted to end it.

"I take it you like the book?" Rosa changed the subject.

Bailey looked at her with the same eyes Adam did. She could see his feelings in them. He made no attempt to hide his, while Adam often did. "I expect the party today will be full of presents, most of them useless, but no matter what else I get, nothing will compare with this. Thank you."

Rosa felt a lump in her throat. But she managed a tight "You're welcome."

"Look at him." Bailey pointed to the picture of

Adam. Rosa looked. "I remember when I was his age. I was a hell-raiser. So was Adam in his teens. By the time I was thirty I'd settled down, but it was the prime of my life. It was the time for making memories. I got married. We had Adam. Lived."

"You don't think Adam is doing that?" It was a statement.

Bailey shook his head. "Rosa, you're young. Adam is young. You're supposed to pursue your dreams when you're young, not sit around and wait for people to die."

"Adam isn't waiting for you to die."

"What would you call it? He's refusing all offers for a job he wants. One that is perfect for him. He's putting everything on hold until I'm gone. Then his life can begin. That's no way to live. Day by day it'll eat at him and he'll end up a bitter old man. And who knows how long that'll be? By the time he's ready, the opportunity may be gone."

Rosa looked down at the image of Adam. "I understand his dilemma," she said. "My mother died of a heart attack a couple of years ago." Rosa felt the emotion in her throat and forced it down. "I was there at the time, but I regret spending so much time away from home. I wished I could have been with my mother, making memories, having as much time as possible with her before she died. Instead, I was off in the capitals of the world wearing clothes most people can't afford."

"She wouldn't have wanted that."

"Maybe not," Rosa said. "But I wanted it."

Neither of them knew Adam was standing outside the door. He'd come into the house only moments ago, but long enough to hear Rosa speaking of her mother. He'd been thinking of returning to Washington, taking the job that Ben offered him.

But hearing her, he made his decision. He didn't want to have the regrets Rosa had. She was luckier than he was. She had brothers and a sister. There were other siblings to be with her parents while she was away.

Bailey only had him.

The library had the largest hall in the Valley if you didn't count the high school gym. The main salon had once been the central ballroom of the mansion that Luke and Clara Evans lived in. Generally the room was used for events. There were a few bookshelves along the walls, but it mainly reflected its former glory, period furniture and early American paintings. Streamers hung from the ceiling, along with balloons and colored lights. A huge happy birthday sign covered the entrance, announcing the evening's festivities. Presents were stacked in another room, too many to open.

The original floor was wooden, but a dance floor had been constructed over it to protect it from the many feet that would celebrate Bailey's seventh decade. The Valley put on its finest for the party. Women sparkled in sequined-covered dresses and men sported tuxedos. They twisted and twirled to the music. Bailey was the man of the hour in his tux and Medea had changed into a gown of gray lace with pearls covering the bodice.

Rosa's breath had caught in her throat earlier when she opened the door and Adam stood there dressed as if he were about to enter the White House reception room.

We're a couple, she thought. Her brother Owen had said it. Rosa was poised to deny it then, but not tonight. Adam took her in his arms and danced her around the floor of the house that his great-grandparents had moved into as newlyweds. His hand touched her back where there was no fabric, only skin. His fingers aroused her. Rosa was amazed at how Adam's touch could send her into flights of fantasy. She leaned her head back to smile up at him.

"You'd better stop that," Rosa said. "You don't want the whole town to see what you're doing to me."

Adam raised a single eyebrow. "Isn't that why you wore this dress, so I could put my hands on you?"

Rosa didn't get to answer. The music ended then and Adam's hands snaked down her arms until his fingers reached hers. Together they walked off the floor. Along the back wall was a bar. They headed for it. Adam snagged two glasses of wine and gave one to her.

"It's loud in here. Why don't we find a quiet place?"

"I get it. You just want to be alone with me," she teased.

"You found me out." He took her hand just as Tommie stopped in front of them.

"Adam, Rosa," Tommie said. "Did you see the pictures? They came today. They are gorgeous. And Crawford is working on a job for me in New York."

"Calm down, Tommie," Adam said. "You don't want to fly away before you get the chance to get to New York."

"Congratulations," Rosa said, and hugged her. "I know you'll do a good job."

"I can't thank you and Vida enough."

Vida and Mike arrived as if on cue. "Did I hear my name?" Vida said.

"I was telling them about the photos," Tommie explained.

"We knew you'd be good, Tommie," Vida told her.

"I'll drop by with the photos," Tommie said to Rosa and moved off toward a small group that included several young men.

"Ah, the energy," Vida said. "Remember when we were that enthusiastic?"

"I still am," Rosa said.

"I know," Vida said. "You'll be leaving us in just a couple of weeks. I can't believe the summer has gone by so fast."

Rosa wasn't looking at Adam, but she felt his body tighten. Unconsciously, she reached for his hand. Finding it, she squeezed it.

"How are the wedding plans coming?" Rosa changed the subject. She didn't want to think about leaving tonight. She knew she had to go, but she could put off the inevitable for a few more days.

"Now that I've gotten over the stress, they're going well."

Vida had finally finished the design of her gown. It had taken her nearly a week. And her office took the brunt of her frustration. But after a while, she found the right lines and coupled them with pearl and lace accessories that she thought would enhance the dress and that special day. When Rosa saw the final design, she gasped at the perfection of it. Immediately she wanted to model it, but this one was for only one model.

"I'm so glad the gown is done. Hercules is

going to make it for me. He's given it a high priority since the ceremony is so close."

"Hercules?" Adam repeated.

"He's the greatest tailor in the world," Vida said. "Designers vie for his services."

"Come on, Vida, let's dance." Mike took his fiancée's arm. "If I don't stop her now, she'll keep up the wedding talk all night."

"I *will* not," Vida objected, but she let Mike lead her to the dance floor.

Rosa sipped her wine. She and Adam strolled around the room, speaking to friends and watching the dancers on the floor, but neither made a move to join them. At the door to the main entry room of the library, they passed through it. They gravitated to the seats where they'd met before. She wondered if Adam remembered.

"You know you're going to be missed in there," Rosa said.

"Not as much as your absence will be noticed. All eyes were on you, not me."

Rosa looked around the room. She loved the smell of books. Eventually, when she settled and stopped traveling so much, she planned to have a library full of books. "I'm glad I came to the Valley for the summer."

"We are a colorful lot," Adam acknowledged.

"You are," she agreed, her attention coming back to where he stood.

"Small towns are great places to get to know people," Adam said.

"True," Rosa said. "Big towns are impersonal. You'd never meet anyone there."

"You're mocking me?"

Rosa sobered. "Of course I am. I know all my neighbors."

"Yeah, but you'd be noticed no matter where you lived."

"I live in New York. When are you going to accept that job in D.C.? You know you want it."

"What did my father say to you?"

"When?"

"This morning, after breakfast, when the two of you were in the great room."

Rosa had to think a moment. Then she remembered. "He said we were young people. That it was our time for making memories."

"And you said you wished you'd made more memories with your mother."

"You were listening." She stared at him, her eyes opening wide at the realization.

"Only the end of the conversation. I came in just before Joel came running down the stairs."

"What I said is true, but I thought about it after I left Bailey. I have a wealth of memories with my mother. I hadn't thought about them in a while. We talked a lot while I was away on trips. My brother Dean insisted we use these video conference machines. Later we switched to the Internet. The talks we had probably made us better friends than if I'd been with her every day. I'm very fond of that time. I wouldn't give it up for anything."

"You're suggesting I get video equipment?"

"Not quite. You can use the Internet. This way you can see your father on the screen."

"But I can't keep him from doing things he's not supposed to do from sixteen hundred miles away."

"He's not a child, Adam. And how good a job are you doing by being here? When he had the heart attack, you were only a few miles away, but you weren't with him. You can't always be with him."

He weighed her words a second before answering, "I just want him around as long as possible."

"Then you have to let him live."

"Can we not talk about this now? There's a party going on."

Rosa looked down. "Of course, we can drop it."

He spun her around as if to begin dancing, but at the last moment pulled her into his arms and kissed her.

"We should meet here and kiss like this every year," he said, letting her know that he remembered the kiss they had shared almost on the very spot where they stood.

"A kind of *Same Time, Next Year* for this millennium?"

"Uh-huh." He kissed her again.

"Does that mean we'll both have somewhere to be returning from?"

He nodded. "I suppose it could."

"Good," she said. "Because I have a message for you."

"You do?" The sexual innuendo was evident as he leaned toward her again.

Rosa placed her hand on his chest and stopped him. "It not that kind of message. And it might bring the same subject up again."

"Oh?" His eyebrow went up.

"You got a phone call tonight."

His expression changed and he stood up straight. "Don't tell me Ben called the house number again?"

"He did."

Adam sighed. "What is the message?"

"Since you are going to Washington over Joel's custody, he'd like to take you to dinner."

"How does he know about Joel?"

"He didn't say. But from what I've heard, Washington is like the Valley. It's a place where there are no secrets."

"You're right about that. Ben doesn't want to have dinner with me. He wants to try and convince me to return to the anchor's chair."

"Is there anything so wrong in that?" Rosa whispered. "You'd be—"

"Rosa, it's my dad," Adam interrupted.

"No, it's not," she stated. "Your dad has a condition, a potentially life-threatening condition, but look at him." They glanced through the doorway. Bailey was dancing and laughing as if he were a teenager. "He's living every day. Can you say the same?" She didn't wait for him to answer. "You're using Bailey as a marker to hide behind. And now there's Joel. You can use him as a shield, too."

"I'm not hiding."

"What is it you're doing, then?"

Adam stared at her for a long moment. "I'm not hiding," he said quietly.

"I don't know why," Rosa said. "But it all seems to have begun with Maureen's death. You once told me you weren't in love with her, but you were on your way to being in love. Maybe you were wrong and you really are in love with her."

Rosa moved toward the door that would lead them back to the party. Adam stopped her with an arm going around her waist. He pulled her body back against his.

"I'm not in love with Maureen," he told her. "I'm in love with you."

Rosa didn't have time to react. She didn't know what she would have said, but the opportunity was taken away from her when Bailey spoke.

"Adam, what are you two doing over there?" Bailey stood several feet away. "I thought I'd get a dance with Rosa, but you seem to be monopolizing her."

Rosa turned in Adam's arms. Her face felt hot. Her heart hammered. Her hands didn't seem to know where to go. The music in the background was only white noise to the whirling sound in her ears. Adam released her. "Go on, dance with him. We'll talk later."

But she didn't. Her arms went around his neck and she stood on her toes to reach him. She kissed him, oblivious of everything except those three little words.

"I love you."

Chapter 13

The Mayflower Hotel was an old established building that sat in a fashionable part of Connecticut Avenue in the District of Columbia. Adam and Rosa arrived and checked in. He'd planned to make the trip alone, but when she offered to travel with him, he didn't have the will to leave her behind.

Funny, Adam thought, he'd been to hundreds of functions at the Mayflower, but he'd never spent the night. His apartment wasn't far from here. It was farther up on Sixteenth Street, within walking distance of the studio on M Street. He liked the District, loved the pace. Montana was quiet, slow moving, but the District hummed. He didn't know how much he'd missed it in the last two years. Yet it only took him a second to remember the traffic, the streets, the crowds.

"I'm leaving now," he called to Rosa. She came to the bathroom door, fresh from her shower. Adam felt a pull of arousal. He didn't want to leave her. She'd always been the most beautiful woman he'd ever seen, but that was when she'd

applied the perfect makeup and wore the latest
fashions. Standing in the doorway, free of any
adornments except those rendered by nature,
made her the most beautiful woman in the
world. No magazine would refuse this fresh all-
American-woman look. And he was sorry he had
to leave.

"Are you sure you don't want me to come with
you?"

He did want her with him. He never wanted to
be anywhere without her, but he shook his head.
"I need to do this alone. And you have people to
see, too."

She nodded. Rosa had told him she was going
to see Crawford first and then meet some friends
for lunch. She came forward. His arms automat-
ically opened for her. She smelled like soap,
clean and fresh and ready for lovemaking. He
kissed her quickly.

"I'll see you when you get back," she said.

Adam left then. He walked along Connecticut
Avenue. The humidity was something else he'd
forgotten about D.C., but it quickly reminded
him that summer in the city was a humid undertaking. The attorney's office wasn't far away. He
supposed that, like medical people, lawyers also
took up residence in the same area. K Street NW
was the place for law offices. All kinds of lawyers
had offices there, everything from patents and
governmental attorneys to criminal and family
law. It was family law that interested Adam.

The proceedings took very little time and
Adam left the offices with a much lighter step
than the one he'd come in with. Lillian sat across
the long mahogany table from him with her
lawyer. Adam sat with his. Surprisingly she didn't

oppose the change in custody. Adam watched her. Something didn't seem right about her, but she signed all the papers and he walked out of there with what Maureen had wanted. It had only taken two years for it to happen. And the report he had from Simon Thalberg had never been mentioned.

Adam didn't head back to the hotel. Rosa was out with her friends. He went down in the subway and got on one of the cars. He didn't plan to go there, but when he came up he was in the Ayerst section of town. This was where Maureen had died. The place hadn't changed much since that day. The ground was still dirty, the houses burned out or boarded up. Addicts hung out on the corners, some of them begging for loose change.

He walked around the house that Maureen had been photographing. He'd seen the tape that was in her camera the night she died. In two years, the place still looked the same, brick house, broken windows, cracked stairs. This was the dirty side of life. Adam knew it. He'd lived inside its walls, rubbed shoulders with it. And Maureen had given her life to it.

Why should he come back here? Why should he return to this life? To reporting it? To sitting behind a desk with a camera in his face, while people like Maureen gave their lives . . . for what?

"Adam."

He turned quickly, hearing his name.

"What are you doing here?" he asked. He looked both ways, then grabbed Rosa's arm and turned her back toward the subway.

She stopped him. "This is where Maureen died."

"How did you know?"

"I looked up the story online. It wasn't hard to find."

"Why did you come here?"

"I knew you'd be here."

"I'm not in love with her," Adam said. "I don't even know why I'm here. Only that I had to come. She was part of my life for a long time. I have her son to rear. We were friends, the best of friends. And I value that."

"Adam, do you think I'm trying to take something away from you? That's not why I'm here. I came because I thought you might need someone. I know you miss her. She died too soon."

He hugged her. "I miss it, Rosa. I didn't think I would, but I do. I miss the work, digging for the truth. And I feel like I've let a dear friend down."

"You want to come back."

He nodded. "But what about Dad?"

"Talk to him. I'm sure you'll find out that both of you will be all right with your decision."

"I will."

They started for the subway again. "You said you'll be rearing Joel. What happened at the lawyer's office?"

"Maureen won."

Vida's office looked better than it did the last time Rosa saw it. There were no papers on the floor. It was as neat as its owner. Her huge desk faced the room, allowing the sunlight from a huge window and that of a skylight to shower the desk. She sat on a high stool working. Rosa paced about, holding a cup of coffee, looking at some of the designs that lay on various counters.

"How was the trip?" Vida asked.

"From what Adam said, Lillian had no objections. She signed the papers giving him custody. She has visitation rights for a week in the summer if both Joel and Adam approve."

Vida looked up. "Gee, that was gracious of her."

"Extremely," Rosa said. "I believe Joel knows more than he's saying and that if he does talk, she stands to lose more than she wants to. I doubt she'll ever ask to exercise the visitation rights."

"You don't think he was abused, do you?"

Rosa shook her head. "Sexually, no. Adam specifically asked the doctor to check Joel thoroughly. He found nothing and Joel would have told Adam if anything like that had occurred."

Vida sighed in relief. "That's good. It'll probably take him some time to get used to being here, but he'll be fine."

Rosa nodded. "He's got a great support system. Bailey has him calling him grandfather and I can already see him fitting in."

"You don't sound like it's a good thing," Vida said. She turned away from the drawing on the desk and stared at Rosa. "What's wrong?"

"Nothing," Rosa sighed, and dropped into a comfortable chair opposite Vida's drawing table.

"Does nothing come in the form of Adam Osborne?" she asked.

"Isn't it always a man?" Rosa answered.

"I thought you and Adam were heading in the same direction as Mike and I." Vida stated it.

"Nobody could be in that direction." She smiled. "I think you two have carved out your own road."

Vida smiled, too, only her face flushed. After a moment she said, "Tell me what's happening."

"Not much. I supposed I thought coming here for the summer would mean a lot of solitary enjoyment of the scenery, some horseback riding, visit with you and nothing more. I didn't expect to become part of the community, getting involved in other people's lives, and . . ."

"And falling in love."

"And falling in love."

"Rosa, falling in love isn't a disaster. Most people think it's great."

"I know. Those people follow the straight line, though."

"Love is not a straight line. Look at Mike and me. We've been dancing around each other for years."

"But there are no obstacles between you. You're a designer now and you'll be pretty much in the same town for most of the year."

Vida would only need to travel to fashion shows, design conferences, and corporate meetings if she decided to sell her designs exclusively. Mostly she could choose her own schedule.

"What obstacles are between you and Adam?"

"Space is going to be the first one. I'll be somewhere in the world and he'll be here. We both know how difficult it is to maintain a relationship long distance. Then there's his family."

"Bailey?"

"Bailey *and* Joel."

"You object to Joel?"

"Of course not! He's a precious little boy."

"Then you object to Bailey."

"No."

"So how can his family be an obstacle?"

"This is where Adam's energy is. He's got to build a relationship with Joel. Even though they had one in the past, two years and lots of growing have separated them. Kids need attention."

"Rosa, you sound like no woman every married a man with a father and a child."

"He hasn't asked me to marry him."

"You could ask him."

"It wouldn't work. He'll be here and I'll be in New York or parts unknown. My first assignment when I leave here is in Finland. I'll make a quick stop in New York to drop the things I have here and then I'm off for three weeks. After that it's—"

"You can stop." Vida raised her hands. "I know the routine. Have you thought of giving it up?"

"Modeling? It's my job. I have contracts. I can't give it up."

"Sure you can. Maybe not immediately, but you haven't mentioned anything that can't be fixed."

"Maybe I'm oversimplifying it, but I don't see it working when I'm not in the same place he is. And he has a family to take care of."

"Well, think about this. Is this how you want your life to be? Always on the road, never staying in one place long enough to get to know people? You've probably been in the Valley for a longer amount of time than you've been anywhere else except Texas."

Rosa nodded.

"And you see what it's like to have neighbors who care about you. How to put down roots."

"I have roots."

"But you have wanderlust, too. It's what took you out of Texas and around the world."

"You'd still be traveling, too, if it weren't for the accident."

"The accident was a wake-up call. At first I was angry, but Mike helped me realize that I had other talents, that I could still do many other things without having to be on a runway."

"Vida, I am truly happy for you and Mike. And I can't leave modeling until after your collection comes out."

The computer and screen were back in the boxes. Rosa had called a delivery service and they were due any minute to pick up the boxes and ship them to her condo in New York. Her clothes were packed and she'd turned in the rental car. The only thing left was to say good-bye to Bailey, Adam, and Joel and go to the airport.

Vida and Mike were taking her this time. There was no mixup, no emergencies that took Mike away, no illness that prevented Vida from driving. Rosa looked around the room. She'd spent a lifetime in this house, even though she'd only been here for three short months. It felt as if she'd lived her entire life in this small space.

She could feel Adam here. They'd shared meals at the kitchen counter, spent evenings on the terrace, and made passionate love in the loft. She looked up, imagining Adam looking at her over the banister. Again she saw the design in it. She had planned to ask him what it was, but never got around to it. Now she was leaving. She'd return the keys to Liam Wilkerson on her way out of town.

The doorbell rang and Rosa quickly dispatched the packed boxes. Vida and Mike were due in an hour. It was time to see Adam for the last time.

Rosa didn't often walk in the Valley. She'd ridden the horses or spun around in the Corvette, but today she was without both. Gathering the box with Maureen's cameras, she set out for the Osborne Ranch.

"Rosa, come on in," Medea said when Rosa appeared at her kitchen door. Medea pushed the screen open and let her pass.

Rosa set the camera box on the floor near the door. "I came to good-bye. My plane leaves in a few hours."

Medea hugged her. "I heard you were leaving us, but I thought you'd be around for a little longer."

The two women sat down at the big table where Rosa had shared several meals. "Work calls."

"You'll be back?" she asked.

"I feel at home here," Rosa answered honestly.

"Good, whenever you need us, you just come on back. There'll always be a hot meal . . . or a salad . . . waiting for you here."

The two women laughed.

"Hey, I thought I heard your voice." Bailey came in.

Rosa stood up and hugged him.

"All ready to go?"

She nodded. A sudden lump lodged in her throat and tears gathered in her eyes, but Rosa held them back.

"I'm sorry to see you leave. You made me remember some of the best times in my life. And that birthday present was the best ever. I thought you and Adam . . ." He stopped. "Well, I thought things would work out differently."

"I thought so, too, but he has a lot to do and there's Joel now to care for. I have things to do, too. So it's all for the best."

"Not to this ole man's eyes."

"Where are Joel and Adam?"

"Joel is upstairs and Adam is out riding."

Rosa's face fell. She had no idea where he would go to ride. She wanted to see him, but it might not happen. After what they had shared, all the time they'd spent together, maybe saying good-bye was too much for both of them. Rosa wasn't looking forward to walking away from him. Maybe he was making it easier for her by not being there. And maybe he was running away from his feelings.

"Oh, the box," Rosa said. She'd nearly forgotten it. "It's for Adam. He loaned it to me." She looked at the worn box, remembering Adam's face as he'd given it to her. "I'll go see Joel."

"He's in his room," Bailey said, standing aside.

Mist gathered in Rosa's eyes. She wiped it away as she mounted the stairs. She'd never been upstairs before and didn't know which room was Joel's or which one belonged to Adam. The hall was huge, the way they used to build them before development housing and cookie-cutter buildings took over. The walls were white, but the molding was dark. Rosa heard music coming from one room and knew that must be where Joel was.

Before reaching Joel, she passed an open door. It was Adam's room. His boots lay on the floor near a window. She recognized them and stood at the door. The bed was huge, with a dark brown coverlet. The furniture was dark wood. There was a bookcase jam-packed with books against one wall. A computer desk sat in the corner. Newspapers the height of the desk leaned against it. Papers were littered over the desk; otherwise the room was neat.

Rosa took in a breath. She could smell Adam's presence here. She closed her eyes, taking in the scent of him. She held it, hoping she'd be able to remember it when she was huddled around a fire in Finland or some other distant land.

"Rosa?"

She jumped as if she'd been caught doing something wrong. It was wrong. Adam had never invited her to his room. She was invading his privacy.

"I thought I heard someone."

"I came to say good-bye." She recovered, but her voice sounded a little strained. "I'm leaving for the airport in a little while. I wanted to tell you what a pleasure it was to meet you and spend some time with you."

She didn't approach him, but he came closer to her.

"Are you leaving?" He sounded hurt, like he didn't know.

"It's time. I have to go back to my home and then to some jobs."

"I guessed you would." He lowered his head. Rosa took a step toward him.

"You're going to be all right, Joel. You have Adam and your grandfather. The community here is wonderful. You'll make new friends and fit right in. School will open soon. In a while you won't even think about all that happened to you."

"I know. People have been very friendly so far."

"And you have my phone number and my family's numbers in case you need to find me."

He nodded.

"See you later, then?"

"See ya."

Rosa turned and walked down the hallway. She was at the top of the stairs when Joel called her name.

She turned and he came running down the hall. He hugged her. "Thank you," he said. "I'm glad you were there when I came."

"Me, too," Rosa said. She pushed back, her body full of emotion and love for the young boy. "You take care of Adam," she told him. "He's going to need a lot of understanding."

Joel laughed. "I will."

Rosa went down the stairs. Time had come to find Adam. He'd be the hardest to leave, but she had to do it. Medea told her Adam was back. He was outside in the barn. Taking a deep breath, she hugged Medea one last time and went out the door.

The barn was only twenty feet from the main house, but it seemed to take her a lifetime to cross the yard. She heard voices before she got there. She recognized Adam and Bailey.

"Listen to me. You can't stay here. You can't bury yourself on my account."

"Dad, there are things you can't do anymore."

"Don't you think I know that?"

"Well, you don't act like it. Look at you, galli-vanting around here on horseback with your heart condition."

"I never had a heart attack on the horse. I had it in the truck and Rosa was there, not you. If you want to take that job, you can go. If you want Joel to stay here, he can. If you want him to go to D.C. with you, he can do that, too. It's your decision, but don't make it on my account. We already have a manager running the ranch. I'll do what

Joy and Rosa have got me started doing. I'll finish writing and recording those memoirs. That will keep me busy."

"I'll think about it, Dad."

"Really think about it?"

"Really think about it."

A moment later, Bailey came out of the barn. When he saw Rosa, he stopped. "He's all yours," he said. "Maybe you can make him see sense."

Bailey stopped and hugged her, then continued toward the house.

Adam came to the door. They looked at each other, neither speaking. Words had flown from Rosa's head. She could think of nothing to say.

"I brought the cameras back," she finally said.

"You could have left them."

"The keys. I'll leave them with Liam on the way to the airport."

Rosa couldn't believe she was talking about boxes and keys when this might be the last time she saw the man she was in love with.

"I saw Joel," she said. "I told him to take care of you. Kids like that. It makes them feel grown-up."

Rosa didn't see Adam move, but in a flash he was in front of her, his arms around her, his mouth on her, hot and seeking. She melted into him, unable to do anything else. She carried nothing in her hands since she'd returned the camera box. Her arms went around his neck and she returned the kiss with as much ardor as Adam showed.

It was like the first time he'd kissed her. The passion and emotion she felt then came to her now. The knowledge of her leaving was clear in the kiss. It was good-bye forever. She seared her mouth to his, accepting his invading tongue.

The fire of his hands on her back as they roamed up and down her frame set her soul burning. She wanted it to go on forever, have the world stop at this moment and never resume its forward spin.

But she knew that wouldn't happen. Adam slid his mouth from hers and Rosa lay limply in his arms, her head on his shoulder, her breath shallow. After a moment, she found the strength to push herself back.

"I have to go now."

He dropped his arms and stepped back. Rosa took a step back also. She couldn't say good-bye. Her voice wouldn't allow her to speak over the huge knot in her throat. She turned and began walking.

At the fence, before she reached the road that would lead back to the rented house, she realized Adam hadn't uttered a single word.

Chapter 14

Everything about New York seemed louder when Rosa arrived at her condo. While she wasn't on a major thoroughfare, she heard noise she hadn't noticed in the past. Rambling around the rooms, she thought of nothing but Adam for days. She was going crazy, wanting to call him, wanting to hear the sound of his voice. She'd pick up the phone and then return it to its cradle.

She didn't have to be in Finland for another week. Usually she savored this time, getting things in order, preparing for something new, but her past, the past summer, was on her mind. Unable to take it any longer, she called the airport and got the first flight to Dallas.

Stephanie picked her up. "This was a surprise," she said as Rosa threw her overnight bag in the back and got into the decorating van Stephanie used for her business. "Aren't you leaving for Europe in a few days?"

"Yes, but I needed some time with family."

"And would family's name be Adam Osborne?"

Rosa glanced sideways at her sister-in-law as

she pulled into the traffic exiting the airport. Rosa saw right away she wasn't going to be able to hide her feelings from her perceptive sisters-in-law. What one knew, they all knew. And that meant Luanne and Mark, her sister and brother-in-law, knew, too. And possibly her brothers. No, certainly her brothers.

"Adam has issues of his own to work through."

"Fell hard, did you?"

"I don't want to talk about it," Rosa said.

"Okay." Stephanie immediately stopped asking questions. Rosa liked that about her. Initially the two of them had not been friends, mainly because of Rosa protecting her brother Owen from what she thought might be heartache. Now she knew no one could protect another person from love.

"How is everyone? I saw Owen and Dean," Rosa said to fill the air with something other than her thoughts of Adam.

"Yes, they told me they came to visit you this summer and met Adam."

"They only stayed a short while. We had dinner together and then they were gone."

"Everyone else is fine. Luanne, Mark, and the baby were here a week ago. He's getting very big. Erin and Digger came for the art gallery exhibit. They brought Samantha, who's quite a young lady now." Since Stephanie and Owen met at a private showing at the Women's Museum, they go back each year.

They didn't talk anymore until Stephanie parked in the driveway of the house where Rosa had grown up. Not much about it had changed since her last visit. Owen had redone the inside, but the outside and the main rooms were the same. Rosa felt good that something in her life remained constant and unchanging.

"Do you have to go back to work?"

Stephanie got out of the van and opened the door to get Rosa's suitcase.

"It's nearly closing now and my assistant, Marian, is closing up today. But I do have to run to the grocery store and pick up some things for dinner."

"We could have stopped on the way. I can go with you."

"Oh no, you go on in and unpack. I'll be right back."

Rosa took her suitcase and walked up the steps to the front door. She saw Clare almost as soon as she closed the door. Clare was the carving on the newel post that Digger had done when he was thirteen. They all rubbed it when leaving the house for good luck.

Rosa approached Clare and rubbed her head. "Maybe you'll be lucky for me coming, too," she said aloud. It was a superstition of the family, rubbing Clare for good luck.

"She was for me."

Rosa's eyes flashed up at the sound of the voice. Adam stood in the doorway leading to the living room. She blinked to make sure she was seeing reality and not some poltergeist that her mind had created.

"Adam?" she said tentatively.

"I couldn't live without you," he said.

"Adam," she repeated.

"I'm here. I'm real."

Rosa started running. Tears streamed from her eyes as she crashed into him. Her arms circling his neck, their mouths merging.

"How did you know I'd be here?" she asked several moments later when she came up for air.

"You didn't answer your home phone. Joel gave me your cell number, only he got it wrong and I called here. Stephanie told me you were on your way. I got on the first plane."

"Why?"

"Rosa, I'm in love with you."

"But your dad? Joel?"

"I had a talk with Dad. And I understand what you told me. I can't live his life and he can't live mine. I want to be with you, wherever you are."

"I'm going to be traveling for the next couple of years. I have contracts to fulfill. I'm not accepting any more. After they're finished, I'm quitting. It's time. People like Tommie can take over. I'll recommend her."

Adam kissed her. "I'm glad to hear that. I'm taking the job in D.C. Wanna move there and marry me?"

"What?"

"I know you understand the question."

"Yes . . . I mean no."

"Come on, sit down and I'll explain it."

Rosa was familiar with the room. The piano her mother used to play. The photos of all her brothers and sister at various stages of growth. The furniture was different than it had been when she was growing up, but Owen and Stephanie, an architect and a designer, lived here now, and the room had taken on a new look. She sat on the sofa. Adam sat next to her, his arm around her shoulders.

"I'll be taking Joel and moving into the company condo until I can find a place, a house. The anchor's position starts next month."

"What about Bailey?"

Dear Reader,

Last Night's Kiss is the fifth and final book in the Claytons series. When the previous book, *On My Terms*, was released, the mail was overwhelming for the series. Thank you all for loving the Claytons and for wanting more. I'm happy to say the Claytons are enjoying a worldwide audience. Translated editions of my books are available in Spain, Iceland, and Chile, and omnibus editions are available in England and Australia.

There will be other clans and other series for you to fall in love with. I'm developing one now, but can't spill the details just yet.

Thanks again and y'all come back for more adventures in love. If you'd like to hear more about *Last Night's Kiss*, and other books I've written or upcoming releases, please send a business-size, self-addressed, stamped envelope to me at the following address:

Shirley Hailstock
P.O. Box 513
Plainsboro, NJ 08536

You can also visit my Web page at the following address. Also, take a moment to join my e-newsletter.
http://www.geocities.com/shailstock.

Sincerely yours,

Shirley Hailstock